behind the frame

gordon bonnet

To Dave Allen

who once told me he'd kick my butt if I continued doubting myself.

1. rose-colored glasses

. . .

K it McIntyre sat up in bed, his green eyes snapping open, the light summer blanket sliding from his bare shoulders. A tremor rippled through his body, and he reached up, running his fingers through long sandy hair, tangled from a night's sleep. He watched his own arm moving in a slow, dreamlike fashion and frowned at it in confusion.

My body is somewhere else. This is not me.

Then the world righted itself. He blinked a couple of times, took a long, deep breath, and fell back against his bed.

Ordinarily, Kit woke up slowly. A sound sleeper, his mother said that he could sleep through an air raid. And while it was true that he could be difficult to wake up, it was clear that he thrashed around a good bit in his sleep, to judge by the usual tangled condition of his blankets in the morning.

Kit never mentioned to his mother his nightly restlessness, which sometimes was so severe that it dumped him bodily onto the floor. Ever since boyhood, Kit had been the unwilling victim of frequent, and extremely vivid, dreams. Normally they did not wake him. The only trace left of the mental rollercoasters he rode at night were a vague unease and sometimes physical stiffness when he woke up. Most often, he only remembered odd, assorted fragments of his dreams upon waking, and even those faded to nothing by the time he ate breakfast.

This morning was different.

His dream was still there, floating behind his eyelids. At first, he had the illusory sense that it was real—a memory, not a dream. He'd lived with strange dreams his entire life, though, and that confusion was fleeting. He was still in his bedroom in a third-floor apartment in Issaquah, Washington, which he shared with his mother and younger sister.

Yet, when he closed his eyes, clear, crisp images flooded back into his brain.

He stood on the sill of a window, at least forty feet off the ground. It was an old building—that, at least, he could tell by the gray and weathered wood under his feet. He would have had to turn in order to see what kind of building it was, and that was impossible. His back was against the exterior wall and the sill was too narrow to turn around safely.

He squinted at the land spreading away from him, the terrain unfamiliar. Instead of the craggy backdrop of the Cascade Mountains with which he had grown up, the distance was clad in rolling hills. Even the trees were strange. Not the Douglas firs and spruces of the Northwest, but broad-leafed trees for which he had no names. There were at least five people on the ground, screaming threats, shaking their fists at him and shouting in voices incomprehensible with anger and distance. As he watched, two of them disappeared from his field of vision and he was sure that they had run into the building. Somehow, there was something different about those people, but looking down at them from above—along with the peculiar mix of extreme clarity and blurred senses which is typical of dreams—he couldn't see what was wrong with them, frantically scurrying around.

He was acutely aware of his own fear, like a cold stone in his belly. Anything, even fighting the mysterious screamers who he was certain were now coming to get him, would be better than jumping off the top of a building. On the verge of trying to climb back through the window, another familiar voice from behind him whispered, "Jump, Kit. You know you must jump." He looked at the ground. Forty feet? It now looked more like a thousand.

But he jumped.

But it wasn't the feeling of falling—the nemesis of so many dreamers—that woke Kit up. It was that, as he fell, a strong hand had grabbed his. Instead of the hand saving him, pulling him back, he swung the hand's unseen owner out into the empty air with him, and they fell together.

"God, what a dream." He shuddered again. He knew, although he had no memory of it, that this was only a fragment of the total dream. Heaven only knew what had occurred in the first part.

He swung his legs, nut-brown from the summer sun, out of bed and pulled on a pair of shorts. Grabbing a t-shirt from his dresser, he paused in front of his mirror and flexed before slipping it on.

He padded barefoot down the hall to the bathroom, stopping briefly to wash his face and run a brush through his tousled mop of hair. The aromatic smell of frying sausage wafted from the kitchen, and from the living room came the low murmur of the radio playing something edgy from the nineties. Linkin Park? The ordinariness of the morning reassured him, but he still couldn't shake the odd feeling of upset that his dream had left him with. There was something about it more than the usual surreality. He had experienced many strange dreams, but this one was different in some way he couldn't quite put his finger on.

Kit walked into the kitchen. "Morning, Mom."

Alison McIntyre turned and gave her son a wan smile. She was a thin, dark-haired woman whose worry lines and harried expression made her look older than her forty-three years.

"Morning, honey. I wondered if you'd be up before I left. I have to go in to the office early today. Marnie Cousins called in sick."

"Dr. G. can't answer his own phones for an hour?" Kit sat down at the table and poured himself some orange juice.

Alison simply smiled again and turned back to the stove. "Are you going down to the high school to play soccer today?"

"Maybe this afternoon. This morning I promised Philip I'd check in on him and hear his latest book idea. He said he wanted my advice."

"Now, don't you be bothering Mr. Amirault. What's a published writer like him want with ideas from a seventeen-year-old boy?"

Kit frowned at his mother's back, his pride stung by her condescension. "How should I know? He asked me to come, not the other way around."

Mrs. McIntyre turned off the stove and carried the plate of steaming sausage to the table. "Now, don't get your dander up, Christopher McIntyre. Mr. Amirault is a very nice man and I don't want you to wear out your welcome."

Kit rolled his eyes and helped himself to toast and sausage. "Geez, give me credit for some intelligence, Mom. Where's Laurie, by the way? It's not like her to miss breakfast."

"I heard that," replied a girl of thirteen, walking into the kitchen from the hall. "You haven't been missing many meals yourself, Kit."

"I didn't mean you were fat, Laurie."

"You'd better not have." Indeed, Laurie McIntyre had inherited her mother's black hair, small stature, and slenderness. There was nothing of timidity about her, however. People who judged her toughness on her size made that mistake only once. She had a temper and sharp wit that came straight from their father, who had been a master at slicing people up with words.

… and probably still was. Kit sighed and then realized he was being spoken to.

"What were you doing last night?"

It seemed such an incongruous question that he simply stared at Laurie. "What?"

"I said, what were you doing last night? Or this morning, really. Around three a.m. it sounded like *The Walking Dead* in there. You were moaning and bumping into the wall. Scared me half to death."

Kit looked at his sister. She looked a little irritated, but mostly curious. "I must have been dreaming." His voice sounded strained and thin.

"What about?"

He glanced up at his mother. Mrs. McIntyre was frowning at him—she had heard the strange note in his voice. Kit knew his mother was a born worrier. If she thought anything was bothering him, she would have it out of him even if it meant that she ran late for work and had to take all sorts of crap from Dr. William 'Arrogant-Jerk' Garrison for the remainder of the day.

Kit shrugged and grabbed another sausage. "No idea. Probably just one of those crazy dreams that make no sense."

"I have those, too. Just last week, I dreamed Karen Petrovich turned into a big bird and flew away, and then all of a sudden, I was at school and Mrs. Markover—you remember Mrs. Markover? Well, she was…."

Mrs. McIntyre, distracted by Laurie's chatter, glanced down at her watch, gave an exclamation of dismay, and stood up. She wiped her hands on her napkin, walking over to kiss both of her children.

"Goodbye, you two. If you need anything and you can't reach me, go get Mrs. Lorenzo down the hall."

Both Kit and Laurie only listened with half an ear. This speech was a summer ritual, given every time their mother left them alone for any length of time.

"If you go any farther than the high school, let her know where you're going and when you'll be back. I should be home by five o'clock. Love you."

"Love you, too, Mom."

Both children continued their breakfast in silence until the front door closed and their mother's footsteps could be heard receding down the hall. They faintly heard the swish of the elevator door opening, then shutting. Kit glanced at Laurie. She was staring right at him, an intent glitter in her dark eyes.

"So, what were you really dreaming about? At first, I thought you were just dreaming you were kissing Andy Halloran, but I finally decided that you didn't sound like you were having a good time, so it must have been something else."

"Cute, squirt."

"Yeah, I'm all about cute."

"I don't have a crush on Andy Halloran. And even if I did, I'm sure he's one hundred percent straight."

"I don't know how you're so sure, given that you're too scared to ask anyone out." She gestured at him with her fork. "Now, what were you dreaming about?"

Kit sighed. It was nearly impossible to evade his sister's questions without walking out of the room. "Okay, promise you won't laugh? It sounds pretty stupid."

"Can't promise, but I'll try."

Kit outlined his dream, which by now was becoming fuzzy and indistinct. He had a hard time rationalizing why it had given him such an ungodly scare. Still, he remembered it clearly enough to tell his sister the essential images.

"Funny," Laurie commented, but didn't laugh. "All I know is I was almost worried enough to check on you. I know you dream a lot...."

"How do you know that?"

"I hear you talking and bumping around. I've known that *forever*. What do you think I am, an idiot?"

"I suppose not."

"I also know you don't want to tell Mom about it, and I'm sorry I pushed you earlier. I was just worried."

Kit didn't answer. He crumpled up his napkin and stood up.

"You *are* okay, aren't you, Kit?" For all of her self-assurance, Laurie suddenly looked very young.

"Yeah, Laurie, I'm fine. Really. Like I said before, it really was just a crazy dream. I'm sorry I woke you up." He glanced at the clock above the kitchen window and swore under his breath. "Oh, no, I'm late. I told Philip I'd be there by nine." He picked up his plate and dumped it into the sink.

"Why would Philip care if you're a little late?" Laurie's gaze followed her brother as he dashed back to his room to grab his watch and keys.

"I don't know, he just does." He ran back down the hall. "You know how he is. He's a funny guy. And I like him. I don't want to tick him off for no good reason." Kit grabbed a pair of rubber-soled slip-ons from the shoe rack inside the coat closet and pulled them on. "I'll be back by lunch." He ran out the front door.

Philip Amirault lived in the apartment directly below Kit and his family. Kit ran past the elevator, which was slower than the stairs, then down one floor and up the hall to Philip's door.

A series of noises—a bang, followed by a sliding crash—emanated from behind the door in response to his knock. Finally, Kit heard the sound of shuffling footsteps and the door opened. Just a crack at first, and then wider.

"Kit, yes, come in," a quiet voice came from within and the door opened, although it was still impossible to see the voice's owner. Kit walked in without hesitation and the door shut behind him.

Kit turned to look at his friend. Philip Amirault was one of the ugliest men Kit had ever seen. Short, heavy-set, with a great quantity of straggling gray hair on his face with very little on top of his head. He had a large mole on the side of his nose and one eye turned in slightly. This latter characteristic had the unsettling effect of making it nearly impossible to figure out whom Philip was looking at. Philip's grin, certainly meant to be welcoming, revealed a row of yellowed, horsey teeth.

"You're late." Philip continued to grin.

"Sorry. My fault. I wasn't watching the time."

"That was the right answer." Philip, with a casual motion of one hand, turned and made his way into his apartment.

In terms of floor plan, Philip's apartment was a carbon copy of Kit's, but it would have taken someone with incredible powers of observation to draw that conclusion. Philip's apartment was a continual source of fascination for Kit, and he knew he was one of the very few people who had ever seen the inside of it. The windows were all but blocked by thick tapestries, which Philip claimed kept the cold out.

"If it was good enough for Charlemagne, it's good enough for me," he had once told Kit.

The result? The apartment looked like a disorderly attic. Clutter, dust, and little light. Thousands of books—everything from *The Decameron* to psychological thrillers by Andrew Butters—lined bookshelves and lay tumbled on the floor, table, and chairs. A moth-eaten stuffed coyote sat at attention by the front door, casting its dusty glass gaze on any newcomers. A huge Ugandan tribal drum occupied the same corner of the apartment where, one floor up, the McIntyres' stereo dwelt. The walls were hung with various *objets d'art*, most of them African or Native American, although some were simply weird—such as a necklace of galvanized wing nuts carefully wound into a piece of jute twine hanging on a nail next to the kitchen light switch. Kit had once asked Philip where he had gotten that and what it was for.

"Heck if I know," Philip responded. "If I ever need to know, I suppose I'll remember."

Kit had spent many hours in this apartment, conversing with the old man. The ritual was set. They first shared a cup of tea. Never plain tea, of course, always some sort of herbal tea Philip had concocted himself. Some of the herbs he used, Kit knew well enough. Catnip, lemon balm, spearmint—his mother had grown them in their vegetable garden when he was little, before his parents split. Others were strange, with wonderful and mysterious names. Wood betony, pennyroyal, angelica, fenugreek, elecampane. The last was administered when Kit came for a visit while suffering from a cold, and docilely consumed, even though Kit later reported to his sister it tasted like stewed horse crap. He did admit it had helped his sneezing and coughing, but afterwards he carefully avoided visits when he was ill.

Today it was chamomile tea, which was sweet, fruity, and pleasant. They drank it in silence, and Kit waited for Philip to bring up the subject of why he had been invited. The old man had to do things in his own time.

Philip drained his cup with a noisy slurp and sat back, looking at Kit with one dark, intelligent eye. The other seemed to gaze over Kit's right shoulder.

"I want your opinion on something." He gave no preamble at all.

Kit did not respond but waited for his host to complete his thought.

"Some years ago, I made an acquisition which I never have attempted to test thoroughly or explain. As you know, I tend to be rather skeptical of claims of the paranormal and other such hocus-pocus." He stood up, left the kitchen, and returned a moment later with a long, rectangular black box of considerable age. He dropped into his chair with a grunt and continued. "Bought these in a second-hand book store in San Antonio, Texas, three years ago. Was there for an interview— book tour, you know, when *The Broken Coin* hit number one." *The Broken Coin* was Philip's most recent book. "TV reporter took one look at me and had second thoughts about putting me on his show." He chuckled under his breath. "Guess he felt ugly people shouldn't write bestsellers."

Kit started to object, but Philip cut him off before he could get a word out. "Look, Kit old man, I've lived with this face for a few years. God knows I have to look at it in the mirror every morning. Don't argue with me. Anyway, I had some time on my hands and found a used book store. Guy behind the counter said I looked like a man who could use these."

He opened up the box, and inside were five pairs of old wire-rim glasses. "He called them the original rose-colored glasses. My opinion is, he was a jackass who wanted to turn a quick buck and had no idea what they were. I tried them on, but you know my eyes are completely shot. I'm blind in one of them and not much better in the other. I could only see fuzz. Some rose-colored glasses. I don't know what I expected —they'd give me my twenty-twenty vision back, or what. Stupid of me.

"Still, the idea appealed to me. Don't know why. Superstitious nonsense is just that, and I've never subscribed to it. I thought I might be able to use the idea in a story or something, and he only wanted thirty dollars for them, so I paid him and took them home. Then I lost them for a couple of years and generally forgot about them, and found them again last week. I thought—maybe Kit will be interested, and at least he could put them on and tell me what he sees. If he sees Brigadoon or the Pearly Gates, then he and I can sell them for a million dollars and split the money."

Kit looked at the old, tarnished spectacles with their round glass lenses. They were thin and perfectly flat, like costume glasses used on stage. They seemed completely unremarkable. Without speaking, he picked up a pair, unfolded the arms, and slipped them on.

As he put the glasses on, he was looking at the table, set with two empty teacups, the black box with two more pairs of glasses, and several books. The flat lenses, as he expected, didn't distort what he saw. It looked just like it did before, only a little smeared and dusty. He looked up, to tell Philip that his magic glasses didn't work, but stopped mid-sentence.

Philip was gone.

Kit stood up and put out his hand, knocking over his teacup. "Philip?"

All of the sounds, including his own voice, were distant and thin, like an echo from fifty miles away. Kit stared at Philip's empty chair, and as he watched, the chair began to shift shape, melting. The table sagged in the middle, like it was made of thick syrup, and the cups, books, and the box with the glasses slid down into a hole in the center, stretching and distorting like a Dali painting before slipping into nothing.

"Philip!" he screamed, but his voice sounded to him no louder than a whisper.

He heard, or thought he did, a paper-thin hissing, a two-dimensional parody of Philip Amirault's voice.

"Take them off... take off the glasses... Kit, take them off...." His hands reached up, but he could not see them and they could not find his face.

Or, perhaps, where his face once was, there was now nothing solid.

Then the walls of the apartment began to twist, like water going down a drain. Kit was caught in the spiral, and, in slow motion, he turned and fell over onto his back as the darkness swallowed him up.

2. erased

. . .

Kit landed flat on his back in cool, wet grass, so hard the breath was knocked out of him. He lay there, gasping for nearly a minute, the glasses still perched on his nose, yanked crooked by his fall. The odd distortion had passed and he now looked up into a deep blue sky dotted with puffy cumulus clouds. A few tree branches extended into his field of view, their leaves rustling in the light breeze. The enormity of what happened momentarily short-circuited his ability for rational thought and it took him several moments to realize if things were still normal, he'd be staring at Philip Amirault's apartment ceiling. He sat up, wincing and swearing under his breath.

He sat in front of an abandoned church. The grass was nearly a foot deep, with bright blue and gold flowers growing in patches and sparkling in the last rays of daylight. Suddenly aware he still wore the glasses, he roughly pulled them off, thinking perhaps they were responsible for this illusion, but everything looked the same without them. He stood up and looked around.

The old church on whose doorstep he had landed sat on a small hill. It was in a state of extreme dilapidation, but had probably once been beautiful, in a nineteenth-century New England sort of way. Wooden, with a tall steeple and belfry, its weathered siding still showed flecks of white and green paint. The windows yawned dark and empty. Right in front of the church was a broken sign, on which could be read the faint legend:

FINN HILL METHODIST CHURCH

Rev. Thomas Cole, Pastor

It was evident Reverend Cole had been away for a while and probably wasn't expected back any time soon. The church didn't look like it had been used in thirty years or more.

At the base of the hill, a dirt road wound away into a thicket of trees on his right. Just discernible in the failing light was the distant silhouette of two houses. One was past the thicket and toward the right, probably a quarter of a mile away. The second, with lights showing in the windows, stood perhaps a mile away, on a rise in the fields to the left and beyond the thicket of trees. Further off was what looked like farm land, perhaps corn or wheat fields.

His first impulse was to call Philip on his phone, to ask him how in the hell he'd done that and to get him home. To tell him okay, joke's over. But he soon realized in his rush to leave the apartment, he hadn't stuck his phone in his pocket. It probably still sat on the coffee table, where he'd left it the previous evening.

He patted his pants pocket, just in case.

Empty. No phone, no wallet. Nothing.

It was now beginning to get dark. Even if he had to spend the night in the open, he had no intention of staying near the abandoned church. Its empty windows looked far too much like eyes. He turned again to look at it. At that point, he realized that he still held the glasses. He glanced down at them. It brought back to him the craziness of the situation and how he had gotten here—wherever *here* was. Swearing again, louder this time, he turned and pitched the glasses at the church. They flipped end over end and were swallowed into the darkness of one of the windows. Kit heard them strike the floor inside and skitter briefly across its surface. Then he turned and walked down the hill toward the road.

Even though the house to the right of the thicket was closer, Kit was lured by the lights in the windows of the farther one. When he reached a fork in the road just inside the confines of the woods, he took the left-hand turn, identified by an old hand-painted sign as "Swenson Road." Crickets and frogs began to sound in the darkness under the trees and he slapped at a mosquito whining briefly near his ear.

Was *this* a dream? If so, it was a pretty realistic one.

Most of his dreams, of course, *were* pretty realistic. It was his memory of them that was not true, that reflected them incompletely. Kit was one of those rare people whose dreams were in full sensory impact and wild technicolor. He'd had dreams this realistic hundreds of times before. He had more than once awakened either laughing hysterically or weeping uncontrollably. Occasionally, he awoke still feeling a pain whose explanation lay in his dream. He had dreams from which he had woken with his fists clenched in anger, face flushed, adrenaline coursing through his veins. Yes, this could easily have been one of his dreams.

But looking around him—no, he didn't think it was a dream. Of course, anybody inside a dream would probably say the same thing.

Still, something felt solidly real about where he was, despite the unfamiliarity of his surroundings. Kit had grown up in a densely populated area—the I-5 corridor, in Seattle suburbia. Even his hometown, the once isolated village of Issaquah, had virtually been absorbed by the sprawling outgrowth of greater Seattle, collectively referred to as "the Eastside." The great wash of humanity, roaring up from the Puget Sound Basin, lapped at the feet of the Cascades, and as a result, Kit had never experienced real silence. He had been camping before, but always with friends or family, never alone. He slept in a bedroom overlooking Second Avenue Southeast, one of the busiest streets in Issaquah. He was never far from human noise. Cars, the babble of voices, airplanes from Sea-Tac airport.

Here, the lack of that noise was almost itself a real, solid entity. Crickets and frogs ruled this place. The dirt road, puddled and muddy from a recent shower, showed no signs of cars passing—there was even grass encroaching in places. As far as he could tell, it hadn't seen an automobile in months. If he hadn't seen the lights on in the distant farmhouse, he would have believed himself the only human within a thousand miles.

By the time Kit came out from under the trees, the sky had darkened to indigo, pricked by a few glittering white stars. The moon was just past full and hovered near the horizon, illuminating the countryside with a ghostly but surprisingly brilliant light. Ahead of him, the road descended a shallow decline, crossed a wooden bridge over a small stream, and began to rise again. At the top of the rise, less than an eighth of a mile away, was the house, its windows shining a warm yellow.

He walked quickly down the middle of the road, not wanting to take his eyes off the house. Suddenly the absurdity of his situation closed in. He felt that if he looked away, the house would vanish, and he would be alone. The thought terrified him, and when his foot unexpectedly landed on the first plank of the wooden bridge with a loud *bonk*, he gasped and jumped back, and tears came into his eyes. He looked down at the bridge, forced a smile, and wiped his eyes with his sleeve. "Wuss," he hissed at himself and continued to walk.

The stream chattered loudly over the rocks under the bridge, rolling away to his right to somewhere further down the valley. He passed it by, climbed the last hill, and stood before his goal.

It was a white farmhouse, with trim of some dark color indistinguishable from black in the moonlight. A neatly painted mailbox stood at the end of the sidewalk.

Carl & Helen Swenson

6 Swenson Rd.

Kit walked up the sidewalk, between rows of carefully maintained flowers, climbed the three stairs onto the front deck, and knocked on the door.

There was a murmur of voices from inside and then the clear sound of footsteps on a wooden floor. The door opened wide—further convincing Kit he was nowhere near Seattle, no one in the Seattle area flung open his door to a stranger with such nonchalance—revealing a tall man in his fifties, clad in worn jeans and a plaid work shirt. He wore square wire-rimmed bifocal glasses, and his hair, of a nondescript brown, was thin on top.

"Yes?"

Kit had walked nearly a mile, knocked on a stranger's door, and only then did it occur to him that he had no idea what to say.

Hello, my name is Christopher McIntyre, Kit to my friends. Where in the heck am I?

Hi, my name is Kit. I fell through a hole in my friend Philip's dinner table, and I'm trying to find my way back home.

Evening, Mr. Swenson. I just put on some magic rose-colored glasses, and presto-chango and hocus-pocus, here I am. Where is here, anyway?

Finally, he simply asked, "Sir, may I come in?"

The man frowned in a perplexed way but stepped back from the door. "Sure. You one of Adam's friends?"

Kit walked inside and the man shut the door behind him. Kit shook his head. "No. My name is Kit McIntyre. I come from a long way away." He couldn't be sure about this, but it seemed likely. "I got lost, and yours was the first house I came to. I hope I'm not disturbing you."

Kit's hesitancy, and politeness, obviously affected the man positively. "Not at all, not at all. Just didn't expect anyone, least of all a young fellow like yourself, walking down our road at nine o'clock at night. Where do you come from?"

"Washington."

"D.C.?"

"State."

Mr. Swenson whistled. "You're not lying, you come from a ways off. You here visiting friends?"

"Uh… no." Kit looked away and shifted his weight to his other foot.

"Boy, you a runaway?"

Kit looked up and Mr. Swenson's eyes narrowed. "No, I'm not. I'm just a long way from home and need to find my way back."

Mr. Swenson's gaze softened. "Well, I guess there's a lot you're not telling me. But you don't look like a runaway. I suppose we won't have to call Chief of Police Cole just yet."

"Is… is he any relation to Reverend Thomas Cole?"

Mr. Swenson's frown returned. "How do you know about Reverend Cole?"

"I saw his name on a sign in front of an old church."

"Oh. How'd you get up there? That's near the end of the road. All there is up there is thorn bushes, rabbits, and raccoons. Yeah, Johnny Cole, our Chief of Police, is old Reverend Thomas's great grandson."

As they were talking, a tall woman with salt-and-pepper hair tied back in a bun walked into the room from a brightly-lit back area which could only be the kitchen. She walked gracefully, like someone who might once have been a dancer.

"Who's our guest, Carl?" Her face was serious but not unkind. A stern, quiet, country face, all angles and no frills.

Kit stood. "Kit McIntyre." He extended his hand.

She nodded gravely as she shook his hand. "I'm Helen Swenson. Where are you from, Kit McIntyre?"

Mr. Swenson shrugged. "He got lost up by the old Methodist Church. He's originally from Washington State."

"What brings you to our part of the world?"

Internally, Kit itched to shout out, *and what part of the world is this exactly?* But he maintained his calm demeanor. "I just sort of found myself here by accident."

"Perhaps you'd like to call your folks?" suggested Mrs. Swenson.

"Yes." Kit realized with a sudden shock that his mom would probably have every policeman in the state of Washington on full red alert by now. "Yes, that would be great. I lost my phone somehow." He paused. "It's long distance… I mean, obviously."

"No problem to us. We don't get many visitors needing to call other states. Let me show you the phone."

Mrs. Swenson led the way into a large farm kitchen, with an immaculate pale, yellow tile floor, polished slate counters, and shiny orange-brown pinewood cabinets. An old push-button landline phone sat on the edge of one of the counters, near a door that evidently led out into the back yard. She gestured toward the phone, then tactfully retreated back into the living room.

Kit picked up the receiver and dialed the number. There were two rings and then a click.

"I'm sorry," came the mechanical voice of a recorded operator. "The number you have dialed is no longer in service. Please hang up, check the number, and dial again. Thank you."

Must have slipped and dialed a digit wrong. All this craziness had made him careless. He tried again. Two rings and a click.

"I'm sorry, the number you have dialed is no longer…."

He hung up. Could he be remembering his phone number

incorrectly? He stopped, closed his eyes, and went through it. No, that was what he had dialed.

Time to try another tack. He picked up the receiver again and dialed directory assistance. Two rings and a click.

"Directory assistance, this is Clara. What city, please?"

"Issaquah, Washington."

"Could you spell that, please?"

Kit did.

"I'm sorry, sir, we have no listing for an Issaquah, Washington. Do you know the area code for the number you are trying to reach?"

No listing for Issaquah? How could that be? Mechanically, he answered, "Area code 206."

"And what name?"

"Alison McIntyre."

A pause. "I'm sorry, there is no listing for an Alison McIntyre in the 206 area code."

His breathing sped up, but he didn't respond.

"Is that all, sir?"

"Uh… no. Philip Amirault. Same area code."

"Spell the last name, please."

Kit did.

"I'm sorry, there is no listing for a Philip Amirault in this area code."

"Oh my god," he murmured. "Try Harley Claiborne." Harley Claiborne was the principal of Issaquah High School, a member of Rotary and every other service organization in the area, and generally a pillar of the community.

"I'm sorry, there is no listing for…." He gently placed the receiver on the phone.

For a moment, he stood, staring into space. What had happened? What, in heaven's name, happened when he had put on those glasses? No Mom, no Laurie, no Philip…. Where was he and what happened to everyone he knew?

If he told these people, they'd think he was crazy and

probably throw him out. Kit realized the truth was so unutterably weird that no one—particularly a farmer and his wife from Outer Sticksville, Tennessee, or wherever this was—would ever believe him. Still, what did he have to lose? If they threw him out, there was at least one other house within walking distance where he could beg shelter, and failing that, it was a nice warm night and he'd never minded sleeping outside.

He walked back into the living room. Helen and Carl Swenson both looked at him in a slightly embarrassed way, leaving him little doubt they'd overheard his phone conversation. "My mom's phone has been disconnected."

"I'm sorry." The embarrassment in Mrs. Swenson's face deepened to actual discomfort. This heightened the severity of her expression to the point it could have been mistaken for anger.

"I guess I ought to tell you how I got here."

Mr. and Mrs. Swenson remained silent.

Kit's voice became tense with emotion. "What I'm telling you is the truth—you've got to believe me. It's God's honest truth, I swear it."

Mrs. Swenson gave him nod. "Why don't you just tell us, Kit?"

He swallowed. "I was in a friend's apartment, in the same apartment complex I live in. Well, he's not a friend of my age —he's in his seventies, but he's still one of my best friends. Anyway, he gave me some old glasses to try on and I guess I passed out. When I woke up, I was here. Actually, I mean I was over in front of the Methodist church and I walked here."

The Swensons looked at Kit for a moment in silence, their faces registering no emotion.

Mr. Swenson crossed his arms. "What you're telling me is that you were in your friend's apartment—in the state of Washington—and you passed out, and woke up here a few moments later?"

"Yes, I guess so… only, I don't know how many moments it was. It was morning when I was there, so maybe twelve hours. I don't know."

"Twelve hours." Mr. Swenson huffed, and his eyes met his wife's for a moment. "Are you sure it wasn't a week? You might be suffering from… whatcha call it, amnesia?"

Kit looked startled. He hadn't considered that. "I guess I could be."

"What date and time was it when you were in your friend's apartment?"

Kit considered. "The time was around nine-thirty, maybe a quarter to ten. It was Tuesday, July… thirteenth, I think. 2015."

Again, the Swensons' eyes met. "Well, you've got the right day. That's today. And that tells me one thing. Son, you're one of the worst liars I've ever met."

Kit froze. "I…."

Mr. Swenson cut him off. "I may be a country hick, but I'm not stupid. You're trying to tell me at nine-thirty this morning you were in the state of Washington, and at nine o'clock tonight you're here? You'd be hard pressed to do that on a jet liner."

"I swear to you…."

"Swear all you like, son. It just isn't possible. Now why don't you tell me how you really got here?"

Kit looked from Mr. Swenson to his wife. Mrs. Swenson would not meet his eye. He cleared his throat. "Sir, where exactly is here?"

"You are near the village limits of the fine burg of Finn Hill, Hamilton County, New York. The nearest big airport is Watertown, about eighty miles as the crow flies and probably twice that by car. You don't look old enough to drive legally, although you might be driving anyhow. Guess you could have left your car somewhere and walked here. State of Washington's on Pacific Time, isn't it, Helen?" Mrs. Swenson nodded. "That's three hours different from here, meaning you got here in about eight and a half hours. How far is it to the nearest airport from your house?"

"Sea-Tac Airport. It's about forty-five minutes to an hour, depending on how bad the traffic is."

"So, that leaves maybe seven and a half hours. It's probably three and a half hours from Watertown Airport to here, which would leave you only four hours to make a trip by plane from there to here, counting layovers and such like. Now, does that sound likely to you?"

"No. It's impossible. I never claimed I took a plane."

"I know, son, I know." Mr. Swenson's patience was obviously wearing thin. "I'm not trying to prove you did. I'm trying to prove you're lying about having been in Washington state at nine-thirty this morning."

Mrs. Swenson placed a hand on her husband's shoulder. "Carl...."

"No, Helen, I want to know who he is and why he's here."

Kit was ashamed at the tears of impatience that came to his eyes. "I don't have any idea why I'm here!"

There was a noise and all three turned. A boy, about Kit's age, walked down the stairs at the back of the room. He was tall—maybe a little over six feet—with an athletic build. He had brown eyes, short, curly dark brown hair, and finely-cut, sensitive features. He met Kit's eyes for a moment, then gave Mr. and Mrs. Swenson a curious look. "What's going on down here, Dad?"

"Don't worry, Malachi. I was just about to show our visitor out." He stood up.

"Please, Mr. Swenson." Kit's voice was raw. "Please, you've got to believe me."

Mrs. Swenson shook her head. "What are you asking us to believe?"

"I have no idea how I got here. I swear, I swear I'm telling the truth. I don't understand any of this. My mom's phone number doesn't work and until you told me, I had no idea where I was. I don't know how I'm going to get back. Please, just let me stay the night…. I'll sleep on the couch, I swear I won't cause any trouble, and I'll leave tomorrow morning…."

Now that it became obvious the Swensons were going to throw him out, Kit's earlier breezy acceptance of his other options was clean gone. He couldn't face a night alone in this unfamiliar country, with nothing to think about but why and what and how could he get out of here? Malachi, the Swensons' son, watched him. His expression was one of intelligent curiosity. He seemed to be evaluating Kit.

Mr. Swenson's face softened and he pulled out a handkerchief and handed it to Kit. "Look, son, I just want to get at the truth here. You can see how your story…."

"Sounds ridiculous," Kit finished.

Mr. Swenson chuckled, but his eyes still retained their skepticism, and one eyebrow was raised. "You might say that. You know, though, you don't strike me as a liar. That's why I'm so miffed. I don't like being taken for a fool. Too many people think country means dumb. Now, I'm pretty good at spotting liars and I don't especially want to miss one." He looked at his wife. "I won't say I'm convinced, not just yet. Helen, we still got that road atlas?"

"I believe so." She walked over to a tall antique oak cabinet standing against the back wall.

"What town you said you were from?"

"Issaquah, Washington. About twenty-five miles east of Seattle. But the operator said…." Kit stopped. What the operator had said, he didn't want to think about.

Mrs. Swenson brought an old, battered paperback road atlas to her husband, and he opened it near the back, and then flipped a few pages. "Here we are. State of Washington. Well, there's Seattle."

Kit came over and stood next to him, looking over his shoulder.

"Let's see. East of Seattle, there's a lake."

"That's Lake Washington. We're east of there, along Interstate 90."

"Yes, I see. Lake Washington. Then there's a couple of little towns—Greene, Canton, Denny Creek."

Amazement showed in Kit's eyes and the amazement deepened to disbelief. "What?" His voice was strangled. "I've never heard of any of those places."

Mr. Swenson pointed at the map and Kit's gaze followed his finger. Kit knew all of their eyes were on him. Mr. Swenson's, doubtful, eyebrows raised. Mrs. Swenson's, still stern, disturbed by the insinuation of falsehood. Malachi's, probing, thoughtful, clearly trying to decide for himself what to make of their strange evening visitor.

Kit tried to keep the dismay out of his face and failed miserably. That, more than anything else, was probably what convinced Mr. Swenson Kit hadn't been lying. No one but an experienced actor could possibly have faked his horrified expression. For all of the towns Kit had grown up knowing—Kirkland, Bellevue, Carnation, Renton, Kent—were missing. The City of Seattle was still there, and a few of the geographical landmarks—Lake Washington, the Cascade Mountains—but the suburban towns at the periphery were completely different. Even a few of the rivers and smaller lakes had different names. It was like someone had glanced at a map and had reconstructed it from memory. The major features were identified correctly, but the remainder of the places had been filled in with random names. And where his home was, the town of Issaquah, was nothing but a blank space.

Kit, his eyes still registering disbelief, took the map from Mr. Swenson, and flipped to the index. His eyes scanned down to the "I" names listed there. Innsmouth – D-14; Ireland – C-2; Island County – D-10; Ivanhoe – H-9. And that was all. No Issaquah. His entire hometown, including his mother, his sister, and his friend Philip, had been erased.

3. crow's eyes

. . .

At the same time Kit was lying on his back in the wet grass in front of the Finn Hill Methodist Church, attempting to get his breath back and figure out where he was, a young woman in her mid-twenties was in her yard, about a quarter of a mile to the southwest, trying to use the last bit of daylight to finish planting her geraniums. Hers was the house Kit would see from the hill a few minutes later, whose darkened windows pointed him in the direction of the welcoming lights at the Swensons'.

Christina Thorne had spent the afternoon and early evening preparing a new garden for these particular flowers. She was not a person to be dissuaded by the onset of night. Now that she was done with the hard work, she wanted to get the plants in the ground and have something nice to show for her time.

When Christina and her husband Adam moved to Finn Hill from Cincinnati, Ohio, two years earlier, small-town tongues began to wag. The village men commented on Christina's remarkable beauty and the village women on the effect of Christina's presence on their husbands, boyfriends, brothers, and sons. The women also commented about

Adam's Greek god physique, complete with curly blond hair and a surf-n-sun grin that could charm summer back in January. Marie Bedford, the cashier of the Finn Hill Nice 'n' Easy Grocery Store and Kwik Fill, was of the opinion they were too good to be true and that there had to be something wrong with two people who seemed so perfect. She derisively called them "Ken and Barbie" behind their backs and darkly hinted that Adam beat Christina or she cheated on him, 'just you wait and see if it isn't true.' In spite of this, Marie's co-workers noticed and took every occasion to point out, when Adam came into the Nice 'n' Easy, Marie was friendlier to him than she was to her own husband.

Two years passed, and Marie's dire predictions showed no signs of coming true. In fact, Adam and Christina were model citizens who made every attempt not to disturb the life of the tiny village they had entered. Adam was hired to teach physical education and coach track at the regional high school. Christina found work as an assistant librarian in the village of Carnahan, fifteen miles west of Finn Hill.

The head librarian noted in an amused way how the use of the Carnahan Public Library by boys from the high school skyrocketed when word got out Mrs. Thorne worked there, something Christina overheard and didn't mind in the least.

Still, the Thornes were private people, and chose a house up on Old Church Road, out in the wooded area north of the village center. Christina had grown up in Cincinnati and didn't trust people easily, an attitude she was well aware of and didn't see any reason to change. Adam stayed at school only as long as it took to discharge his duties as teacher and coach. He was nice, as far as it went, and a great favorite with his female students, but he didn't socialize with his coworkers. Neither of them made any real friends in the two years they had lived there, and to the village folks, they were still somewhat of an enigma. After two years, they continued to rely only on each other, and no one in the village really knew them.

Tonight, Christina, clad in a halter top and very short shorts, planted geraniums. A huge pile of weeds sat behind her, the remains of the part of lawn that she had excavated that afternoon. Darkness had nearly fallen, and she was attending to her task with her usual intensity.

It took her some time to notice the crow.

She finally turned her head, for no real reason—just that feeling, perhaps, of eyes on her back which nearly everyone has experienced and no one has ever been able to explain. There, sitting right there on the weed pile, was a large crow, watching her. It gazed at her curiously, its eyes intelligent and completely fearless, glittering like beads of black glass. She stared back at it. The bird was no more than four feet away and, in Christina's kneeling position, was slightly higher than she was, looking down at her. Except for a slight breeze ruffling its wing's feathers, it was completely still.

Christina stood up and the crow's head moved smoothly, like it was being pulled with a string, to follow her motion. This was unnerving. She waved her arms and shouted, "Boo! Go away!" The crow didn't move and didn't even show a sign of having been startled by her behavior.

This was too much. Christina took a step backward, treading on one of her carefully planted flowers. Without taking her eyes off the crow, she shouted, "Adam?" Even now, she wasn't actually scared. Her feeling was one of annoyance, of irritation at being harassed by a bird and losing the last precious minutes of daylight.

Adam came around the side of the house, where he had been repairing the deck, his broad and bronzed chest covered with sweat and flecked with sawdust. As soon as he appeared, the crow's head swiveled around to look at him, and when he was about ten feet away, it gave a squawk and flew away with a loud flutter.

"What's up, babe?"

"Did you see that crow?"

"Yes. Not very afraid of people, was it?"

"No. It was watching me. It was only a few feet away, watching me." Christina's voice sounded thin and her eyes were not on Adam, but on the weed pile.

"Pretty strange." Adam didn't sound overly concerned and that defused some of Christina's vague annoyance. She wasn't afraid of it. It was only a bird.

No, not afraid at all.

She turned, looked at her husband and then looked down at her feet.

"Geez! I stepped on one of my geraniums."

"How can you see anything in this darkness? At least I have the flood lights to help me. Maybe we ought to put in flood lights out here and you could work in your garden at midnight if you wanted to." He paused. "But don't you think it's time to take a break? You've been working all afternoon."

"I wanted to get finished." She looked at her plants, at the pile of weeds, and thought again of the crow. A little shiver vibrated over her skin. "I guess it could just as easily be left until tomorrow."

"Good. I need some dinner, woman." Adam caught her around the waist and picked her up as if she were a child. His grin flashed out in the shadows.

She slapped at his chest. "Put me down, you brute. You're getting me all sweaty."

"Men are supposed to be sweaty. Didn't you know that?"

She laughed out loud and he turned and strode to the door, pushing it open with his foot. They went inside, their voices and laughter receding into the interior of the house.

As soon as the door closed, there was a fluttering sound and a rustling in the branches of a nearby beech tree. A shape, broad and diffuse and blacker than the sky from which it descended, settled down into the Thornes' yard like a blanket of darkness. It hovered for a moment over Christina's garden, and then it shrank, the vague shadow congealing into a definite shape. A crow landed on the weed pile and swiveled its head to look at the house with its polished black eyes.

It was almost midnight. Christina woke up in pitch darkness, lying curled up on her side in their king-sized bed. Her heart pounded, although she did not know why. She felt Adam's body next to hers, one arm thrown protectively over her, his breathing soft and regular.

Had some noise awakened her? She was a sound sleeper, and though she was only covered by a thin sheet, it was a warm night and she did not feel chilled. As if in answer, she heard a soft tapping and she suddenly knew this was the sound that had disturbed her sleep.

There it was again—just a clicking sound, like a pencil tapped on a stone. Five clicks and then nothing. Then again, seven clicks. More curious than afraid, Christina extricated herself from beneath her husband's arm and stood. She reached for her robe and, pulling it on, walked out into the dark upstairs hallway.

There it was again. Four clicks, then silence. She looked down the shadowy stairway, its end invisible in the darkness of the living room below. After a moment, she began to descend the steps.

When she reached the bottom, she clicked on the light and stood silently for a moment. Nothing looked out of the ordinary. She was about to shut off the light and return to bed when it came again. Several clicks, this time coming unmistakably from behind the curtained living room window.

Christina suppressed a shudder. It was probably a June beetle, trapped between the curtain and the glass, trying to get out. Her pride in her unflappability would not allow her to summon Adam or return to bed without finding out the source of the sound. Steeling herself, she walked over to the window, reached out, and pulled the drawstring.

There, sitting on the edge of a window box full of flowers, was the crow. As she watched, it leaned forward and gave several sharp taps on the window glass.

Fear vanished in a red haze of anger. How dare this damned bird scare her like this—not once, but twice? What had she ever done to it? Christina swore beneath her breath, whirled around and went to the living room closet, where Adam kept his pellet gun. She shook it to make sure it was loaded and then unlocked the lever, all the time keeping her eye on the crow. The bird showed no sign of leaving. It watched her intently as she pumped the chamber a number of times and followed her with its eyes as she cautiously made her way back to the window.

She reached out and took hold of the slide bolt that locked the window and lifted it. As she did so, a hint of fear returned, making its cold touch felt through her irrational rage. Why not let the crow be? It wasn't hurting anything.

She knew she was just dissembling. Her sudden reluctance had nothing to do with protecting innocent wildlife. She was scared.

Badly.

"Toughen up," she said quietly, and took a deep breath. Okay, so she was scared. Big deal. Everyone gets scared sometimes.

Still, something inside her couldn't just go back to bed without somehow dealing with the situation. It was too much like letting the crow win.

But at least she'd go get Adam first. She took a step back.

As she did so, the crow lunged forward and struck the glass a sharp blow with its beak. The safety glass pane immediately shattered into a thousand pieces, crackling like popcorn over a flame. For a few seconds, the window held together and in that moment, Christina could see multiple images of the crow through the crazed glass, like a view through the multiple facets of a fly's eye. Then the window collapsed inward.

The crow hopped forward, landing on the window frame. Christina recoiled and cried out with terror and raised the gun. She did not have a chance to fire. The last thing she saw was two arms, darker than the crow's plumage, reaching out toward her—and eyes, which started out small and birdlike but rapidly metamorphosed into something unrecognizable, gazing down into hers.

4. searching in the dark

. . .

I t was well after ten o'clock in the Swenson household and they were all still awake.

Kit quickly got the impression that being up late was an unusual occurrence. Mrs. Swenson kept surreptitiously looking at the clock and Mr. Swenson yawned more than once, but it was evident there would be no putting this aside until Kit's fate had been decided.

Malachi seemed the most sympathetic to Kit's cause and Mr. Swenson the most skeptical. Mrs. Swenson's opinion was unclear. Upon some family discussion out of Kit's earshot, it was finally decided he would be allowed to spend the night. Mr. Swenson ended the discussion with, "and then we'll see." Malachi seemed satisfied with the outcome, gave him a quick, enigmatic smile, and vanished upstairs. Kit was shown into a guest bedroom on the first floor. Exhausted from the evening's crazy occurrences, he pulled his shirt off, climbed into bed and fell asleep almost instantly.

He awoke in the pitch darkness. Lying on his back in the Swenson's bed, he was acutely aware that there was something wrong. He was groggy and disoriented and had the strange sensation he had spent the entire night blindfolded and wearing earplugs.

He reconsidered. It was more as if he were immersed in a dark pool of water. His conscious mind tried to evaluate this image unsuccessfully and he chided himself.

Of course it was dark. It was nighttime.

Then, suddenly, he realized what the difference was.

He had not dreamed.

While thinking about that new and amazing piece of information, he heard again the sound that had has awoken him. Someone was pounding on the front door. He wondered if anyone heard it except him. There was no sound from the upstairs indicating they had. The Swensons must be sound sleepers. He got up, pulled on his shirt, and turned on the light. A battered digital clock on the nightstand stood at two-fifty. Kit opened the bedroom door just as Carl Swenson came stumbling down the stairs in an old plaid terry cloth bathrobe, looking much less than half awake.

Mr. Swenson went to the front door and opened it. He blocked Kit's view, so the person outside could not be seen at first. Mrs. Swenson came down the stairs together, Mrs. Swenson was also clad in a robe. Malachi, Kit noted with approval, was wearing only a pair of pajama bottoms.

"Adam, what's wrong? Come in."

Adam Thorne came into the room. His face was streaked with tears. It looked out of place on his near-perfect features. "Carl, you've got to help me. Something's happened to Christina."

"What happened?"

"I was asleep and I heard a crash. A window breaking downstairs. I woke up and Christina wasn't in bed. I guess she had gotten up before. Then I heard a scream... it was her, it was Christina. I ran downstairs and the living room window was shattered and she was gone. Carl, there's blood on the window and there was this snagged on the window latch." He opened his fist, which had been clenched tightly, to show a small fragment of cloth. "It's from her robe."

"Did you call Johnny Cole?"

"Yes. I told him that I was going to go get you and if you're willing to help, we'd meet him back at my house. Will you… please, Carl…." His voice cracked.

"Of course, son, of course. Let me just get dressed." He turned to run back up the stairs.

"Mr. Swenson!" Moved by some sudden impulse, Kit reached out and touched the older man's arm. "I'd like to help, too."

Mr. Swenson gave him a curious look. From behind them, Adam gave Kit a suspicious glance. "Who are you?"

Kit turned. "I'm Kit McIntyre, from Issaquah, Washington."

"He's our guest, Adam." Now it was Kit's turn to give his host a surprised glance. Mr. Swenson continued, "I suppose it's okay, Kit, if you want to. Malachi, you come along, too. If Cole says it's okay, you can both help."

Kit returned to his room to put his shoes on as Mr. Swenson and Malachi went upstairs to dress.

Fifteen minutes later, Kit, Malachi, and the two men arrived at Adam Thorne's house. As predicted, Chief of Police Cole was already there. Johnny Cole was a beanpole of a man, with a long, angular face, a prominent Adam's apple, and brown hair worn in an unflattering crewcut. He nodded his greetings at Adam, Malachi, and Mr. Swenson, and then he saw Kit.

"Who are you?" He asked this bluntly, much as Adam had.

"His name is Kit McIntyre. He's visiting us from Washington State." He motioned the officer aside and there was a quick whispered conversation.

Twice the policeman looked over at Kit and seemed to be appraising him. Finally, he grunted. "Okay, Kit, you can help out, but keep an eye on him, Carl. And Malachi, you be careful, too. We don't know what we're dealing with here. My guess is some sort of animal—a bear, maybe. We got to look for any signs of Christina. The sooner we do, the more likely we'll find her. I've put in calls to two of my deputies, but one lives in Carnahan and the other out North Hanville way, so it'll be at least a half hour before they're here. Meanwhile, we ought to have a look around the house. If you see anything, shout out. I've got flashlights and I brought two rifles." He walked over to his car, opened the trunk, and retrieved a heavy-duty metal flashlight for each of them. Carl Swenson was given one of the rifles and Police Chief Cole shouldered the other. "If you see any dangerous-looking animal, shoot it. If you yell for help, or hesitate, you may not get a second chance."

Five flashlight beams, crossing and recrossing, swept the ground, the bushes, and Christina's unfinished garden, silently illuminating the yard and the woods which surrounded it. The living room window had looked out over the deck where Adam had been working that evening. Most of the glass had fallen into the house, but Cole found more fragments of fabric caught on the edge of the window box, and there were several drops of blood on the deck. One of Adam's paint cans had been knocked over and had rolled off the deck into the bushes, but that alone was not enough to tell which way Christina had been taken.

The three men and two boys made as complete a search as was possible in the dark, without finding any more evidence. Except for the front drive, the Thornes' house was completely surrounded by bushes and trees, and none of the vegetation showed any sign of disturbance. There was not so much as a bent twig to give any hint as to which direction Christina's abductor had taken her.

Seven people gathered on the deck after an hour and a half's fruitless search—the four who had begun the search, and the two deputies, who had arrived about forty-five minutes earlier. Adam Thorne was nearly sick with grief and exhaustion.

"We've done all we can for tonight. I've put out a call to the state police investigators and they should be here by morning. You're gonna come home with me, Adam. Leslie and me got room. You need to sleep if you can and being in this house tonight won't be right for that. Thanks for helping, Carl, Mal. You too, Kit."

Kit nodded his head solemnly and leaned against the deck railing, wrapping his fingers around the back of the railing. Then he jerked his hand away.

"Splinter?"

"Yeah, several." Kit took his flashlight and bent over and looked under the rail. "Didn't Mr. Thorne say he'd just put in this rail?"

Mr. Swenson nodded.

"The wood's all splintered under here."

Cole and Carl Swenson looked underneath the rail. On both of the lower angles of the two-by-six which formed the top of the deck rail, there were deep gouges. On the outward-facing edge, there were three deep scars, each about six inches apart, and about a foot away an identical set of three. The inward facing edge only had two, spaced about a foot and a half apart, roughly lined up with the center of the corresponding sets of scars on the outer edge.

"Now what could'a done that?" Cole's brow furrowed. "Adam, you use a new two-by-six on this rail?"

"Yes, of course."

"And you didn't damage it putting it up?"

"I don't think so."

He pointed at the scars. "Then where did those come from?"

"I haven't got any idea."

Kit frowned at the gouges. "They look like claw marks."

Cole scowled at him. "What kind of animal can leave claw marks underneath something it's walking on?"

Kit shrugged. "Maybe something like a bird, that wraps its feet around whatever it's sitting on."

One of the deputies snickered. "It'd have to be a pretty big freakin' bird. Sucker'd have to have feet nearly a foot across."

"Shut up, Jenks. I don't hear you makin' any better suggestions. Well, I'll have the state investigators look at these marks when they get here. Until then, gentlemen, get some sleep."

The six dispersed to their various cars. Adam Thorne locked his house before leaving, though a lot of good that'd do, with a busted-out window.

Adam climbed into the passenger side of the Chief of Police's car, and put his hands over his face.

Malachi said to Kit in a low voice, "That was good spotting."

"What?"

"The claw marks."

"Thanks."

They were about to get into the Swensons' car when Kit paused. Cole was talking to Mr. Swenson in low tones.

"You really think that kid is a runaway?"

"Doggoned if I know."

"I'll put his name in the computer tomorrow and see what we can pull up. Of course, it may not be his real name."

"I know that."

"Gotta say one more thing, Carl. You've known me ever since you used to beat me up in elementary school and you'd say I was a pretty good judge of character, wouldn't you?"

Mr. Swenson chuckled. "You'd beat me up if I didn't."

"You got that right. Well, you take this for what it's worth, but I'd bet my next paycheck this kid isn't a liar. I've dealt with my share of runaways and most of 'em have 'runaway' pasted across their faces in ten-inch letters. I'd say that kid is in trouble, yes. He certainly don't know what to do next. But I don't think he's run away. Whatever his problem is, I don't think it's that. I'd say he's a good kid who's run afoul of the world somehow."

"Maybe you're right, Johnny."

Cole gave Mr. Swenson a sour look. "Yeah, I may just be, you stubborn old goat. I can tell you gonna do what you always do, which is to say Carl Swenson is right and to heck with everybody else's opinion. You better go on home, before I do beat you up. And keep an eye on that kid."

When Kit, Malachi, and Mr. Swenson arrived back at the Swensons' house, Mrs. Swenson made hot coffee and buttered toast for them and then sat down to watch them consume it. Twice Kit looked up at Malachi and got the same quirky smile as before, but each time, the other boy looked away without speaking. For a time, the only noises in the big farm kitchen were the sounds of eating and the ticking of an imitation Swiss pendulum clock on the wall, which hung above an old embroidered sampler. The sampler, much yellowed from age, showed a picture of a house and garden and bore the legend "Carl Swenson and Helen Parker, married August 15, 1975." Kit tried to picture the Swensons as newlyweds and failed utterly.

It was almost five o'clock and Mr. Swenson was clearly not intending to return to bed. "I'd have to get up in an hour anyhow. I need to overhaul the engine of my tractor this morning. She's been running rough." He took a sip of coffee.

"Strangest thing out there at Thorne's. It's like Christina just vanished into nothing."

"Didn't Adam say the window was broken?" Mrs. Swenson stood at the sink, rinsing the coffee pot.

"Yeah, but after that there's no trace of her. I'd'a sworn Johnny Cole could follow the track of a mouse over a five-acre parking lot, but he didn't see anything. Christina's not a big woman, but whatever carried her off darn sure should've left some tracks."

"It was dark, Carl."

"If the signs had been there, Johnny'd have seen them."

"How is Adam doing?"

"He's awful torn up. I don't think there's anything else that'd get at him like this has."

"He must really love her."

Mr. Swenson grunted his assent and took a bite of toast.

"Why is Johnny so sure it was an animal?"

"I guess it's hard to imagine why a man would break the window, climb in, grab her, and then drag her back out the same window when there was a door only a few feet away. And besides, Hamilton County isn't exactly a hotbed of crime."

"Would a bear really do that?" Kit asked.

Mr. Swenson frowned. "I've never heard tell of anything like it, but I don't know as I'd put it past one. Bears are unpredictable. The few times I've seen one, I've always given it plenty of room. I know there've been cases of bears attacking campers." He paused and downed the last of his coffee. "Until someone shows me another explanation, I guess I'll believe that's what happened." Mr. Swenson stood and brought his cup and plate to the sink. "Well, I'd better get to work. Time's wasting." He turned, then winced and his hand went to his side.

Mrs. Swenson moved to his side. "What's wrong?"

"Don't know. Just a twinge when I turned. Comes of not

enough sleep, I guess." He dried his hands on a towel hanging over the oven handle and went out into the back yard.

Kit yawned.

"You don't have to be awake just because my husband won't go back to bed and get enough rest himself. There's no reason for you to stay up. That goes for you, too, Malachi."

"I don't think you'll have to ask me twice, Mom," Malachi said with a smile.

"Maybe I'll take you up on that, too, Mrs. Swenson," Kit said. "Thanks."

"Good. Don't worry about breakfast. I'll fix you both something when you get up."

Kit stood and his smile vanished. "You believe me, don't you? You believe I'm telling the truth."

Mrs. Swenson looked at him thoughtfully. "I'm trying to, Kit."

"I really am. I haven't lied to you."

"I'd guess you haven't told us the whole truth, either."

He didn't respond.

"If you want someone to trust you, you should trust them with the whole truth. A half of a true story sometimes sounds more false than an outright lie."

"I don't know. If I told you the whole story, you'd probably think I was completely insane."

"I don't know about that. But I think you're in the position of having to trust us to make that judgment."

Kit shrugged. "Maybe you're right. But I'd like to tell you all together. When will Mr. Swenson come back in?"

"He'll be back in around noon, for lunch."

He smiled again. "Thanks for the coffee and toast." She nodded and returned his smile. Kit realized that it was the first time he had seen her smile and it lessened the angular harshness of her stern country face. The transformation was rather startling and Kit immediately saw her resemblance to her son.

Kit returned to the bedroom where he had slept, kicked off his shoes, and lay down on the bed fully clothed. He was asleep in five minutes.

But he still didn't dream, and the early morning hours flowed over him like a slow river of dark water.

5. thunder approaching

. . .

When Kit awoke, sunlight streamed through the window, and the black alarm clock stood at nearly ten in the morning. He stretched and sat up, feeling punchy and not fully awake. He was again aware of the absence of his usual dreams. He was sure when he awoke he lay in exactly the same position as he had fallen asleep in.

Oddly, he found himself missing the nightly rollercoaster. As much as he disliked the bruised shins and bumped heads from his tumbles out of bed in the past, he was even more acutely distressed by the silence. The two times he had fallen asleep since his arrival here were too much like his half-formed ideas about death.

A slow fall into a pitch black and empty nothingness.

The feeling of dismay had lessened by the time he exited the bedroom. He crossed the living room and the tiled kitchen, both of which were empty, and looked out the back window. Mrs. Swenson was outside, hanging up laundry. Malachi was a little farther off, dressed in shorts and a tank-top, hoeing a large and immaculate vegetable garden. Corn, beans, and tomatoes stood straight and tall, in ruler-straight rows, and hills of squash and pumpkins occupied an area just beyond.

If he were a corn plant in Mrs. Swenson's garden, he'd stand at attention too. Helen Swenson looked like the type who brooked no nonsense. However, as she stood pinning laundry to the line, there was that dancer's grace about her movements he had noticed when he had first seen her. It struck him as an odd contrast to her angular face.

He opened the door, and both Malachi and Mrs. Swenson turned. "Have they found Mrs. Thorne?"

Mrs. Swenson shook her head. "Not that we've heard. It's kind of you to ask. You must be hungry. There's cereal in the pantry next to the stove, and milk and juice in the refrigerator. Help yourself. I know I promised I'd fix you something better, but Wednesday's wash day, and the weather report on the radio says we're in for rain this afternoon. I have to get these clothes hung."

"No problem." He turned to go in, but not before he saw that Malachi had propped his hoe against the gate and was watching him.

Kit was halfway through his second bowl of cereal when Malachi came inside and silently sat down at the table. He waited for him to say something, but for a moment he just watched him, an intelligent curiosity in his dark eyes. Finally he smiled.

"Mom wasn't sure about my coming in to talk to you. I had to prove to her all of my chores were finished, and I wasn't swept away by the mystery of your arrival here. I think she thinks you might be not be trustworthy."

"I thought she believed what I said was the truth."

"It's not that. She doesn't trust city boys."

Kit blushed.

"When I go to college, I want to go somewhere urban. I don't dislike it here, but there's not much to it, you know? But Mom is worried I'll get eaten alive."

"It's not like that."

"I know. But that's not why I came in here. I wanted to tell you I believe your story."

Kit felt a rush of relief wash over him. "You do?"

"You seem pretty surprised. Don't you believe it yourself?"

"Of course. But why do you?"

"Several things. I tried to think about what I would do if I ran away, and it didn't make any sense. I took your story a piece at a time. If it was me, I'd probably give a fake name, so, I thought, maybe Kit McIntyre isn't your real name. I listened to you while you were on the phone last night..." Kit winced, and Malachi continued. "It was impossible not to. My bedroom's right above the kitchen, and voices come right up the heat ducts. My parents learned years ago not to discuss secrets in the kitchen. Besides, your voice carries. Anyway, you asked for somebody McIntyre, a woman's name..."

"Alison."

"Yeah. And I figured that might be a made up name, supposed to be your mother."

"She *is* my mother."

"Okay, but I didn't know that for sure at the time. If I'd been a runaway, I'd have called some random number, or something, once, and then have left it at that. Then, I'd have told the people whose house I was in 'my mom isn't home.' At first you did that, but then you called information, and asked for two people with really weird names..."

"Philip Amirault and Harley Claiborne. Philip's a friend of mine and Doc Claiborne is the principal at the high school I go to."

"So I said to myself, would someone make up those names, and call information about them, knowing they weren't real? Why do that? And besides, I immediately knew Harley Claiborne couldn't be made up. No one our age would make up a name that dorky."

Kit grinned. "Doc's a nice guy, actually."

"He probably is. And then there's the thing about your home town. Why make up a town? Make up a fake name for yourself, yes. But a whole town? It's too easy to check. You seemed too smart to make a mistake like that. And you seemed so surprised when it wasn't on the map. I didn't see how you could possibly have faked that. You looked like you'd been kicked by a horse."

"I felt like it."

"And maybe I just have Dad's touch for spotting liars. You look like you're telling the truth."

"Then why doesn't your father believe me?"

"I think he does, but he doesn't want to. Dad doesn't like mysteries. Things have to be straightforward and fit the routine. You don't fit." He stood. "Anyway, I'd like to show you around the village later, if you want."

"You think your mom will be okay with that?"

"It shouldn't be hard. She doesn't think you're going to beat me up and steal my wallet, or something. It's not about that kind of trust."

"But you trust me, right?"

He nodded.

"Why?"

"There you go again, arguing against yourself. I *know* you're trustworthy. I'm not sure why." He got up and walked to the door. "You really have never been in the village?"

"I thought you believed my story."

He smiled. "Right. I'd forgotten. I guess you should know where things are around here. Give me a half-hour to finish in the garden, and you can see everything you've missed by not visiting the metropolis of Finn Hill, New York." His smile widened into a grin. "Which will take even less than a half-hour."

Kit was washing his breakfast dishes when Mrs. Swenson came in, carrying the empty laundry basket. She regarded him with her usual gravity, and then walked into the laundry room, which opened off the kitchen.

"My son has asked if he can show you around." She returned from the laundry room, having stood the basket in the corner.

Kit nodded.

"I have agreed, although against my better judgment. I hardly know you."

"Mrs. Swenson..."

She held up one hand. "I'm not trying to insinuate you are up to no good. I am merely a cautious old woman, and don't wish to take any unnecessary risks with my only child."

"If you don't think it's okay, then we don't have to go together. I can go walking myself, and show myself around."

"Kit, there's something you need to understand. Malachi... he hasn't had an easy time in school for the last year. He trusts people too easily and too quickly, and has gotten hurt because of it. He's been bullied quite badly. Carl and I, we've tried to help him, but the fact is, he's barely got any friends. He's physically strong, I know that, but he's got such a soft heart, and it's been bruised a lot."

Kit nodded. How would she respond if he said, *I understand, I'm not exactly Mr. Popularity, either?* Would it make her even more suspicious of him?

In the end, all he said was, "I get it."

"You understand why I'm telling you this, and have no problem with it?"

"Yes, I understand. And no problem at all." He paused. "I would have treated him kindly even if you hadn't asked."

She gave him a grave nod. "Kit, I'm only bringing this up because I want you to know how serious I think it is. Mal is on the threshold of adulthood, but I can't help worrying that he's in for a lot more hurt, and I have to do what I can to protect him. I do trust you—God alone knows why—but you need to understand how difficult it is for me to rely on that trust."

"I appreciate that."

"I suspect Malachi's father might see things differently than I do. That's also something you should know."

Kit didn't respond.

"Anyway, have fun and be careful." One corner of her mouth curled. "Actually, I suppose if you were looking for somewhere to get into trouble around here, you would have to look hard. Finn Hill is a wide spot in the road."

Kit grinned. "I like it."

"You haven't seen it yet."

Kit and Malachi left on foot fifteen minutes later. The dirt road that ran in front of the Swensons' house was deserted. Clearly not much traffic came this way. Kit could see the bridge he had crossed at the bottom of the hill, and in the distance the steeple of the abandoned church poked up above the tops of several trees. They took the other direction, and soon both were lost to view as they topped the hill and began to descend into a small valley. Only about a mile ahead the road joined a paved street, but most of it was hidden by woods. Ahead were several houses, widely spaced and well sheltered by thickets of trees and bushes, two on the right and three on the left. The nearest one was in a state of some dilapidation. A rusted car sat on four flat tires in the side yard, and an old refrigerator leaned against the house, its door sagging open. A dented mailbox was sloppily painted with the legend "5 – Addison."

Malachi's brow furrowed with distaste. "I wish the Addisons would move out of Finn Hill. They're the only really horrible family in the village, and they live right next door to us."

Kit smiled at his definition of "right next door." In the Seattle area, "right next door" meant you shared a wall. "What's wrong with them?"

"Cleve Addison is a gross excuse for a human being. He has a huge beer belly and chain smokes." He paused. "No one ever sees Maureen Addison, his wife. I think he beats her. It would be in character. They've got about ten children. Trent is in my grade. He's third to oldest, and he's just like his father except a little thinner."

"Geez."

"It's terrible." The Addison house was now behind them, hidden by a row of poplars. "I don't even like walking past that house, although of course I do it when I have to. I always feel like some of the Addisons are staring at me as I walk by. They bullied me a lot in elementary school, especially Trent's older brothers, until Dad went and talked to Mr. Addison and told him if he heard of any more trouble from them, he'd have the police on their doorstep. It worked, I guess, although Trent still acts like a jerk sometimes."

"How long have you lived here?"

"Forever. Both my parents were born in this village. Dad's father, Lars Swenson, came here from Sweden and married a woman from the village. He once owned all of this land. Mom's family, the Parkers, have been here since the village was settled."

"So none of you ever lived anywhere else?"

"Mom spent some time in New York City before she

married Dad. She wanted to be an actress. I guess it didn't work out, and she came back."

"What happened?"

"I don't really know. She doesn't talk about it much."

They were approaching another house, this one considerably better kept. The mailbox had "4 Swenson Road" on it in adhesive stickers, but there was a tile hanging next to the door with hand-painted flowers on it, and "The Gallaghers" written underneath.

"Mr. Gallagher lives there," said Malachi.

"I see that."

"He's the real estate agent. Mr. Gallagher's a nice guy. His wife died last year in a car accident during a snowstorm. I feel sorry for him. Since she died he doesn't like guests. Mom has tried to invite him to dinner, but he always refuses." Shortly beyond Mr. Gallagher's house there was a neatly-kept cottage on the opposite side of the road. In the front yard a woman in her mid-thirties knelt, yanking at a clump of crabgrass in the middle of a large and untidy garden. She wore a sunhat and a flowered blouse with khaki shorts. She glanced up as they approached, revealing a face distorted and made owl-like by large, thick glasses.

She grinned and waved. Malachi returned the wave. "Hi, Miss Garvey."

Miss Garvey stood, pulled off her gloves, and walked over to meet them. "Hi, Mal. Who's your friend?"

"This is Kit McIntyre, from Washington State."

Miss Garvey stretched out a hand, and Kit shook it. "What brings you to New York?"

Kit glanced at Malachi. "I'm just visiting."

"Welcome. I hope you have a nice stay. Is Malachi showing you around?"

Kit nodded.

"Why don't you stop on the way back? I can make some

lemonade. I'd love to hear about Washington State. I'm afraid the farthest west I've been is Ohio."

"Thanks," Malachi said. "That sounds great."

"Better than pulling crabgrass, anyway." She grinned. "Have a nice walk."

They walked on. "Miss Garvey teaches in the elementary school. She was my second grade teacher."

Kit smiled. "Do you know everyone around here?"

"Of course." He seemed surprised at the question.

"Geez, I don't even know all the people who live on my floor in our apartment building."

"I can't imagine that. What do you do, walk around all the time without talking to anyone?

"Pretty much. Maybe people are just more private in the city."

"Do you like that?"

"I don't think about it much, I guess. Doesn't it bother you that everyone knows all about you?"

Malachi laughed. "Why should it? I haven't done anything wrong."

By this time they had reached the paved road Kit had glimpsed from the Swenson's house. To the left it curved away around the base of the broad hill they had just descended. To the right, it curved the opposite way and continued downhill, into a valley where a few buildings were clustered, maybe a half-mile away. Kit noticed that past the village, over the crest of some faraway tree-covered hills, there were a few dark clouds gathering, the first sign of the approaching rain Mrs. Swenson had mentioned earlier. For the time being, however, the sunlight still cascaded through the leaves of the maple trees that lined the street.

They turned toward the village and walked in silence. Kit realized, for the first time since his impromptu arrival, he was feeling relaxed and happy. It was a beautiful warm day, and he was delighted with Malachi's trust in him. He was no closer to figuring out what had happened to him, but just having someone who believed his story—what he had told him of it—made a huge difference.

And the fact that he was handsome and had a great smile didn't hurt either.

The center of the village of Finn Hill, New York seemed to be nothing more than a post office, a gas station, a grocery store, a hardware and feed store, and a tiny library. A few other small businesses were clustered on the opposite side. Several side streets ran off the main road, and a handful of widely-spaced houses could be seen among the trees. It was clean and well-kept and, to Kit's city eyes, entirely charming. Past the hardware store on the far end of the village, set apart from the rest of the buildings and separated from the main road by a fence, was a complex of low brick buildings that could only be a school.

"Finn Hill Elementary." Malachi pointed in the opposite direction. "I go to North Hamilton Regional High School, about four miles up that way."

As they walked down the sidewalk which bordered the road, Kit became aware that they were being watched by an old man who stood in front of an ancient structure, leaning on a broom. The shop carried a sign saying "Antiques." It was an appropriate label for the store itself, which could easily have been vintage 1800. The man didn't smile, but his gaze followed them as they walked. Kit became uncomfortable, and kept glancing at the man.

Malachi seemed to have an unusual knack for sensing what Kit thought. "Don't pay any attention to him. That's Mr. Averill Parker. He owns the antique store, and is the crankiest old geezer you've ever met. He hates anything new. He's some distant kin of Mom's, but she doesn't claim him. He doesn't like outsiders, even though they're the only ones who buy his antiques. He always keeps his eye on everything. Dad once told him he should sell his shop and start a business as a private detective. That made him pretty mad, and he hasn't spoken to Dad since." Malachi grinned. "I think Mr. Parker thinks Dad is an outsider because his father wasn't born in the village. Pretty crazy."

With little warning, the dark clouds Kit had seen on the horizon swallowed up the sun. The temperature seemed to drop ten degrees in a matter of seconds. There was a sound of thunder in the hills, distant, followed by a louder and nearer clap.

"Uh-oh," said Malachi. "I'm glad I got the garden done."

A few large drops of water came down, and there was the sudden sharp odor of wet pavement. Then the sky opened up, and sheets of rain came sluicing down. Kit had never seen rain this hard, nor this sudden. The difference between this and the typical Pacific Northwest drizzle was like the difference between a spring breeze and a tornado. They were soaking wet within the first minute. Malachi clapped Kit on the shoulder and together they broke into a run. They crossed the street, which already flowed like a river, and burst into the door of the Nice 'n' Easy Grocery Store, where they stood, laughing and dripping. Thunder boomed, and the panes rattled. A middle-aged woman, slightly overweight and with gray-brown hair in an untidy bun, stood behind the counter grinning at them.

"Lord, you two look like drowned rats. Who's your friend, Mal?"

"His name's Kit. He's visiting, and I'm showing him around. Kit, this is Mrs. Bedford."

"Hi."

"Hi yourself." Mrs. Bedford's grin widened. "Malachi Swenson, your mama's gonna be worried sick with you out in this thunder. You want to call her?"

"She knows I have enough sense to come in out of the rain."

Marie chuckled. "Don't look like you do."

Kit glanced around the store. Except for Marie Bedford behind the counter and themselves, the store seemed empty. Then there was a dull clunk as one of the doors shut on a refrigerated compartment in the back, and a tall, heavy-set boy with a sullen expression walked out from behind a shelf, carrying a package of Twinkies and a bottle of Coke. He looked over in their direction. His eyes ran over Malachi, and his mouth twisted in disdain. Malachi stared at him levelly for a second—the challenge was obvious—then turned toward Kit in a deliberate fashion. The boy only then seemed to notice Kit, and his eyes narrowed.

Malachi put his hand on Kit's upper arm, and gave him a smile that looked a little forced. "The rain's letting up. We're already wet, you want to keep walking?"

The boy turned away and plunked his Twinkies and Coke down on the counter, but still kept throwing them sidewise glances. Kit and Malachi walked out of the store.

The rain had decreased to a stiff drizzle. The storm itself seemed to have already moved farther up the valley. They stood for a moment on the sidewalk.

"Trent Addison." Malachi wasn't smiling anymore.

"Looks like a real creep."

They began to walk back up Main Street, the way they had come, but on the opposite side of the road. They passed under the awning of the antique shop. The rain seemed to have dampened Mr. Averill Parker's inquisitiveness, and he was nowhere to be seen. They continued walking past the village clerk's office, the post office, and the library, and on up the maple-lined sidewalk toward Swenson Road.

They walked in silence. Somehow the encounter with Trent Addison had spoiled the sweetness of the day. Kit's mind had returned to his dilemma, and the strangeness of his being here at all—his mother, who was probably having a nervous breakdown by now, and Philip, who must be wondering what had happened to him, if he had not had a heart attack outright when Kit vanished. By this time the rain had stopped, but the trees still dripped chilly rainwater as they passed, and farther down the valley they heard more thunder. Another shower was on its way.

He looked over at Malachi, trying to recapture some of what he'd felt earlier, but the other boy seemed lost in thought, and wouldn't meet his eyes.

They had just turned onto the dirt road leading up to the Swensons' house when a bicycle bore down on them from behind, and struck a mud puddle, splattering them both. The rider swerved in front of them to block their way, and ground to a halt, grinning insolently.

"Got yourself a boyfriend, Malachi Swenson?"

"Get out of our way, Trent." Malachi's face was closed and his eyes clouded with anger. The transformation was instantaneous. It was a side of him Kit had not yet seen.

"He looks gayer than you are, and that's saying something. Maybe Jim, Andy and I should give him a haircut."

Kit flushed. "Try it."

Trent's head swiveled toward Kit, and his grin vanished. "Okay. Maybe I should give you a haircut and something else, too."

There was a gust of wind, and a shower of droplets fell from the trees above them. Kit did not move, and his eyes never left the other boy's face. "Like I said. Try it."

"Kit." Malachi put his hand on his arm.

"'Kit,'" Trent mocked. "Gay name, too."

"Touch him, Trent, and Dad'll have the Chief of Police on your doorstep before noon."

"Your queer little boyfriend told me to try it himself." He shrugged. "Asked me to. Tell your Dad that." With a motion quicker than looked possible for someone so heavy, he swung his leg over the seat of his bicycle and at the same time launched a meaty fist at Kit's face. Trent was fat but strong, and his strike would probably have blackened Kit's eye, if not worse. But the blow never landed. Kit took a graceful step backwards, and his left arm came up and deflected the punch. An instant later, Kit's right fist connected with Trent's breastbone.

The breath came out of the larger boy in a wheezing gust. His face purpled, but he stammered out a few hoarse obscenities and tried another punch. An easy sidestep, and this one missed entirely. Kit's body pivoted, his left foot swiveling smoothly on the wet ground. His right foot shot upward and across, making solid contact with Trent's face. Trent staggered backward, tripped over his bicycle, and fell flat on his back in the mud.

Kit looked at Trent for a moment, waiting to see if he'd get up. He didn't. He was winded and hurt, and apparently not used to anyone being able to withstand his size and strength advantage. He glared at Kit and Malachi, and they gazed calmly back. Finally Kit spoke in a disgusted voice. "Let's get out of here." They walked around Trent and his toppled bike. Trent began struggling to his feet, his eyes dark with fury, but he did not follow them.

As soon as they passed out of earshot, Malachi whispered, "What was that?"

"Tae Kwon Do." Kit felt strangely like laughing. It was the first time he had ever used it to defend himself. "Me and some of my friends take classes three times a week. I'm only a blue belt. You should see my sister—she's three years younger than I am and started at the same time as I did, but she's only one step from black belt. She could kick my butt any day of the week."

"Wow. I'm... I'm really impressed." Malachi looked over at Kit, a blush rising in his cheeks. "I'm sorry, though. Kit, I'm..." He looked up, and took a deep breath. "Trent thinks 'gay' is the worst insult there is. Most people around here don't think like that, but he and his family—well, they've been calling me that for years. I'm sorry, I didn't want you to have to… you know, deal with guilt by association."

"Don't worry about me." He paused. "It's not like I don't have to deal with that sometimes myself."

Malachi met his eyes, and gave a solemn nod.

Kit was on the verge of saying, *Look, I understand, I'm gay.* But in the end he just said, "Homophobes are idiots."

Something in Malachi's face relaxed, and he closed his eyes for a moment and took another deep breath. "I'm sorry about what Trent did. I wish… I wish your first impression of the village didn't involve him."

"It's okay. There are idiots wherever you go. And plenty of nice people, you know? You can't let the morons make you hate everyone."

Malachi nodded, and they continued their walk up the road in silence.

Finally Malachi laughed again. "I can't wait to tell Dad you punched Trent Addison."

Kit frowned. "Will it make him mad?"

Malachi's laugh turned into a deep guffaw. "On the contrary. The only thing that would make Dad happier than your punching Trent Addison is if you had punched his father and all his brothers, one after the other."

6. skin deep

. . .

When Kit and Malachi arrived back at the Swensons' house, Mr. Swenson stood at the kitchen sink washing his hands. He wore an oil-stained flannel shirt and a pair of old blue jeans, still with large dark patches on the shoulders, back, and legs where the rain had caught him before he'd run for cover. He turned as they entered the kitchen, and looked at them nearsightedly. His wire-rimmed glasses sat on the counter, waiting their turn for cleaning and drying.

"Got rained on." Kit wasn't sure if he was referring to them or himself.

"You sure have big storms in this part of the country," said Kit.

"Just a squall. I've seen worse." He pointed out toward the barn. "Two years ago, storm knocked over a big old silver maple tree right onto the barn roof. That was a heck of a storm. Haven't seen wind like that before or since."

"Dad," said Malachi. "On the way back from the village, Kit got in a fight."

Kit gave him an alarmed look, but he would not meet his eye.

Mr. Swenson's eyebrows rose. "Who you been fighting with, son?" His voice was level, but cold. "I don't hold with anyone coming into our village and stirring up trouble."

"It was Trent." Malachi's voice sounded like he was struggling not to burst into wild peals of laughter. "Trent Addison. He threatened both of us, and I think he really wanted to pick a fight. He threw a punch at Kit, and Kit blocked it and then kicked him across the road."

"Did you now?" Mr. Swenson's eyebrows rose until they nearly met his receding hairline. "Well, now."

"I didn't really kick him that far."

Mr. Swenson cut him off. "Don't worry, son. That boy's had it coming to him for years now. High time somebody stood up to them Addisons. I wouldn't complain if you kicked him all the way to Lake Ontario." He cleared his throat. "Only thing is, you'd better watch your back, next few days. Trent and his brothers'll be out for your blood, if I know them, and likely their father too. Worse than animals, the lot of them. I want you to stay away from them, Kit, and you, too, Malachi. You might be able to handle Trent—sounds like you can look after yourself all right, I guess—but the next time you can bet Trent won't be alone. Couple of years ago, I heard Marty Kern up North Hanville way started talking rough with Trent's brother Andy in a bar, and pretty soon the two of them were shoving each other. Bartender broke it up, but the next day Andy got together with Jim, the oldest of the Addisons, and some of their friends, and they beat up Marty so bad his mother hardly even recognized him. Andy spent a week in the county jail for drunk and disorderly, but Marty wouldn't press charges for assault. Figured next time it'd be a knife or a shotgun, and not just a bunch of fists."

Kit nodded.

"Anyway, son, you watch yourself. Stick around here, and don't go anywhere by yourself, at least until we see how they're gonna react." He paused, and wiped his glasses with a damp rag. A faint smile turned up the corners of his mouth. "But hot dog, I wish I'd been there to see Trent go flying."

"Landed on his back in a mud puddle." Malachi gave his father a gleeful grin.

"Did he? Well now," he clapped Kit on the shoulder, "that's just about the best thing I've heard all day. Makes up for these doggone aches and pains. Spent too long under that tractor in the damp. Your mama's gonna read me the riot act." He scratched absently at a place on his palm where the oil and grime had ground into his skin, beyond the reach of the soap. "Don't help that I'm using up all of her soap washing my hands instead of using my gloves to keep 'em clean. I hate them gloves. Can't feel a thing through 'em."

"I'll fix us some lunch since you're in, Dad. Where's Mom?"

"Believe she went upstairs to put away some of the laundry. She had to use that dryer after all. Rain came sooner than she expected." He winced as the patch of dirty skin on his hand flaked off unexpectedly. "Ouch! Damn."

Helen Swenson walked in, her face in its usual serious set, but one eyebrow was raised. "Carl, I do believe St. Peter will one day have a word with you about your tongue."

"And I'll tell him I've already heard it all from you. Skin on my palm is peeling, and it hurts like mad." He held his palm closer to his eye. A small white patch lay underneath where the skin had come away, but there was no bleeding.

"I'll get you some hand lotion. Although you wouldn't have this problem if you'd only wear your work gloves."

Mr. Swenson half turned his head to Kit and slowly winked one eye. It was at that moment Kit realized that he'd reached some sort of a new level with the Swensons. Maybe things were looking up. Maybe now he could tell them what really happened, and see if he could find out how to get himself home.

As it happened, further discussion of Kit's arrival in Finn Hill, and speculation on how he would get home, was deferred to the evening meal. Mr. Swenson obviously wanted to get back to work outside as quickly as possible after lunch, and Mrs. Swenson had asked Malachi to drive down to Carnahan to pick up some groceries. Kit followed Mr. Swenson out into the field behind the house and helped him as far as was possible for someone with no experience of farm work. However, he provided a good bit of help with lifting, hauling, and fetching, as Mr. Swenson's arthritis was acting up a bit. He moved stiffly and with a lot of grunts and groans. Kit also provided a few moments of unintentional amusement. At one point Mr. Swenson, peering into the interior of his antiquated John Deere tractor, asked Kit if he could find him the big Allen wrench.

"Big Allen who?" Mr. Swenson pulled his head out from under the hood and laughed harder than Kit had yet seen him laugh.

"You *are* a city boy." He pulled out an old handkerchief and wiped his eyes. "I don't know, Kit. 'Big Allen who.' That's pretty good."

Kit flushed with embarrassment. "I..."

"Oh, don't worry about it, son. I'm just having you on. I'm sure you know about all sorts of things that you run into in the city I never heard of. If I was there I probably wouldn't last ten minutes, and in that ten minutes I'd probably make a fool out of myself at least ten times."

He gave Kit his crooked half smile, and Kit grinned back.

The evening meal was obviously a point of pride with Mrs. Swenson. Whether she did this every night or not there was no way to know, but compared to the quick meals Mrs. McIntyre usually threw together, it was a feast. She had baked a chicken with a number of foil-wrapped potatoes, and cooked a large pot of broccoli that only that afternoon had been growing in their garden. Kit didn't tell her he hated broccoli, and told himself he'd eat some with a smile rather than offend her. Several years of politely drinking Philip Amirault's odd herbal tea concoctions had forced him to learn gracious table manners.

After they sat, Mr. Swenson pronounced grace. This was novelty to Kit, whose father was a cheerful atheist and mother was a guilt-ridden lapsed Catholic. For ten minutes they ate in total silence. Kit glanced surreptitiously at the other three, hardly wanting to breathe for fear of doing something unacceptable to his hosts. Mr. Swenson concentrated on his food. Mrs. Swenson sat very upright in her chair, looking every so often at the others to make certain they ate. She herself had taken very small servings. When Kit looked at Malachi, he found that once again he was looking at him, but reddened immediately and looked away. Kit cleared his throat.

"Excuse me." He sounded awkward, but breaking the silence reigning over the Swensons' meal seemed to require an apology.

"Yes?" Mr. Swenson looked up from his steaming baked potato. He set down his knife and fork. Kit swallowed. He'd never been with a family who seemed to find eating and conversation mutually exclusive.

"I want to tell you all exactly what happened yesterday, when I arrived here. Before I arrived, I mean."

Mr. Swenson exchanged a glance with his wife, whose face remained impassive. "Go ahead."

Kit took a deep breath, and began. "I have a friend in Issaquah. His name is Philip Amirault. He's an author, and he lives in the apartment downstairs from mine. He's kind of a strange guy, but he's really nice. Well, yesterday morning he invited me to his apartment. He's a famous author, or at least I guess he is. He's published a bunch of books. He'd said he wanted to talk to me about an idea for a new book he was writing, or something. When I got there, he showed me some glasses he'd picked up in a book store somewhere... somewhere in Texas, I think. Anyway, his eyes are really bad, and he wanted me to try them on. The guy he bought them from had said they were magic glasses. So I put them on. When I did, the whole apartment seemed to melt away, and it made me really dizzy. I couldn't stay on my feet. It's like I couldn't figure out which way was up. I fell down, and passed out for a moment. Or maybe more than a moment, I don't know. Anyhow, I landed on my back in front of that old church. I looked around for a while, and saw your house in the distance, so I walked here."

They stared at him, whether in amazement, disbelief, or both, was impossible to tell. "It's the truth, I swear."

"Don't swear." Mrs. Swenson's voice was quiet, level. "It's not proper."

"But it is true."

Mr. Swenson looked at Kit, his eyes narrowing. "Son, I just don't know what to make of you."

Kit did not respond.

"Where are these glasses?"

"I threw them through the church window. I was mad, and really scared, and I thought they were dangerous, so I took them off and pitched them."

"I see. They'd still be there, then."

Kit shrugged. "I guess they must be."

"Maybe we should go look for them."

"Would you believe me if we found them?"

"I'm not sure I don't believe you now." Mrs. Swenson gave her husband a quick, sharp glance, but he continued. "Now, I know what you told us sounds crazy. But I been thinking about this nearly all day. I been placing myself in your shoes. If I was a runaway, I sure would come up with some sort of plausible story before I tried to ask someone for a night's lodging. You didn't. In fact, you seemed as surprised as we were about all what's happened. Then you do us a good turn by kicking that Addison boy's fat rump when he gave our son some trouble, and help me out all afternoon. Okay, I might do that if I was a runaway, worm my way into the family's good graces, you might say. But then, just when things are going smooth, you tell us some kind of crack-brained story about a pair of magic glasses. Son, I got to tell you. Either you're telling the truth, or you're plain crazy."

"I don't believe in magic," said Mrs. Swenson curtly. Kit noticed that she had balled up her napkin in one fist.

"Me neither," said Mr. Swenson. "And maybe this isn't magic. Maybe this is just something you and me don't know about. There's got to be lots of things out there we don't know about that'd seem like magic to us, and that're just God's way of dealing with a world a lot more complicated than a couple of country hicks like us'll ever know. We don't have to under-stand it, Helen. But like I said. I been thinking about it all day, and I decided he's telling the truth, however impossible his story. I'd lay odds we'd go up to the old church, and those glasses would be somewhere inside."

Mrs. Swenson set her crumpled napkin on the table gently, with a tense but restrained motion, and nervously placed her hand back in her lap.

"Kit." He looked at her, and their eyes met. "I just want you to say it to me. You've said it before, but look at me and say it. Are you lying to us? About anything, anything at all?"

Kit's gaze did not waver. "Mrs. Swenson, I sw... I've told you the truth about everything. What I just told you—about the glasses and all—is the truth. I know it seems crazy. I don't understand it. Right now I just want to go home." Kit suddenly found himself near to crying, and bit the inside of his cheek, hoping the pain would stop it. It didn't work. His eyes spilled over, and several tears tracked down his face. "I miss my mother and my sister so much. They must be worried sick about me. I didn't even get a chance to tell them goodbye, a real goodbye." Malachi looked away from him, his face inscrutable. He seemed to be fighting his own reaction to Kit's pain.

"Son, how can we help you? I mean, if your home town isn't even on the map..."

"I know. I don't understand it. It's like someone took me out of the world I know. Like this is another world, that's sort of like mine, but different in places. I don't know how to get back."

Malachi looked up at him. "When you... found yourself here, were you still wearing the glasses?"

"Yes."

"Did things look different through them? I mean, you said when you put them on in your friend's apartment, everything changed and looked different."

"No. Things looked just the same with them on as with them off. I thought of that, that maybe if I put them on again, they'd bring me back. But having them on here didn't do anything."

There was a silence.

Mr. Swenson finally spoke. "I just don't know how we can get you home when you don't seem to have a home to get to any more."

"What happened when I put on those glasses? How could my putting on a pair of glasses have changed everything?"

"I'd guess that if we could figure that out, we could get you back where you need to be."

Mrs. Swenson abruptly stood. Her angular features were set. "Well, I can't abide this discussion any more. There's something about this that offends me down to the core. It's just not right. Kit, I believe you, but it's beyond me what to make out about how it all happened. I'm sorry for you, and you can stay here as long as you need to, as far as I'm concerned, but this will bring trouble. Mark my words. Someone—maybe that friend of yours, I don't know—has meddled with something that shouldn't be meddled with. I just can't bear to sit here discussing it like... like it was the day's weather. I just can't bear it." She turned to exit the room.

"Helen." Mr. Swenson stood, but as he turned toward her, he gave a gasp of pain, and his face twisted into a grimace. He grasped his side, and clutched the table for support. Malachi shouted, "Dad!" and he and Kit both leaped up from their chairs. Mrs. Swenson, frozen to the spot, shouted, "Carl, what is it?" in a frightened voice.

Mr. Swenson straightened up slowly, wincing as he did so. "God almighty, it hurts," he said in a weak voice. "Not inside. My skin hurts. It's been sensitive all day."

Malachi crossed to him. "Let's see," he said in a firm voice. He obediently untucked his shirt, and pulled it up, exposing his side. Malachi and Kit saw what had happened immediately, and stood horrified. Mrs. Swenson slowly, as if in a dream, walked over to her husband, and then she saw as well. In patches all up and down his side, Mr. Swenson's skin seemed to have become brittle. It had pulled together and split, like the surface of a pond after the first hard freeze of winter. A network of cracks cobwebbed across the surface. Kit was immediately reminded of the dry skin on Mr. Swenson's palm earlier that day, for where it had cracked, it did not bleed at all. And underneath, where the skin had pulled away, his natural ruddy coloration had been replaced by a smooth, pure white.

7. a walk in the woods

. . .

Adam Thorne woke up early Wednesday morning. He had slept soundly, helped no doubt by a dose of sleeping pills which Leslie Cole, the Chief of Police's wife, had dispensed. Adam noticed that she had taken care to lock them up in a cabinet afterwards and pocket the key. Probably afraid he'd take the whole bottle. Actually, he was still so deeply in shock that until then the idea of suicide had not even occurred to him. His mental faculties felt numbed, and he walked through the hours like a zombie. Perhaps when he really realized what had happened, he'd kill himself. Not now. Right now he didn't care if he lived, but he didn't feel like he had the energy to commit suicide.

The state police had come and gone, Christina was listed as a missing person, and an APB was sent out requesting leads. Nothing had come of it in the twenty-four hours since. As Adam dressed, he stared at himself in the mirror. His face was pale beneath his summer tan, his hair disheveled, his eyes dull. He thought about trying to make himself more presentable, then decided he didn't care. He finished buttoning his shirt, pulled on his pants, zipped them, and fastened the snap, all the time watching himself without expression.

Leslie Cole was frying bacon as he entered the kitchen. Sunlight streamed in through the window, past an exuberant variety of lush and well-cared-for house plants.

"Morning, Adam."

He heard the sympathy in her voice. Adam bristled at her tone, then forced the feeling away. Leslie was known throughout the village as one of the most caring people around, and had a hand in almost every good cause she could find, from the Presbyterian Church Bazaar to the SPCA Pet Adoption Program in Carnahan, fifteen miles away. Adam once heard a coworker laughingly wonder over the lunch table how "that ugly old buzzard Johnny" had ever captured her heart. Another replied, with some amazement in his voice, that Leslie and Johnny had been sweethearts since high school. Johnny Cole had been the captain of the basketball team up at Regional, and Leslie Preston had split her time between the cheerleading squad, the school chorus, and exciting the awed admiration of almost every senior boy in the school. They were married at nineteen, parents at twenty. They had two children, who were now both away at college—a son downstate in Colville, New York, and a daughter, *way* downstate—at the University of Alabama.

No accounting for taste, the first guy had said. Hardly seemed fair.

That left no real room for any response but a nod, but Adam still remembered the conversation.

So it was no surprise Leslie immediately took him in, even though she hardly knew him. Helping people was a way of life for her.

"Like some bacon? Johnny'll be down in a moment. You can join us for breakfast."

Adam sat down at the table, and filled a glass with orange juice.

Johnny Cole walked in a moment later, straightening his tie. "Morning, honey." He gave Leslie a quick kiss, and added, "Morning, Adam."

Adam cleared his throat. "Good morning."

Cole looked at his wife, and their eyes met momentarily. Then he sat down across the table from Adam. "Before I go off to work, I just want to let you know what's been going on. State police've got an all-points bulletin out on Christina. They've combed the woods, from Main Street all the way to the Haverhill Road. Nothing so far."

Adam didn't respond.

"I'm going back out to your house today. I want to give one more look to the place. It rained pretty hard yesterday afternoon, but I still can't help but think we missed something."

"Do you want me to help?" Adam's voice sounded flat and unemotional.

"If you want to, I won't stop you. But if it's too hard for you to go back just now, I sure wouldn't argue with you on that, either. It's really up to you."

"I'd like to help. When are you going to be there?"

"Oh, probably about ten-thirty, eleven o'clock. I got a bunch of damned paperwork to clean up at the station, but then I can take a drive up to your place, as long as Cleve Addison don't start beating his wife, or Mike Latimer and his friends don't decide to run their dirt bikes through Lem Stutes's cornfield again. If things are quiet, I'll probably give it till lunchtime and see what I can find."

"I'll walk up and meet you."

Leslie frowned. "I can give you a ride, Adam."

Adam smiled wanly, like a shadow of his former life, a life that had effectively ended a day and a half ago. "I think I'd like to walk, thanks. It will give me a chance to think. And to remember."

Adam left at ten o'clock. The Coles lived in a secluded area south of the village, and it was about four miles in a straight line from their house to Adam's. Adam was a fast walker and figured he could make it in about an hour if he took the old hiking path through the woods instead of sticking to the main roads. This would bring him up behind Carl Swenson's fields. He could wade Sterling Creek and strike the road below the old Methodist church, then walk the remaining quarter-mile along the road.

The thunderstorms of the previous afternoon had cleared the air, and it was fresh, cool, and pleasant. It took Adam about ten minutes, walking along a path that skirted corn-fields and a low tree-covered hill, to reach Main Street. Two cars passed him, one of them a red sports car driven by Arnold Kretz, a science teacher at Regional, who waved at him and grinned.

He hadn't heard what happened yet. That was obvious. As soon as people find out about a tragedy, they don't smile at you any more. They don't know what to say. It embarrasses people. He wondered briefly why that was, as he crossed the road. Maybe people feel like when your life changes, you change too, and they don't know you any more.

And maybe they're right.

The trail continued on the other side of the road, but almost immediately curved off into the trees. There were still wet spots from the previous day's rains, but the track was grassy and mud puddles easy to avoid. The midsummer flowers—early asters, butterfly weed, chicory, and goldenrod —were everywhere. Adam passed a red squirrel sitting in the middle of the path, eating a beech nut. It watched him with its bright eyes, waiting until he was only five feet away to run, chattering, up the nearest tree. A pair of woodpeckers drummed on a tree trunk, which had been knocked sideways during a recent storm and had ended propped diagonally against another tree. It was a typical calm, mild summer day in the Adirondacks.

Everything Adam saw, however, simply reinforced the endless tape-loop that had begun playing in his mind that morning, when he awoke to a certainty that Christina was gone, gone forever. He knew they were still looking for her, would be for a while, but in his heart there was no doubt she was dead.

Christina wasn't here to see this.

Beautiful flowers. But who cared? Christina loved flowers, and she wasn't here to enjoy these.

Adam topped a hill, and the trees were thinner there. In the distance he saw the backs of first Tony Gallagher's house, and then the Swensons', past the corn fields that ran behind both houses.

Nice people. All of them were nice people. They should have made more friends here. Adam wished all those nice people had known Christina before it was too late. At least Tony Gallagher would understand. Tony was a widower, too.

Widower. How desperately empty the word sounded.

As he walked, the litany continued. He was powerless to halt the voices in his mind. By this time, he wasn't sure he wanted to. It seemed the only link left with his old life, a life that had suddenly ceased less than twelve hours ago.

Adam descended the other side of the hill, and the houses were lost to view again. The trail dropped into a steep-sided gully with a tiny, nameless trickle of water at its bottom, running down toward Sterling Creek. The trees became denser, and the dappled light gave way to shadow. Ferns sprouted from crevices in the boulders, and there was more underbrush. This was when he first heard the noises—a rustle, at first distant, then nearer. A furtive scrambling. Probably some sort of animal. He wondered if there were bears around here. He had never seen one, but he recalled Chief of Police Cole saying it had probably been a bear that had taken Christina.

He stopped. The rustling was now directly behind him. He turned, and a thicket of bushes he had just passed shivered, and then was still. Wind, he told himself, but his neck prickled, the way it does when you've found that a stranger is staring at you.

Only the wind, he told himself.

The trail, paralleling the gully's downhill course, wound in and out of a group of large lichen-encrusted rock outcrops. It then went down a coarse set of stairs which the village powers-that-be had seen fit to set into the creekside two years ago, after the mayor's wife, leading a gaggle of "underprivileged city kids" from Watertown on a nature walk, had slipped on the steep slope and skidded all the way down the hill on her ample posterior. Adam passed around the boulders and stood on the top step, when he felt that prickly sensation again, and whirled around. In the dense shadow surrounding the outcrops of rock, there was a darker shadow. A somehow misshapen shadow, one that had no corresponding object to account for its presence. Adam blinked once, twice. It was still there. He tried to make out what it could be the shadow of, but its shape corresponded to no known object in his mind. Breathing hard, he turned and walked toward it. Then, as he reached the nearest of the large rocks, the shadow abruptly vanished. When he passed the boulder and looked around it and down the path, there was nothing there.

Fear effectively derailed the revolving litany of tragedy messages in his brain. There was no longer any time for selfpity. He was scared as hell. Something, something large and unseen, followed him. He thought of the gouge-marks on the deck rail, the marks that kid had found. Cole hadn't been able to explain them. Where had they come from? He pondered it for a moment, and then decided at this point, he didn't really care. He turned back toward the steps. Right at the moment, what he wanted was to reach his house safely, and find Cole there. There was a difference between two people facing a mysterious something in the woods, and one person facing it alone. It may have been only a psychological difference, but it was still a difference.

A huge one.

Adam had been a runner for years, and coached track at the high school. In his college days had been a decent sprinter and hurdler, and still raced in local 5Ks, 10Ks, and half-marathons. Almost reflexively he began to run down the trail, and immediately heard the rustling noises, now coupled with cracking of branches, match his speed. He reached the bank of Sterling Creek where the trail struck it at right angles, and jumped in without hesitation. The creek was only about three feet deep at its deepest, but was fast and cold. The clear water was icy on his sneaker-clad feet. He was across it in less than a second, and pelted up the other side.

At this point, he ventured a quick look over his shoulder, and was immediately sorry that he had done so. All he caught was a sidelong glimpse of a shadow on the opposite bank, where he had been only seconds before, but it was enough to bring his heart into his mouth with wild terror. The shadow instantly slipped sideways and vanished into some alder brush near where the trail intersected the creek. Whatever it was, was in those bushes watching him, he was sure. And it wasn't human. No human could move so quickly through underbrush. He was being stalked by some animal, and it was playing with him. At any time it would strike, and have done with him, like a cat tired of releasing and recapturing a mouse, and give him a death blow. Adrenaline poured into his veins, and all of his careless lethargy was gone. He wanted to live—oh, God, he wasn't ready to die, especially not underneath the claws of some predator....

Without warning, a nearby bush shuddered. The creature, whatever it was, had somehow crossed the creek downstream of the trail, and was less than ten feet away. Adam turned and sprinted down the path, his breath whining in his throat. He fled headlong up the trail, the unseen shadow-thing on his heels. Twice he thought he felt a sharp claw snag his shirt and then pop free, but it may have only been low branches of the overhanging trees.

He burst out of the trees and onto Old Church Road, his breath in ragged gasps. He continued to pelt down the road, past the abandoned Methodist Church, his feet kicking up globs of mud. His lungs ached, and sweat streamed from his face and soaked his t-shirt, but he didn't dare stop. Without the cover of the underbrush, he heard nothing following him, but this meant if he turned around, he would see the actual thing itself, pursuing him. He couldn't do that. He couldn't stop and face it. He knew once he got a glimpse of the nightmare that was hunting him, he would lie down in the extremity of his terror and let it rip him to bloody shreds.

He passed the head of Swenson Road, and continued running uphill, toward his house. He had turned the last curve of the road before his driveway when he heard a noise behind him. The noise of a different sort of pursuer. It was not the furtive rustle of whatever had hunted him in the forest, but the hoarse rumble of a car's engine. He stopped and turned, in time to see Chief of Police Cole's car round the bend toward him.

Adam stood and waited, his racing heart pounding in his ribcage, his breaths coming painful and rapid. He bent over, hands on his knees, head hanging downward. He coughed several times and spat into the grass on the side of the road, then looked up again as Cole's car slowed to a stop next to him.

"Jeezly crow." Cole spoke through the open car window. "What the heck happened to you? You look like you seen a ghost!"

Adam leaned his forehead against the frame of the window. "I think I did."

"What do you mean?"

Adam looked back down the road. The summer's day was calm, the trees and bushes undisturbed by anything more violent than a soft and intermittent breeze. "I'm not sure. Something chased me through the woods. I never really saw it clearly, but I heard it. I guess it's gone now."

Cole looked at Adam closely. "You sure you wasn't just thinking about what happened... the other night, and it got the best of you? I mean, it would be understandable if...."

"I'm sure. I heard it, and I saw it, or at least its shadow, several times."

"Holy Moses. No idea what it was? A bear, maybe?"

"If it was a bear, it moved quickly. And it didn't make much noise. I don't think it was very large, from the sound of it, but its shadow was big. It was agile. Good at keeping out of sight."

"All I can say, is you're either fast, or lucky, or both. Let's go up to the house and see what we can find there. Hop in."

Adam opened the car door, but could not resist one more glance down the road. From where they were, the steeple of the Methodist Church could just be seen above the nearest trees.

As he stood there, he got a glimpse of something dark fluttering around the window in the steeple.

He gripped the side of the car door, and without taking his eyes off the steeple, hissed, "Johnny! Look!"

Cole was out of his car in a moment, and looking back in the direction of the steeple. He was able to get only a few seconds' sight of a shadow dancing in front of the steeple window—a shadow that, for a moment, was considerably larger than the window itself. Then, as the two men watched from their vantage point on the road, the darkness gathered itself up, and was swallowed into the window and vanished like a veil of smoke.

8. the knife's edge

. . .

While Adam Thorne prepared to leave Cole's house on the walk that would become a run for his life, Trent Addison was lying in bed palpating a huge bruise over his left cheekbone and plotting revenge.

He had returned home in a black rage the previous day, covered with mud. He ached from his various injuries, and he had trudged back down the road pushing his bicycle and swearing under his breath. He would go home, tell his father and his two older brothers about what had happened, and then that queer weirdo, he'd pay. And so would Malachi, regardless of his threats about what his father and the Chief of Police would do.

Trent's father was three-quarters drunk when he arrived, and so was his eldest brother, Jim. But much to Trent's amazement, and to the immeasurable darkening of his anger, they both laughed at him when he told them what happened. Laughed at him! Cleve Addison had elbowed Jim and pointed at Trent.

"He looks like he been wallowing around with the pigs," he bellowed, and both laughed.

Trent scowled. "I didn't know he knew karate or whatever. Took me by surprise. But it won't happen again. And I know he won't be able to stand up to all of us together."

Cleve sneered at his son. "Don't know, boy. You can't handle your own problems, don't ask us to take care of 'em for you."

"Dad...."

"Cryin' home to daddy," snickered Jim, who was twenty-three and worked at the Carnahan Texaco Station when he wasn't on an overnighter in jail for drunk and disorderly conduct. He took another swallow of beer, and he and his father both laughed again.

Trent stared at them in disbelief for a moment, and then stormed out of the room and upstairs to his bedroom. He had been slapped both physically and emotionally so many times by his father and older brothers that he should have been used to it by now. But even so, this time he was taken totally off guard. It seemed like whenever Jim or Andy, the two oldest brothers, had asked for help, his male relatives were usually only too happy to gang up on anyone who had injured the family pride. Trent realized at that moment he was still looked upon as a child, an object of scorn. It infuriated him even more. He far preferred to be punched than laughed at. The punches he had received in the past from his father and brothers had almost been worn as badges of honor. They were rites of passage, things to impress the other kids with on the middle school playground.

Look at this black eye and busted lip. My father beat the crap out of me last night, but I didn't cry.

Laughter, however, only left scars inside, and to show scars like those or complain about them only invoked further laughter. He flopped down on his bed, where he remained the rest of the day, nursing his anger and planning his revenge. If anyone noticed his absence from dinner, they certainly didn't spend any time looking for him.

Evening came, and he lay in bed listening to the usual

nightly horrors of the Addison household. Raised voices of Jim and Andy and their father, all three by now drunk out of their gourds. The whimpering, pleading, defeated voice of their mother. The squalling of Crystal, the baby, who was only ten months old, followed by a yell from one of the three men —Trent couldn't tell which, they all sounded the same after a few beers—to "get that brat to shut her mouth."

Trent had heard all this since he was a baby himself, and he gave no thought to it now. His diffuse hurt and anger against his father and brother for their treatment of him that afternoon had focused into a single, needle-sharp thought—to make Kit and Malachi pay. They were the ones who were responsible for how he felt. He'd get even with them. He'd show his family he could take care of himself. Trent Addison didn't just come crying home to daddy.

He lay on his back, indulging in bitter fantasies of tying Kit up and making him watch as he punched the hell out of Malachi. Then maybe he'd do the opposite. The idea of making Malachi plead for his boyfriend was especially attractive. The mental pictures of violence against his imagined victims, however, provided no comfort. They only served to heighten his emptiness and anger. His fury had been white hot that afternoon. Now it was cold, and dark. He willed the darkness into him, and it obeyed.

The next day he'd show them. No one messed with Trent Addison. It was with that thought that he fell asleep, and the vicious images that were such frequent visitors to his brain were swallowed up by a thick, tarry blackness which seemed to have no end, and into which no dreams—good or bad— could come.

Trent awakened the next morning, and his mind immediately refilled itself with his icy, bitter anger. He lay there, gently feeling the large purple bruise above his left cheekbone, and trying to decide what to do. Trent's mind was not a subtle one, and he had gotten no farther than plans to beat the snot out of Kit and Malachi both.

He got out of bed, got dressed, and exited his room. The house was quiet. Trent knew his father was probably still asleep, and equally probable was the likelihood that he'd wake with a splitting headache and a black temper. The Addison children learned early to avoid Cleve's meaty fists under these circumstances. Only his wife, Maureen, never seemed to learn, and bore her bruises with an air of defeat. This fact excited no sympathy in Trent—rather, he felt disdainful of his mother's submission. Even Chuck, who was eight and certainly no Rhodes Scholar, had learned to get out of Cleve Addison's way when he had a hangover. Maureen's injuries only reinforced the older boys' attitude that women were worthy of no better.

The house remained quiet as Trent descended the old wooden staircase. He passed through the living room. His brother Andy, clad only in boxers, lay sprawled on the couch, his head lolling backwards, mouth wide open. As Trent passed, he gave a harsh snore. His arm came up and then fell limply back onto his bare chest. Trent jumped, and immediately felt ashamed at his own fear. This made him even angrier.

Trent, however, was justified in his reaction to his brother. Andy was easily the most dangerous of the older Addison boys. He was certainly the most intelligent, and used that intelligence in a vicious and predatory manner. He harassed his younger siblings incessantly, especially eight-year-old Chuck, and he had participated in numerous acts of violence in his twenty years. Trent remembered when he was twelve and Andy was just turned seventeen. Andy had told him in painstaking detail of beating up a bum while cruising with some friends in Watertown. "It was just a worthless bum, anyway." That was his only statement even remotely defensive of his actions. The rest of the conversation had been a gleefully meticulous recounting of every blow, every kick, every scream.

Trent was both repelled and fascinated by his brother's amorality. Trent lacked Andy's drive and intelligence—his violent actions were limited by a fundamental laziness both of body and of intellect. But he wanted to leave marks on Kit that would never fade.

Cleve Addison kept a hunting knife in the hall closet, which he had used in the days when he was still physically fit enough to hunt. Trent opened the closet door silently, unhooked the sheath from where it hung, and slipped it into his pocket, snapping the sheath onto his belt. Then he walked out of the front door, closing it quietly behind him.

The sky was a fresh blue, streaked with the wispy mares' tails clouds common on summer days in the Adirondacks. Trent turned up Swenson Road toward Malachi's house, and reached the crest of the hill at just about the same time that Adam Thorne, only a quarter of a mile away, was making his first acquaintance with the shadow behind the rocks.

Trent jumped across the ditch opposite to the Swensons' house, into a narrow thicket of ash and maple saplings bordering a cornfield, and then turned and looked back through the narrow trunks at the house. He sat with his back to the largest tree in the thicket, watching and waiting, occupying his mind with the violent images that always took up much of his imagination. Today, many of them involved Kit and Malachi. He felt the knife, still in its sheath in his pocket, and smiled as he pictured himself using the razor-sharp tip to carve his name across Kit's chest.

Trent was normally not a patient person. It was surprising even to himself how long he was willing to wait for his revenge. Under usual circumstances, he would have given up and gone home in twenty minutes, and taken his fury out on one of his younger siblings. Today was different. Trent Addison sat, cool and focused, for almost two hours before the prime focus of his irrational hate walked out of the Swensons' front door. Kit carried a trash can. Trent froze when the door opened, and silently watched Kit walk down the sidewalk. Evidently he was enough a part of their household already that they didn't mind asking him to do chores.

This, for some reason, made Trent even angrier. His heart pounded and black anger poured through his veins. When Kit reached the end of the sidewalk and had set down the garbage can, Trent called quietly, "Kit."

Kit looked up, and gazed across the road. He did not see Trent at first, and took a step forward, shading his eyes from the sun, which was now almost at its zenith. Then he saw who had called, and stopped short.

Trent stood. "Hey, Kit. Come here."

"No." Kit's voice held no fear, but his answer was unequivocal.

Trent stepped out from the thicket. "Look, I just wanted to tell you I was sorry. I didn't act real nice yesterday. I'm sorry."

"Okay." The wariness in his voice made it clear that he knew Trent was lying. "Apology accepted."

Trent walked out into the road. Kit still didn't move, but his eyes never left the bigger boy's face. Trent worked to mold his features into a passable impression of good intent.

Trent was now only about ten feet away, and still walking slowly toward Kit, who stood stock-still. "Look, I don't want any trouble."

Inwardly, Trent laughed. No one but a coward would say that. It was a sign of weakness and fear. This was going to be fun.

Five steps away. Kit's right leg moved smoothly backward, and his body pivoted into profile. Trent thought he was preparing to run away. He was less than three feet away now. Without warning, Trent leapt forward, intending to use his weight advantage to knock Kit down, and then when he was down, to beat him senseless. It was a ploy he had used before, always successfully.

Trent's forward leap came to an abrupt and unexpected halt. Kit had taken a half step back, and then popped forward and upward with his left foot, faster than the eye could follow, and caught Trent right under the chin. His teeth clicked shut on the tip of his tongue, and the pain was so instantaneous and overwhelming that for a moment he almost blacked out. Then a white-hot fury shook him back to consciousness. Even more than the indignity of being beaten by a kid forty pounds lighter than he was, the knowledge of his father's and brothers' reactions to a second beating from the same adversary gripped his brain with a mix of rage, anguish, and terror. Kit stood watching Trent, his eyes on the blood streaming from his mouth, amazed at himself at having hurt the other boy. Then, before he knew what was happening, Trent lashed out, and there was a rip of fabric and a glistening scarlet stain spread across Kit's shirt.

"Didn't know I had a knife, didja, you fag? Didja?"

Kit gasped, and dodged a second sweep of the blade. Trent grinned maniacally, his mouth metallic with the taste of his own blood. Kit attempted to land another kick, but missed. The pain, coupled with the difficulty of avoiding Trent's knife, was eroding his ability to defend himself.

Trent kept slashing savagely at Kit with the knife, and Kit was slowly being forced up the Swensons' sidewalk toward the house. Then Trent's face suddenly changed, and Kit saw him glance up over Kit's right shoulder. Malachi Swenson had come to look out into the front yard to see what the commotion was, and his face was framed in the window, his eyes wide with horror. When Trent noticed him, he gave him a huge grin and spat blood onto the sidewalk, then slurred out, "You're next, gayboy."

Kit took advantage of the split second when his adversary

was not looking at him, and snapped a kick at his right forearm, the one holding the knife. He heard a distinct crack, and the knife sailed up, end over end, sparkling in the blue sky, and landed in the ditch. Trent howled with pain, clutching his arm, and bared his teeth at Kit and growled. Kit struck him across the face with a lazy, graceful backhand that made Trent's head rock back and spattered Mrs. Swenson's neat row of marigolds with droplets of blood.

Without warning, a commanding voice spoke from the porch behind Kit. "Trent Addison, you go home. We've called the police. Get off our property!" As if in answer, there was a sound of a police siren.

Trent looked down the road like a hunted animal, and then fled, still clutching his right arm. He jumped the ditch, the jar to his arm making him give an involuntary, shivering yelp of pain, and vanished into the cornfield.

Mrs. Swenson came up to Kit, and put her arm around him. Kit looked down for the first time. The lower half of his shirt was soaked with blood. The combination of adrenaline, fear, and blood loss struck him all at once. The world grayed out momentarily, and he swayed, taking a step back. Then he steadied, and with Mrs. Swenson's help, he walked up the steps and into the house.

Cole and one of his deputies were there within minutes, and after asking a few questions and ascertaining that Kit was not mortally wounded, they left again to look for Trent Addison. Mrs. Swenson had removed Kit's ruined shirt, and he lay on his back on the sofa, a damp towel pressed against the knife wound. It was long but not especially deep, beginning just underneath his left nipple and traveling downward at an angle all the way across his chest. Malachi sat on a chair nearby, his face pale.

"Kit McIntyre," Mrs. Swenson said, "you've no lack of courage, I'll give you that."

Kit smiled faintly. "I wasn't thinking of being brave. Actually, my only thought was, how can I keep from getting killed?"

Mrs. Swenson stood. "Dr. Westfall will be here in a little while. He was coming anyway to look at Carl, and I suppose he'd better have a look at you as well." She left the room, and went up the staircase.

Kit guessed she was going to tell Mr. Swenson about their guest's most recent encounter with Trent Addison. Judging by their conversation the previous evening, it would no doubt cheer him up. He hadn't been out of bed yet that day, which Kit knew was a bad sign.

He tipped his head backwards, and glanced at Malachi. "I seem to have turned things upside down around here."

"Kit, I'm afraid."

"Of what? The police will catch Trent and that will be that."

"It's not that. It's what's happening to this place. Finn Hill used to be a quiet village. People used to complain because nothing ever happened here."

"And then I arrived."

"Kit, don't misunderstand. I like you... I mean..." He reddened and shrugged, but continued. "So do my parents. We just want to know why, all of a sudden, things... aren't right. Trent looked like he'd lost his mind today. I mean, he's always been obnoxious, but today he looked..." He faltered.

"Looked what?"

"Possessed. Evil. Kit, it's like you're a carrier. You're good yourself—you don't want bad things to happen. But still, somehow you've changed things here. Christina vanishing. And what's... what's happening to Dad. I'm sorry, I know it isn't your fault, you never meant to come here. But I think Mom's right. Somehow it's all connected. You've got to get back to your home, and maybe everything will be okay again. Part of me wants you to stay. I think we could be friends if you stayed. Good friends."

Kit smiled, but his eyes were troubled. "I don't know how to go home, Malachi."

"I know."

***

Dr. Abel Westfall was a short, stocky man, with a close-cropped crew cut of white hair and a neatly-trimmed beard and mustache. He was an extremely serious person, who had seldom been seen to smile. His gruff, straightforward manner, coupled with a high degree of skill in treating the usual range of maladies encountered in general practice, met with the approval of the majority of his patients. Most of them were farmers and their families, glad to be served by a native Upstater, especially one who treated them with the same direct honesty with which they usually treated each other. He had served Finn Hill and its environs for nearly thirty years, and fully intended to serve it for at least thirty more.

Malachi had followed his mother upstairs, while the doctor sat on the edge of the couch, gently probing the cut across Kit's chest. "Boy, if you stay very much longer in Finn Hill," he told Kit as he dabbed antiseptic on the wound, "somebody's going to have to have a talk with you about messing with Addisons."

"Mr. Swenson already did. Trent messed with me, not the other way around."

"That's as may be. Just you be careful. Trent tells his brother Andy, and the next time I'll probably have to clean up your guts off the sidewalk instead of just disinfecting a cut." He carefully taped a gauze bandage over the wound. "It's going to hurt like crazy when I take this off in a couple of days. Just thought I'd let you know."

"Thanks."

"Just be thankful you don't have much chest hair yet. Makes it even more fun."

Kit laughed.

Dr. Westfall stood. "Well, I guess I better go look after that old codger upstairs."

<hr>

Malachi gave Kit one of his t-shirts to replace his, and Kit slipped it over his head as soon as Dr. Westfall left the room. The doctor vanished into the upstairs, and Kit looked up the dimly-lit staircase. Mr. Swenson had gone upstairs the previous night after his attack of—what? Kit had never seen nor heard of anything even remotely like it. Leprosy, maybe… wasn't that supposed to make your skin fall off?

In any case, Kit hadn't seen anything of him since. Curiosity, mixed with a fair measure of genuine regard, made him want to know what was going on in that upstairs bedroom. Finally, he couldn't stand it any longer, and he padded barefoot across the living room and up the stairs.

The door to the Swensons' bedroom stood open, and Kit saw Malachi's back framed within it. He quietly approached, and touched his shoulder. Malachi turned and gave him a quick, anguished glance, and then his eyes returned to his father's prone form, lying under a thin sheet on the bed. Kit remained out in the hall, in the shadows.

Mr. Swenson's face and hands, the only parts of him exposed, were now criss-crossed with a tracery of fine white lines, like cracks in a windowpane. The doctor sat on the bed and touched his skin gently. At each touch, Mr. Swenson winced.

"Strangest thing I've ever seen," Dr. Westfall finally said.

"What could it be, Abel?" Mr. Swenson's voice sounded slurred and cottony. "Hurts like mad."

"I'll bet it does. Where the skin is flaking away, it's exposing the dermis, the layer underneath. Sort of what a brush burn does. What I'm wondering is what could cause this. You been handling any organic solvents lately?"

"Like what?"

"Gasoline, turpentine, xylene, toluene, urethane. Something like that."

"Course I've handled gasoline. None of the others, not recently. Don't even know what xylene is."

"Doesn't matter. Have you gotten anything on your hands and face lately? Been splattered with gasoline, or maybe an oil-based paint? Anything?"

"No."

"That rules out some sort of contact dermatitis. You're not running a fever. Sometimes people's skin will flake off if they've had a really high fever. Haven't been sick lately, I suppose?"

"No."

"I got to say it's like nothing I've ever seen, and I thought in thirty years I'd seen it all. Last thing I thought I'd be doing today is treating Carl Swenson for galloping dandruff. My advice is to take some medication for the pain. I'll write you a prescription, and Helen or Malachi can run up to the pharmacy in Carnahan and pick it up for you. Use lotion on it, something mild, but discontinue if it seems to make it worse. Mostly just lay low and give it another day or two. If it doesn't improve, or gets worse, I think I'd advise a trip to Watertown Hospital."

Mr. Swenson's forehead wrinkled in dismay, but he winced and didn't protest.

"Now, when I say lay low, I mean it. Helen and Malachi, and that young fellow Kit, can do whatever it takes to keep this place going for a couple of days. You stay in bed. Let 'em wait on you."

"How is Kit?"

"Just an ugly cut. He'll probably have a nice scar to brag to his girlfriends about, but nothing worse."

Kit turned and silently retreated down the stairs. His head whirled. What was happening to this place? Were Malachi and Mrs. Swenson right—was it somehow connected to his arrival? And how could he get back home when according to everything he had seen, his home no longer existed?

He walked across the living room to the cabinet where the road atlas was stored, the one they had looked at on his first night here. He opened it to the map of the state of Washington, and once again stared at the blank spot on Interstate 90 where his hometown should have been.

When he got home home—he corrected his mental voice —*if* he got home, he was going to look in a road atlas of New York State. He'd lay odds that Finn Hill wouldn't be on it. How many other places he'd heard about here wouldn't be on the map either? Carnahan? North Hanville? Hamilton County? Watertown? All of them, maybe. Not real, not part of his world, just like he was not supposed to be part of this world.

Then he thought about running across the street in the thunderstorm, and Malachi's warm, friendly smile.

I like you, Malachi had said. *I think we could be friends if you stayed. Good friends.*

No. Malachi was real. He had to be. And if he was, then the rest had to be, too.

He snapped the atlas shut, and tossed it back in the drawer.

Or maybe it was just a dream. But if it was, why couldn't he wake up? Maybe he hadn't awakened because he'd finally found a dream he liked better than he liked reality.

Was that it? Kit had always felt like he was a fairly happy person. He was a moderately good student, a decent soccer player, a fair second trumpet in the school band. His home life was okay—there were no major upheavals between him, his mother, or sister, especially since his parents had separated six years previous and his volatile father had moved to California with a girlfriend. There'd been a few bumps when he'd come out as gay two years ago, but that had smoothed over soon enough. Other than that, all nice, all even-keeled, no highs or lows.

In other words, bland. Boring. Dull.

And here... here things were exciting. A mysterious disappearance, a crazy adversary who Kit had successfully beaten twice, a man with a strange and undiagnosable disease, and a handsome boy who obviously liked Kit very much, and whom Kit had more than a few suspicions might be gay or bi himself. The more Kit thought about it, the more logical it seemed. He was dreaming, another of his wild, irrational, vivid dreams.

Kit lay down on the sofa. Okay, if this was a dream, he should at least learn something from it. When he woke up, he was going to take more chances and have more fun.

When he woke up.

If he woke up.

9. the girl in the box

. . .

Trent Addison, still hugging his injured arm to his body, and whimpering slightly at each footfall, plunged through the cornfield across from the Swensons' house. The sirens were getting louder. He was sure that any moment now, he'd hear a crashing, roaring sound, and look back, and see the police cruiser plowing its way through the cornfield.

The thought filled him with fear and black hatred. The older Addisons hated most everyone in Finn Hill, but Chief of Police Johnny Cole was near the top of the list. He was the only one whom they perceived as a real threat, and every time one of the Addisons had been hauled off to spend a few days in jail, it had been another strike against their opinion of the Chief of Police.

However, the basic cowardliness of the Addisons had prevented them from doing anything about it other than minor disrespect. The three older boys gave Johnny Cole the finger behind his back whenever they could, and once Andy had partially deflated one of the Chief of Police's tires when he had stopped at the Nice 'n' Easy for a can of Pepsi. But the fact remained, they were all really afraid of Johnny Cole. It was the only real fear they had, except of each other.

Trent had run quite a long way when he realized the sirens had stopped, and the police car was not following him. He turned, but couldn't see over the tall cornstalks. Perhaps they had followed him on foot? He was sure that kid would tell the police who had attacked him. God, but it made him mad. Wildly irrational thoughts began to spin through his head. A few inches farther, and the knife would have gone between Kit's ribs rather than just skipping across his chest, and there'd have been no one to tell the police. Oh, no, there was that simpering little gayboy, Malachi Swenson, but he was too afraid to testify against him. Now he was in real trouble. Maybe he'd get sent to the juvenile detention center. He didn't want to end up in juvie. Here, he was the bully-in-chief, a position of fear and respect. There, he'd be just another one of the toughs. He gingerly licked his lips, grimacing at the pain and the metallic taste of blood in his mouth. No, juvie was not the place to be, among other kids just like himself.

Trent Addison was not someone who liked working on an equal playing field.

Home. He'd go home. His father and brothers wouldn't laugh now. Now, they'd do something about that kid. Broke his arm, that's what it felt like. It was already purple and swollen. Nobody, *nobody* broke an Addison's arm and got away with it. Jim'd hold Kit down while Andy slowly broke every bone in his entire body. Teach that queer to mess with the Addisons. They'd fix it so he'd never mess with anyone again.

Trent limped along, down one of the corn rows, heading toward the edge of the field so he could find his way back home. He finally reached the edge and stepped into a fallow field, where the soil had been turned up but not planted. A few weeds, dandelion, chicory, and Queen Anne's lace, sprang up from among the rough clods of dirt. He stumbled along, following the edge of the corn, heading home. He still cradled his swollen arm, only once reaching up to wipe the blood away from his mouth. His brain felt electrified, and a high-voltage wire of madness lay behind his eyes. It had not been there yesterday, when his only intention had been to bully and humiliate someone he thought was a weaker adversary. Something was different now. Something in him had changed.

And he liked it.

In the distance, he saw his house, its unkempt back yard lost in a thicket of broken-down sumac bushes and wild rose. He'd wait till his father and brothers were awake, he'd tell them what happened, and then, there'd be a nice payback for Kit McIntyre.

He was almost all the way to the house before he saw the police car parked in the driveway. He ducked behind the old junked refrigerator that leaned against the side of the house, as quickly as his injuries would allow. His intake of breath had sounded loud enough in his ears to alert anyone within a half-mile radius, but the voices on the porch—Cole and his father, he thought—didn't miss a beat.

"Haven't seen him all day. Got no idea where he is," Cleve was saying. His voice was surly, and it sounded like he might have been awakened by the visit.

"When did you last see him?"

"How'd you expect me to know? I can't keep track of the kid. He's always off somewhere."

"You don't know when you last saw him?" Cole's voice was patient and persistent.

An annoyed grunt from Cleve. "Maybe yesterday afternoon some time. What's all this about?"

"Looks like your boy's been causing trouble up at Carl Swenson's. Attacked a guest of theirs with a knife. Cut him bad. And I understand it's not the first time Trent's tried to rough up this young fellow. He tried to push him around yesterday, too."

Cleve's voice darkened. "Yeah, Cole, and I guess you don't know this kid kicked my son in the face. Or maybe it's all right to knock around an Addison, but it's not all right for us to defend ourselves."

"I'm not gonna stand here arguing about defending yourselves, Cleve Addison. You know as well as I do that your boys cause most of the trouble they get into. I don't think Kit did anything to warrant being attacked with a knife. You just keep that in mind. I'm gonna take that son of yours in, and if I find out you were hiding him, I'll see what I can do about hitting you with obstructing a police officer in the line of duty."

The door slammed, and Trent guessed that Cleve Addison had gotten it as close to Johnny Cole's face as possible. He grinned, in spite of his pain. Cole had done him a real service. Only a visit from the Chief of Police could unify the Addisons. The very fact that he was wanted by the police for assaulting Kit McIntyre would turn Trent into a hero, and Kit McIntyre into the villain. Also, anyone who had eluded Cole for any length of time would win Cleve Addison's admiration. Kit, as the root cause of the whole issue and someone under police protection, would be a fine target for any sort of revenge they could dream up.

The engine of the squad car started up, and there was the crunch of gravel as it backed down the driveway. Trent had to control a hysterical bray of laughter welling up from his ample gut.

He stood up stiffly, and stepped out from behind the refrigerator. Its door sagged on one rusted hinge, and as he passed he glanced sidelong into its darkened compartment.

Except it wasn't dark. Trent did a double take, and then jumped, making the pain in his arm sing. Where there should have been shadows, and perhaps a glimpse of a rusted shelf, there was light. A clear, warm sunlight, streaming from inside. He leaned forward, his forehead wrinkling up in disbelief.

He pulled at the door, which creaked and groaned but swung open. Inside, hanging like an improbable still life across the middle of the old refrigerator, was a landscape he had never seen before. It was an idyllic forest glade, with dappled sunlight spilling through trees, small woodland flowers nodding on slender stalks, and a carpet of old leaves underneath the thicker parts of the forest canopy.

"Geez," he mumbled under his breath. "That looks almost real."

As if his words had activated it, a lazy breath of air stirred the scene, and the leaves of the trees rustled, making the patches of sunlight dance on the ground. He stared at it stupidly, his pain, anger, and fear forgotten for a moment.

It is likely that most people, presented with such an impossible enigma, would have immediately begun wondering what exactly was going on, or would at least have begun looking for evidence that someone was playing an elaborate joke. That thought never crossed Trent Addison's mind. He was not the type who pondered reasons. Ever since he was born, he had been dealt with in a capricious, irrational fashion, and he had finally stopped expecting the universe to make sense. A butterfly flickered across the scene, and then passed out of view, and still he simply stared.

Without warning, a figure stepped into the scene, so close he could have reached out and touched it. It was a woman, her back to him. She was slender, and was dressed in a gauzy gray material tied with a narrow belt made of interlocked silver links. She had flowers braided into her smooth brown hair, and her feet were bare. His expression became suddenly more focused, and his eyes lost their diffuse gaze, but his forehead wrinkled up in complete incomprehension. Finally, he said, in a whisper, "Geez."

At this, she turned around, and smiled at him. Her face

was angelic, and seemed to shine with an unearthly luminescence, which made both the dappled sunlight of the scene inside and the full sunlight of the reality outside seem dingy and dull by comparison. She beckoned to him, and reached out her hand. The fabric whispered against her skin as she moved her arm.

"Come inside." Her voice was cool, almost inaudible, but it echoed in Trent's brain like a struck bell.

"W-what?" he stammered. His injured tongue was swollen enough to slur his speech.

Her face clouded with a sincere sympathy. Her expression was heartbreaking, the very essence of pure empathy. "You're hurt."

He nodded.

She took a step closer to him, coming so close he could not see her feet. She leaned forward, and her face seemed to touch the edge of the scene. It rippled like a reflection in a pool of water. "I can help," she whispered in the same cool voice. "Let me show you. Kiss me."

Trent stared at her in disbelief. "W-what?" he said again.

"I can help," she repeated. "Kiss me."

Trent leaned over, and eagerly pressed his blood-stained mouth against hers. If she felt any revulsion, she did not show it. The kiss seemed to go on forever. Trent certainly wished it to.

Finally she pulled away, and again he saw the rippling, as if she had just gently kissed her own reflection. As addled as he was, he noticed her lips were not stained with the blood covering his mouth. It was only then that he noticed a second, and even more amazing thing.

His tongue was healed.

Not partially healed, but totally smooth and unscarred, and the pain completely gone. He ran his tongue along his teeth, expecting to feel the throbbing ache return.

Nothing. It was as if the injury had never happened.

Trent gaped at her, but she just smiled. "You have other hurts. I can heal those, too. But you must come inside. I can fix the hurt in your arm and your face. I can make you feel well, better than you ever have felt." And she once again held out her hand to him, welcoming, infinitely beckoning.

"Geez," Trent said for the third time.

She turned, and walked a few steps away from him, then turned and looked back. "Come on. I can heal you here. You will never have to leave."

This was too much for him. He stepped into the old refrigerator, his foot making a dull thud on the plastic bottom. He ducked his head, and for a moment was crouched inside, half inside and half outside of reality. Then he stepped over the boundary, and down into the glade.

His feet touched ground with a crunch, and startled, he looked down at the brown carpet of dry leaves scattered beneath the boughs of the trees. A soft breeze touched his face, with a sweet forest smell completely unlike the sharp farmyard scent which, while not exactly unpleasant, was never far away in his part of New York. He looked up, expecting to see the angelic woman standing in front of him with her arms wide, beckoning him.

She was gone. He stood still, staring, his mouth slightly open. A bird twittered in the trees, but other than that and the sighing of the leaves, there was no sound.

"Where'd you go?" he asked, his voice sounding pitiful and very young.

There was no answer. He walked forward into the trees, and never thought to turn around and see if the way back into his own world was still there, hanging in mid-air. Perhaps it was already too late, and he could not have returned home even then. But in any case, it was only much later that the idea occurred to him, and by then he would be far beyond anyone's help—even if anyone had been inclined to help him.

Many hours later, exhausted and ravenously hungry, he gave up his search for the woman and sat down under a tree. His fundamental laziness would have stopped his searching long before had it not been for the considerable pain from his fractured arm, which she had promised to cure. The bone ached like a rotten tooth, and every step, regardless of how gently it was set down, seemed to jar it horribly. Finally, however, he realized she was gone, and he was completely and inextricably lost.

Earlier he had found a clearing in the woods, near a large, reed-enclosed pond. Trent stepped into the clearing, glad for the sunshine and to get out from under the omnipresent trees, and then rushed to the water and drank deeply. But upon looking up, he received the most severe shock yet on this strange, strange day. It was then that he realized he was farther from home than he had thought, or even thought possible. He stood, and then turned as if to shut out the sight, whimpering like a trapped animal, and ran back underneath the cover of the trees.

There were two suns in this world—a large, orange-colored one, and a smaller but intensely bright bluish one. Trent knew nothing about double stars, and the idea of another solar system would have meant nothing to him. All he deduced from this apparition was that he certainly wasn't in Finn Hill any longer, nor anywhere nearby, for the sky to look so strange. This alone was enough to terrify him.

The other thing contributing to his fear was the fact that the two suns were near to setting, and the idea of spending a night alone in a dark, unfamiliar woods horrified him. As he walked, he had seen no food of any kind, not even a berry or nut. He had no idea how to get home, and the direction back to the door through which he had stepped was impossible to determine. Except for the small clearing near the pond from which he had seen the double sun, all there seemed to be here were trees, trees, trees. He even began to doubt his memory of the woman, although something certainly had happened just before he stepped through the door, because his tongue was still sound. But if she was real, where was she? And what had been her purpose in coaxing him through the door? And finally, where was he?

So, in despair, he sat down underneath a large tree, and began to cry. Tears were not a common thing for Trent Addison, but nothing about his situation was common, either. As he sat, weeping softly, the suns set, and a swift darkness fell under the silent forest—a forest that, for all he knew, might completely encircle this strange world in another galaxy, thousands of light years from the village in the Adirondacks where he had been born.

And neither did he know of the creatures inhabiting this planet, human in shape but part of a far older race, who create portals into other places to lure in the hapless inhabitants into one of the many worlds they govern. Afterwards they wait until dark, for it is only then that they hunt—to give their prey the advantage of a cover of darkness, although the outcome is of course always the same. Trent knew nothing about this, yet, but he would find out soon.

Back in Finn Hill, New York, however, had anyone watched Trent Addison step through that refrigerator door into another place and time, they would never have found out anything at all—for as they watched they would have seen only his first tentative steps into the forest, and then the image would have slipped sideways and vanished into nothing. All they would have seen after was a momentary view of the interior of a dark, rusty, dirty refrigerator, exactly what Trent had expected to see minutes earlier.

Then the door swung shut.

10. a voice from the static

. . .

Mr. Tony Gallagher sat in his house at 4 Swenson Road, his tie askew, his face expressionless. His hand held a can of Coke, but he had not taken a drink from it since opening it ten minutes ago. A television, its screen as blank as his eyes, faced him.

This was his evening ritual. He wore what he called his "happy-happy face" all day, as he showed his clients property and houses all over northern Hamilton County, then came home. The smile melted from his face as he pulled into his driveway, after he was sure no one would see him drive past and wave, and expect a grin and a wave back. By the time the door closed behind him, his expression had gone as still and emotionless as a doll's.

The happy-happy face worked, however much it was an assumed persona. Tony had received awards from his realty's parent company three times for his sale volume, which was doubly amazing considering the fact that he lived in one of the most sparsely populated counties in New York State. The fact that much of the property in the county was officially part of Adirondack Park often horrendously complicated land purchases. He was good at what he did.

Part of his success was his ability to project warmth and personality. His clients felt his sincerity. He really seemed to want to find them the best deal on the market, and to meet their needs. He always had a friendly smile on his face, which held no trace of what he called the "gladhander's grin," all too common in his profession. His expression and his voice indicated that he was a good guy, an honest and caring person who also happened to be a realtor.

On some level, this was true. While Claire was alive, it had been completely true, because he had been deliriously happy. The day they married, back in June of 2005, was the high point of his life. She energized him, fulfilled him, supported him, and he gave her everything she wanted, including all of his heart. He kept none for himself. That was why, on a snowy evening last December, his life had ended when Claire's car hit a patch of ice, slid off the road, and flipped into a gully. She held his heart, and when she died, it did too.

Tony had been quite a talented actor in high school and starred in the school play his junior and senior years. It stood him in good stead. The week after Claire was buried, still firmly clutching his cold, dead heart, he returned to work. Everyone commented how strong he was, how well he was carrying on after the terrible tragedy of his young wife's death. He waited a seemly interval before smiling too much, before joking with his secretary and clients, but even then, no one knew he was acting—his most convincing role ever. He was a dead man portraying a living being. Nobody knew about the evenings, the infinite nights alone, sitting in a recliner in front of a dead television.

That Thursday, three hours after Trent Addison made his first acquaintance with the woman in the refrigerator, Tony Gallagher sat clutching his Coke can in nerveless fingers. There were times in the evening that the thought occurred to him that if he could cry, and lay open his soul like a surgeon cutting deep into an infected wound, perhaps he could start to heal. Perhaps not. Several times recently he found he was near tears, but he forced them back. He was afraid, the first real emotion he had experienced in over eight months, afraid if he began to cry, he wouldn't be able to stop. Afraid the tears would scald, leaving blistered tracks across his face, forcing him to feel a pain that he had thought was permanently anesthetized.

The room was dark, as it always was, and that was why the spark seemed so bright. It flashed through the wall, a tiny piece of rainbow-colored lightning, coming from the north— the direction of the Addisons' and Swensons' houses, the direction in which lay the abandoned Methodist church in whose front yard Kit had first appeared. It lit up the room with a faint multicolored sparkle, which probably would have been unnoticeable if the lights had been on. In less than the blink of an eye had whizzed past Tony's left ear, bounced off an elaborate gilt-framed mirror Claire had bought the previous summer at a garage sale, and struck the screen of the television set. There was a momentary flicker on the dusty glass surface of the screen, and then darkness.

And then the television came on.

Tony sat upright in his chair, and the can of Coke fell to the floor, pouring out a fizzy brown puddle onto the carpet. A screen full of snow hissed across the television. He stood, and walked to the set, and pushed the "on-off" button.

Nothing happened.

He did it several more times, and got no response. His heart pounding, he went around to the rear of the set and pulled the plug.

The hissing continued, and when he looked around the front of the television, the snow still swirled across the screen. Tony Gallagher stared at it for nearly a minute, his mouth slightly open, breathing hard.

"What the devil?"

Then he heard the voice. At first, it was mostly obscured

in the static. It sounded like the voice of a distant radio broadcaster, almost beyond the range of reception—fading in and out, hardly understandable.

"Tony."

"Dear God."

"Tony, I need to speak to you."

"What is it? Who are you?" He fell to his knees and placed his ear next to the speaker.

"Tony. Dear Tony. You know my voice, don't you?"

"It can't be," he whispered. Then his voice rose to a shout. "Claire! My dear lord, Claire! Where are you?"

There was a crackle of static which obscured the next few words, and then, "…trapped here."

"This can't be real."

"It is. You can't say you doubt me, Tony, not when we've already lost so much."

"Where are you?" he said again.

"Alone in the dark. Frozen in time, like a butterfly in amber."

Something about the way she said it sounded like an accusation. "I'm alone, too, Claire. Completely alone."

"Your being alone is by choice. Mine is not."

The tears finally came, spilling over, streaming down his cheeks, splattering onto the carpet. "I know. I know. I can't go on without you."

"You must. You have. I'm the one who has no future."

"How is this… how is this happening? How can I be hearing your voice?"

"The doors are open. All manner of things are getting in, things that never should be. I'm one of them. I'm supposed to be here, stay here, silent forever."

"I would do anything to get you back. You know that."

"Even admit that you caused my death?"

He stopped for a moment, struck dumb, then he gasped

out, "I didn't... I didn't cause you to die! You can't possibly think I wanted..."

"You were why I was hurrying home that evening." The accusatory tone became even sharper. "If it hadn't been for you, I would still be alive."

He frowned at the silver-gray static on the television screen, aghast. "Claire," he said in a near whisper, "I don't believe it. This can't really be you."

"Why are you saying that, Tony? Because you don't want to hear what I'm saying?"

"No." He choked back a sob. "No. Because you would... because *Claire* would never treat me this way. Claire would never say something like that to me."

A long pause, with only the hiss of white noise filling the dark room. "Maybe she should have," came the voice. "Maybe you deserved it."

Tony didn't answer, but stared at the floor, continuing his soundless weeping.

"Do you want me to come and talk to you some more?" Now she spoke in silky, seductive tones, again so unlike the real Claire that all Tony could do was stare at the screen in incomprehension. The voice was Claire's; the inflection, the cadence, sounded demonic. "I could tell you other things. Better things. As long as the door is open, we can talk sometimes."

Tony looked up. "What door?"

"It was an accident that opened it..."

"The accident?"

"No, not my accident, Tony. Another. The door is opened, and it created a link between worlds. That gateway is the only thing that's letting me to speak to you. As long as it is open I can get through, a little. The worlds are joined while it's open." She paused. "They are coming, Tony. Soon. They will ask you to help close it."

"They?" Who is they?"

"Police Chief Cole. Malachi Swenson. Others. They will tell you that horrors are coming through as well, and that you need to help them close the gateway."

"Not if it means shutting you back in!"

"I thought you might feel that way. Then when they try to get you to help, you must refuse. There is a boy, a boy named Kit. He doesn't belong here. If he goes back through, it will seal the door and I will be gone. Really, truly gone forever."

"How can I stop him? I don't understand."

"It all began at the old church, up near Adam Thorne's house. It all radiates from there. You must find Kit, and do whatever you can to keep him away from the old church. Only he can stop this."

"Claire, I don't know how to do what you're asking!"

"You must." The voice went cold.

"Don't speak to me that way. Please." Tony knelt on the floor, his arms wrapped around his chest, rocking himself like a small child. "You don't know how lonely I've been. It's horrible, always smiling, laughing, like a clockwork puppet who's been wound up and sent on his way, but empty inside —nothing but springs and gears, cold, dead metal. I can't do anything without you. Please don't leave me again. Why did you leave me? Why? I'm so alone, so alone."

The snow continued hissing on the set, but there was no answer.

"Claire?"

Nothing. And suddenly, the snow-filled screen winked out and went dead and dark. A hundred yards away, through the open window of her cottage, Ann Garvey heard his cry of "NO!" and looked up from the crossword puzzle in the evening newspaper, a frown crossing her plain, kind face. She listened for a moment more, and when nothing more was heard she looked back down again, deciding that it was probably some sort of fracas over at the Addisons' house up the road.

Tony stared at the television from a kneeling position for more than an hour, every few minutes whispering, "Claire?" to its dark screen. There was no response. Finally he stood and went to the bathroom, and opened his medicine cabinet. On the top shelf was a bottle of sedatives, prescribed for him by Dr. Westfall shortly after Claire's death. He had never taken them, not really caring whether he slept or not. Now he shook out about twenty into his palm. He stared at them with an emotionless expression for a moment, and filled a glass with water.

Then, like the clockwork figure he had chosen to become, he began to pop them one by one into his mouth, chasing each down with a swig of water. When they were all gone, he went to his bedroom and lay down, something like the ghost of a smile playing over his lips.

It was only after a few minutes had passed—just before the walls, covered with pictures and mementos of Claire, grayed out for the last time—Tony fuzzily remembered what she had asked him to do. Keep some kid away from the door of the old Methodist church. What kind of crazy request was that? He'd have to ask her about it when he saw her. Find someone named Kit. Stop him from going home.

Whatever that meant. In any case, it didn't matter. If he couldn't bring Claire back to him, he would go to her. All the things she'd asked him to do were irrelevant.

Soon, all of this would be over. The pain and loneliness and fear. It was already working. In fact, he felt great, for the first time in months.

And besides, he didn't know anyone in Finn Hill named Kit.

11. the carrier

. . .

K it got up the next morning after a restless night of black, dreamless sleep broken by intervals of painful waking. He lay for a while in the morning sunshine, his breathing shallow, the gash across his chest still aching miserably. Breathing hurt.

At least Trent Addison hadn't burned the house down during the night. From what Kit had heard about him, he wouldn't have put it past him.

His thoughts returned to the previous day, and the wild, insane look in Trent's eye. He'd heard before of someone having "murder in his eye," but he hadn't understood it until now. Trent had looked crazy, more than willing to kill, baring his scarlet-stained teeth like a wild animal.

If all the Addisons were as homicidal as he was, God help him. It was interesting how little the thought actually scared him. There was still an air of unreality to the whole situation. He was like a visitor from another world, so deep in his own perplexity that the thought of being murdered by a loony kid hardly even impacted his mind.

He sat up, wincing slightly. Another day in Wonderland, who knows what'll happen next? If the White Rabbit had come out of the closet informing him that he was late, he would not really have been surprised. He climbed out of bed, moved carefully as he dressed in his shorts and Malachi's old t-shirt, and ran a comb through his hair. It looked like a fine morning. Perhaps if Mr. Swenson's condition had improved, he would spend the morning helping him. It was a cheering thought, and with that in mind he walked into the living room, just in time to see Mrs. Swenson opening the front door. She heard him and turned. Kit could see new worry lines and paleness in her angular face. Her hair, normally in a neat bun, was unkempt and straggling. She did not smile at him.

"Good morning," he said.

"Morning." Her voice was unwarrantedly cold.

"How is Mr. Swenson?"

"Not well."

"Wasn't the doctor able to help him?"

She laughed, a high, almost hysterical laugh. "Go on, Kit. Go look at him, and tell me what you think the doctor could do for him." She shivered, and only then did he notice that she wore a heavy sweater even though the warm breeze of a summer morning blew through the open door. "It's too late. Kit, he's dying. His body is still alive—what is left of it—but he's dying. He asked me to go out and get him some soup. I want to go do it before he's gone." She turned away.

Kit watched her retreating, feeling sickened with shock. "Mrs. Swenson, what can I do to help?"

She turned, and began to stalk back up the sidewalk toward him, a mad light glittering in her eyes. Kit was immediately reminded of his last conversation on that sidewalk, and the crazy light in Trent Addison's eyes.

My God, not you, too.

"Oh, you've done enough." Her hand came up and smoothed her hair back, "you've done enough and plenty, Kit McIntyre from Nonexistent, Washington. You've done this, don't you realize that? It wasn't until you showed up that it all began. Go, go up and see him. See what you've done." She grabbed his arms, and brought her face close to his. To his horror, her hands and breath were chilly. "Go on, go see what you've done to him!" She angrily let him go, tears coming to her eyes, and turned and walked off, leaving him staring after her. Then she climbed into their car and drove away toward the village.

Kit finally turned, his face white, and went back inside. He walked up the stairs, his brain swirling with a tangled mix of emotions, and silently approached Mr. Swenson's bedroom.

The door stood open, and he could see clearly into its interior, with its blue and cream wallpaper, simple blue curtains, and sparse furnishings. On the wall next to the window was a framed photograph of a young woman holding a baby—presumably Mrs. Swenson and Malachi, seventeen years ago. Hanging on the wall next to the bed was an embroidered sampler with the legend "God is Lord." Malachi sat in a chair beside the bed, and his face was red and puffy from crying. Kit stepped forward, and looked straight at the bed for the first time. His anguished eyes turned to him, and at first he himself wasn't sure what he was looking at. Then, like a 3-D image coming into focus, he saw it and understood.

Mr. Swenson lay on the bed, covered to below his shoulders with a rust-colored blanket. Where his body was exposed—his face, arms, and hands—huge sheets of skin had peeled off or were in the process, like someone with a severe sunburn, but beneath the skin was a snowy, featureless white. Over half of his face had peeled, including over one eye, and most horrifying of all, beneath it he had no eye, only an eye-shaped bump like the contour on the face of a mannequin. But this mannequin moved, its head looking this way and that with its one human eye left, its piebald hands whispering restlessly over the fabric of the blanket.

"Good lord," Kit breathed.

Mr. Swenson's blue eye turned in its socket, and finally looked directly at his face. "Kit." His voice sounded like a sigh of the wind, slurred, full of air, difficult to understand. "Look terrible, don't I?"

Kit didn't respond, but Malachi looked imploringly at him, then back at his father, tears coursing down his face.

"Don't know what's gonna become of me. This'll kill Helen if it isn't over quick. Lord almighty, it hurts."

"Dad, you just rest now," said Malachi. "Mom'll be back with some soup soon."

"Need more'n soup. More'n Doc Westfall. Kit, I knew you'd come soon. I have to talk to you. Gotta stop all this." His eye turned and stared at Kit. "It's you, Kit."

Kit felt a chill crawl up his backbone, and the hairs on his neck stood on end. He did not respond.

"Heard what Helen said," Mr. Swenson continued. "Hearing's gotten better with this, I can hear every rustle in the grass outside—although can't see a thing out of my right eye." He paused. "She said it harsh, but you know she's right, son."

"Sir..."

He held up a hand. Three of the fingers and part of the thumb were white and as featureless as porcelain. "You know she's right. Can only be you. You're the one as started all this. Know you didn't mean to, you're as much caught in it as all of us, but it was your coming here as began it. It's you as got to stop it. Back to the church, that's where you go. Where it began. That's where it all's coming from."

"All of what?" Kit felt a tremor shudder through him.

"Who lives closest to the church? Thornes. They were the first as got hit. Then us, though it took a while to show up. Then Addisons, they're next. You stay here, son, and Tony Gallagher and Ann Garvey'll be next, then Roy and Nina Cook, then Matt and Felicia Darnell. Then into the village it'll go, spreading out like a plague."

"What, sir? What will spread? I don't understand."

"You do, you do understand." He paused, and took a thin, whistling breath. "Or if you don't, it's because you don't want to. And I think that in these few days I already know you better than that. You're a good boy, and I know you didn't want this to happen, but wherever you came from—the good lord only knows, son, but you brought something in with you. It's spreading in big circles from the place where it started. You're a carrier."

"No!" Kit backed away toward the door, wanting to shut out that horror on the bed and its hoarse, sighing voice.

Suddenly Mr. Swenson sat up. "Kit, you got to stop it. You're the only one. I thought I would have the time to help you, but I figured it all out too late. You've got to go home."

Kit was crying now, and Malachi turned his face away to hide his own tears. "I don't know how!" he shouted. "Don't you think I'd go if I could? I don't know how to get home!"

Mr. Swenson fell back against the bed, as if the exertion had exhausted him. "You haven't really tried."

Silence fell, and a bird called clear and pure through the open window. A breeze ruffled the blue curtain.

"I don't think you can ask Helen. She's a good woman, none better, but she can't abide anything strange. That's why I hope I'm done and gone quick. If I linger with this, she won't be able to stand it."

"Dad, please," Malachi began.

"No, son." Mr. Swenson's eye turned toward him. "I gotta say it. My voice is going, too, and I may not be able to talk much more. Your mama's about as good a woman as I ever knew. And God alone knows why, but she's put just about her whole heart and soul into raising you and looking after me. To see me go this way is just about the hardest." He paused for breath. "Look after her, Malachi."

"Dad, you're not going to die."

"Maybe not, Malachi. But what there is left of me won't be

me any more, so it'll be just like I did die. Best to think of it as death and let me go. I'm changing, changing into something else. I can feel it shifting inside of me. Pretty soon, I'll be gone, and what'll be here in my place... well, I don't know. But it won't be me, it isn't me. It doesn't scare me—not much—but I just need you to look after your mama. She isn't as tough as she lets on."

"I know."

There was a pause. "I never told you how we met."

"Dad, don't tire yourself."

"Gotta tell you now, or you'll never know. She'd never tell you, too proud." His voice was fading, becoming no more than a whisper. "She grew up here, but didn't want life in the village. Farm girl. Wanted to dance, wanted to act. She went to New York City, was making it. Danced beautifully, she did. Loveliest thing I ever seen." He paused, his breath whistling in his throat. "She came back to spend a summer with her folks, and we fell in love. Hard to imagine us, isn't it?" A smile played over his cracked and ravaged mouth. "Went too far. Helen went back to the city and was only gone a few weeks when she called and told me she was pregnant."

Malachi closed his eyes tightly, his body shaking with sobs.

"Back then, there wasn't much else to do and stay honest folk. We got married as soon as we could, and hoped people wouldn't count backward on their fingers when the baby came."

"Oh, Dad..."

"She came early. Cutest girl baby I ever did see. Mary Marguerite. Only lived four days, but she was a lovely little thing. Doctors tried, but she just came too early, and there wasn't much they could do. Broke your mama's heart. She gave up her dancing and came back here, and settled in to being a farm wife. Gave up her whole dream, for me. I never forgot that, never forgot how much she sacrificed." The one eye looked at Malachi searchingly. "We always wanted kids. Lord didn't agree, I suppose. We had to wait another twenty-three years for you. Your mama was forty-two and I was forty-one, and we just about thought the sun rose and set on you. Still do, in fact." He paused. "I love you, Malachi, and I love your mama dearly. You just look after her."

"I will, Dad." His voice still hiccuped with sobs.

There was a low noise outside—two cars pulling in somewhere down the road, the sounds of doors slamming. Mr. Swenson, with his heightened hearing, swiveled his head toward the window. The skin on his neck cracked and splintered as he did so.

"What's going on?"

Kit walked to the window, and pushed aside the curtain. "There's an ambulance at the house up the road, the one across from the Addisons'."

Malachi turned and peered past him. "Mr. Gallagher's house."

Mr. Swenson closed his one eye, and seemed to sink back into the bed. "It's already gone farther, then." His voice was barely audible. "You've got to stop it. Kit, for all of us. Undo whatever it is you did. Go home, Kit. Go home."

12. a death and a disappearance

. . .

It was ten o'clock that morning, and Johnny Cole sat in his office thinking.

Strange couple of days. The worst things he usually had to deal with as Chief of Police were when some kid from regional tried to shoplift a candy bar at the Nice 'n' Easy, or one of the Addisons got drunk and disorderly. Some sort of weirdness was seeping down from the forested north end of the village, and he didn't like it.

The visit to Adam Thorne's house the previous day had turned up nothing, and worse still, Adam had somehow gotten convinced he'd been chased through the woods by something. And maybe he did, but maybe it was just his grief doing the talking.

They'd searched the area thoroughly, and not found so much as a broken branch. Adam went inside the house, and came out looking like an orphaned child. The whole house probably reminded him of Christina. Adam asked Cole to take him back to the Coles' house. He said that he wanted to get his stuff together and go back home that afternoon.

"Leslie won't like it."

"I want to be here," Adam responded. "Here is where

Christina is, what's left of her. I want to be near her." His voice sounded distant and forlorn, and not completely in touch with reality. But he went anyway. When Cole got off work at five-thirty, he gave Adam a lift back to his house.

And now, the next morning, the Chief of Police sat at his desk, which was covered with an untidy stack of paperwork weighted down by a mug a quarter-full of cold coffee. He drummed his fingers on the surface, and glanced at the photographs of Leslie and their two kids, Tom and Susan, smiling up from their gold-edged frames.

Something had gone seriously wrong in this town.

The telephone rang.

"Finn Hill police, Cole speaking."

What answered him was a woman's voice, almost incomprehensible through the hysterical sobs. "Ma'am, I can't understand you," he said, in a soothing voice. "Now, just slow down, take a breath. Tell me your name."

She hitched a few sobs, but got better control over herself. "This is Tina Lafleur. Oh, God, Johnny, he's dead, he's..." and she dissolved into tears again. This time, she stopped it herself. "It's Tony. Tony Gallagher. He didn't show up for work today, so I called his house, and no one answered. Mort and Amanda said they'd cover the office, so I drove up to his house. I knocked on the door, and nobody answered, but the door was open, so I went in. Oh, Johnny, he's dead, and I think... I think he killed himself. There's an empty bottle of sleeping pills on the floor, and..."

"I'll be right there."

Chief of Police Cole drove the mile from his office to Tony Gallagher's house in a state of deep perplexity. What was happening to the north end of the village? Christina Thorne's disappearance. Carl Swenson's strange disease. Trent

Addison going berserk and attacking some strange out-of-state kid with a knife. Now, poor Tony Gallagher killing himself. He couldn't shake the feeling that something, something unaccountable, was creeping down the road toward the village, attacking house after house, family after family. Who would be next? He made up his mind to watch Ann Garvey pretty closely for the next few days.

He had called an ambulance before he had left, and it arrived before he did. There was an aid car housed at the fire station, and it had been dispatched before he had left the office. Tina Lafleur met him on the front steps, still crying, but at least not hysterical. Tina was Tony Gallagher's secretary, a sweet if not very bright girl who sang in the Presbyterian church choir with Leslie on Sunday mornings. She waited while he did a cursory examination of the inside of the house, not wanting to re-enter it after such a shock. To be honest, Cole was glad she elected to stay outside. Crying women made him uncomfortable. Leslie wasn't a crier, and he was mighty glad about that.

There didn't seem to be anything unusual to be seen. A pretty clear-cut case of suicide by overdose. He motioned to the ambulance drivers to take the body, and rejoined Tina on the porch.

"I never even knew he was depressed," she told him. "Why didn't he tell me? He could have talked to me about it..." She stood back as the door opened, and watched, hand over her mouth, as two men came out, carrying a draped stretcher.

Johnny Cole patted her shoulder. "I'm sure it hit him hard when Claire died."

"But he never showed it!" she shouted. "Never! I told him, just a few weeks after, if he ever needed someone to talk to about it, I'd be happy to listen. He said he was doing fine, it was hard, of course, but he was coping. That's what he said, Johnny, exactly what he said! Oh, how could he have done this... how am I going to tell Amanda and Mort..."

The Chief of Police gave her another pat on the shoulder as the ambulance drove off. "You oughta go tell them now, get it over with, and then go home and take the rest of the day off. I'll ask Leslie to check in on you later." Tina nodded, her mouth trembling, and then turned and walked back to her car. As it was pulling away, Cole went back inside the empty house, and swung the door shut behind him.

Seemed like a tomb inside.

Until that day he had never been in Tony's house, but was immediately struck by the atmosphere of shadow and gloom that pervaded it. All the shades were drawn. There was nothing out of place. No, more than that—it looked as if nothing was ever used. The books on the shelves were perfectly lined up. A thick layer of dust lay on the mantelpiece above the fireplace. As far as he could tell, very little in this house had been touched in the past year.

Since Claire died, it was like Tony had died the same day, and nobody had lived here since.

He entered the den, and it was there that he was first struck by anything odd. A puddle of Coke on the carpet was drying to a sodden brown mass, the can lying beside it. The television wire had been pulled out from behind it, and it lay on the floor, plug pointing outward. He picked up the wire and fingered the plug, frowning thoughtfully.

Then he looked at the screen, and noticed the handprints.

The screen, like the rest of the house, was covered with dust, but the smooth film was broken by handprints, all over its surface. It looked as if someone had tried to claw the screen, to open it up and climb inside.

Deputy Nate Jenks was just walking out of the building as the Chief of Police pulled up. Jenks was a small, wiry man whose Italian ancestry (his mother had been a Cosentini from Brooklyn, and her parents straight from the old country) showed in his dark hair, olive skin, and brown eyes. His father, however, had been pure Adirondack. The Jenkses, Parkers, Goldings, Coles, and a few other families had settled this area in the eighteenth century and many of their progeny were still here. He was neither the most intelligent nor the most reliable deputy Cole ever had, but his last name had been an asset, especially with people like Averill Parker, who wouldn't even speak civilly to someone whose great-grandparents had been born one county over.

"What's up?" asked Cole, stepping out of the car.

"Craziest thing." The deputy paused with his hand on his own door handle. "You'd never guess who just called and wanted us to help her."

"Yeah?"

"Maureen Addison says her son's disappeared."

"All of 'em?"

"Don't get your hopes up. Just the teenager. You know, Trent—the one that beat up that out-of-towner staying up at Swenson's."

"Aw, cripes." If Maureen Addison had actually scraped together what little spunk she had left to ask the police for help, it must be something serious. If he knew Cleve at all, it probably wasn't with his blessing that she'd called and heaven only knew what she risked in order to do it. "I'd better come along. Hop in, Jenks, we'll take my car."

Jenks climbed into the passenger seat. The Chief of Police pulled out onto the highway, drove a quarter-mile, and made the left-hand turn onto Swenson Road. How many times had he made that turn in the last three days? Six times? Seven times? He passed Tony Gallagher's house, lying empty and filled with shadow. From the outside, it was still trim and neat, with its flowered plaque next to the door. Ann Garvey's cottage, across the road from Tony's house, still seemed untouched—her gardens flowered unabated, as if the house sat on an island in a river of flaming color running around the sides and down the walk. He drove on.

From the outside, everything looked normal. No one looking at the Swensons' house would have guessed that sickness lay within, and the Addisons' house was in no worse disrepair than usual. Still, Johnny felt, with a sixth sense that had served him well in the past, something was wrong. The whole area was slipping into a whirlpool of danger, a place where anything could happen.

The wheels of Johnny's car scrunched over the gravel in the Addison's driveway, and he noticed immediately that Cleve Addison's battered blue '88 Ford station wagon was gone. So that was how Maureen had managed it. Cleve was gone, and probably so were Jim and Andy, who were of like enough mind to their father that she would never have dared to call the police in their presence. As soon as Johnny and Nate Jenks climbed out of the car, the front door opened, and Maureen peered out from the shadowed interior. So did three or four small children. Johnny Cole said a silent prayer the kids would hold their tongues. A slipped word about a visit from the police could earn her a thorough beating.

He'd tried to stop it before. Intervening, warning Cleve to keep his fists off his wife and kids, but that resulted in worse beatings—and no one willing to press charges. Then, about three years ago Maureen called him out of the blue, and said one of the only direct and forceful sentences he'd ever heard her utter.

"You stop interferin', you hear?"

"I'm trying to help."

"You're makin' it worse. I need your help, I'll ask you for it. Till then, leave us the hell alone."

She hung up without waiting for a response.

Since then, he'd kept an eye on the Addisons, feeling guilty about what was clearly a case of abuse, but knowing his hands were tied unless Maureen herself asked for help.

And now, apparently, she was asking.

Maureen edged a foot out onto the unpainted front porch, holding her youngest daughter. Maureen Addison was only forty-five, but looked at least sixty. She had two missing teeth —whether from neglect or violence, Johnny didn't know, but he suspected the latter—and short, untidily cut iron-gray hair. She never met either of the men's eyes as she talked. Her gaze kept straying up the road, and there was a furtive, hurried quality about what she said indicating that she was afraid of getting caught.

For good reason.

"I ain't seen Trent since day before yesterday," she said. "It ain't like him to be gone this long. I... need your help. You gotta find him."

"Do you have any idea where he might be?"

"No. You gotta find him. I heard he cut up that kid stayin' up at Swensons'. I'm afraid he'll..." She paused, and peered down the road. A young boy of about three pushed forward past her, and she absent-mindedly shoved him back into the house. He took a step backward, lost his balance, and landed squarely on his rump. He began to cry, but she didn't even seem to notice.

"Find Trent. And tell that boy, that out-of-towner, Cleve's gonna kill him."

What the heck? Everything kept coming back to Kit. "Why's Cleve out for that boy?" he asked Maureen.

But she seemed near the end of her ability to risk being seen with the police, and she withdrew a step, back toward the door. "Jim and Andy too. They gonna get some of their friends up North Hanville way. Mason Sinclair, Tank Anderson and them boys used to work down on Lem Stutes' farm. They gonna cut him up."

"What for?" Johnny felt his head was spinning.

"They said he killed Trent."

"Killed him? Trent isn't dead, far as I know."

She pulled back into the shadows, and her thin, haunted face stared at him out of the gloom. Several smaller faces peered up at Johnny. The three-year-old had stopped crying, so her last words, though almost in a whisper, were clearly audible.

"They said they was gonna cut off his ears and keep 'em as a trophy."

The door closed.

Cole and Jenks stood for a moment, staring at the Addisons' unpainted front door in silence, then turned and walked down the rickety steps and over to Cole's car.

Jenks' normal bantering demeanor was gone. He gave a sidelong glance at his boss as he climbed into the passenger's seat.

"Sweet merciful Jesus," he said under his breath.

"You said it, my friend." Cole backed down the short driveway, but instead of turning back toward the station, he headed up Swenson Road. He pulled to the side in front of the Swensons' house, and shut the engine off.

"Gonna warn that kid, sir?"

"Not yet. Kit knows he's in danger. Trent Addison pretty near put him in the hospital yesterday. What we got to do is try to find Trent before Cleve and his boys make this mess a whole lot worse."

They got out of the car, and walked part way down the Swensons' sidewalk. It had not rained in two days, and there were still small drops of dried blood on the sidewalk. There were no clear marks on the road—the dirt was too packed down—but they found footprints in the soft soil underneath the ash trees where Trent had lain in wait for Kit.

The way Trent blundered through the cornfield in his flight after the fight was clear enough. He had not taken any kind of care as he ran, and bruised and flattened stalks marked a clear path. Johnny cursed himself for not having done this the previous day, but he had been so sure Trent would turn up home sooner or later that he let the matter rest.

Cole and Jenks followed the trail to the other side of the field, and more clear marks showed his turn toward home. The prints were intermittent, but unmistakable. They followed them to within a hundred yards of the Addisons' house, and then stopped. At that point the ground was too hard to hold any marks, and Johnny didn't especially want to provoke a confrontation with Cleve if he had come back in the interim, for Maureen's sake, if nothing else. Still, it seemed obvious Trent had made it almost all the way home.

But not all the way.

And where was he now? What had happened between the last prints, and the house? An eighth of a mile from home, or less, Trent Addison had either turned aside or vanished. And now his father, brother, and their gang were after a boy whose only crime seemed to be knowing enough martial arts to keep from getting the crap beaten out of him.

"Let's go, Jenks." Cole and Nate Jenks turned and walked back toward the cornfield.

God, this job hadn't been any fun the last couple of days. Galloping insanity. Who was gonna get hit next? He'd need to watch the rest of the folk up and down this road, and watch that boy. Nice kid. Wonder how he got himself mixed up with this.

Maureen Addison's last words came back to his mind. *They said they was gonna cut off his ears and keep 'em as a trophy.*

Yep, that kid was gonna take some watching. The rest of the folk too. If this really was some form of contagion, radiating from the old church or somewhere near it, then Ann Garvey would be the next person to get hit by it. He thought again of her cottage with its river of flowers—herself a plain, bespectacled school teacher, but her yard a riot of fiery colors.

Ann also happened to be one of the nicest people in the village. If he could help it, he wouldn't let anything happen to her. He decided to make sure he or Jenks passed by her house at least once an hour. It seemed the logical thing to do.

Not that anything about this situation so far had been logical.

13. lightning

. . .

It was eight o'clock, and the uneasy peace along Swenson Road still reigned. Its inhabitants were restive, sensing perhaps the same threat in the air that had alarmed Chief of Police Cole that afternoon. Each in his or her own way tried to make sense of the occurrences of the past days, and looked ahead to a shadowy future.

Kit McIntyre was in the Swensons' kitchen, fixing himself a simple and belated dinner of tuna fish on rye bread. He had left Malachi with his father earlier, and returned to the living room, where he had spent most of the day, reading and napping on the couch. He didn't feel inclined to go outside. God alone knew which combination of Addisons would be there waiting for him. It was nearly four when he realized, with some alarm, that Mrs. Swenson had not returned.

After some thought, he had looked up the number of the Finn Hill Police Station, and called. The Chief of Police wasn't there, but he told the deputy on duty about Mrs. Swenson.

"How long has she been gone?" the deputy asked.

"Since about nine o'clock this morning."

"Where'd she say she was going?"

"The grocery store."

"Geez Louise," the deputy muttered under his breath. "What the heck's happening up there?"

Kit didn't answer. The deputy finally said, "I'll tell Police Chief Cole. We'll take a look around. I can't imagine she's gone too far. May've just gone up to Carnahan to the pharmacy and run out of gas or something. Carl's sick, isn't he?"

"Yes. He is."

"Poor Malachi's probably out of his mind worrying," he said, more to himself than to Kit. "Okay, then, we'll let you know when we find her."

"Thanks."

He replaced the receiver, and sat staring at it for a while, debating inwardly whether or not to tell Malachi and Mr. Swenson. He didn't really want to return to that ghastly bedroom, and see what further degradation had occurred to its occupant, so he waited until the sun set in a blaze of crimson, scarlet, and orange, and dusk began, Now he sat alone in the big kitchen, listening to the slow ticking of the clock, and wondering what would happen next.

By nine o'clock, when it seemed obvious Malachi was not coming down and Mrs. Swenson wasn't going to return, he went to bed.

Malachi Swenson had fallen asleep in the rocking chair beside what was left of his father, and sat with his hands crossed over his chest in a pose almost of self-protection. His face was troubled, and his eyes moved under his closed lids. He was dreaming, dreaming of falling into a whirlpool, and being spun around like a ragdoll, helpless to stop the inexorable drag toward the center. He'd had this dream before, and it always left him exhausted.

His father, with perhaps his last human thought, moved his bone-china hands toward his son in pity. His one eye, almost all that was left of his original face, released a single tear. It strayed down the chalk-white surface of his cheek before dropping onto his pillow.

Adam Thorne, clad only in his boxers, lay on his bed, weeping silently for his lost wife. He had returned home to find the entire house permeated with Christina. Tony Gallagher—had he still been alive—would have understood his feelings quite well. Perhaps Leslie Cole was right. Maybe it wasn't a good idea to come back this soon.

Near dusk he became convinced he was being watched. He kept looking over his shoulder, all through his meager dinner and afterwards, as he tried to become engrossed in a book. Each time, he was afraid to turn around, sure some ghastly face would be leering in at him. Each time, he tightened his grip on his courage, and turned, and saw... nothing. Eventually, he pulled all of the window shades, climbed the stairs, undressed, and lay down in bed. Their bed. And began to cry.

Cleve, Jim, and Andy Addison, along with various undesirables from all over northern Hamilton County, were piled in Cleve's run-down station wagon. All of them were drunk, and the wagon wove all over the back road from North Hanville to Finn Hill. They were a good fifteen miles from the village, traveling at speeds which varied from forty miles an hour to five. Cleve's vision was lousy even when sober, but he had at least retained enough of his faculties to want to get to Finn Hill without piling his car into an embankment. No, he wanted to get there safe and sound, so he could watch as "the boys" took that kid apart.

He'd make that kid wish he'd never come within a hundred miles of Finn Hill. Got that straight. They'd carve that freak kid up like a Thanksgiving turkey.

As he drove, Cleve Addison began to grin.

Like Kit and Adam Thorne, Ann Garvey had also gone to bed early. She'd felt just horrid ever since finding out about poor Mr. Gallagher, although she really wasn't too surprised. Behind her second-grade-teacher sweetness and mousy appearance, Ann had one of the most perceptive minds in the village. Not much escaped her. She, probably more than anyone else, had seen past Tony Gallagher's happy-happy face. No, she was not really surprised. Saddened, but not surprised.

She lay down, removing her thick glasses and setting them on the bed stand. The entire world vanished into a blur. She was legally blind without them, and the helplessness she felt without them was her one real fear. She sometimes woke in the middle of the night, panicking, feeling around for her glasses, sure someone had crept in while she was asleep and stolen them. She pictured herself crawling around on her hands and knees trying to find them, trying to find the phone to get help, anything. They were always there under her groping hand, but the mere thought of losing them was enough to dump large quantities of adrenaline into her body.

Tonight, she lay there, staring silently and unseeingly at the ceiling. Things didn't seem right. She wasn't sure what was wrong, but something certainly was. More newsworthy events had happened in Finn Hill in the last week than had happened in the previous five years. In the past, just the arrival of the Swensons' visitor from Washington would have been noteworthy. Now, it paled into insignificance.

She thought about Kit, and smiled. It seemed obvious

Malachi was sweet on him. Despite his size, muscular frame, and a creditable intelligence, Malachi Swenson had an innocence that always seemed to Ann to be entirely charming. Just from their short visit, Ann had deduced correctly that Kit was gay, and was just as attracted to Malachi as Malachi was to him. Kit was a lucky boy. She wondered how long he'd be staying, and if maybe she should try her hand at encouraging the two of them to admit to each other how they felt.

Life, after all, was too short to waste time.

It was with that pleasant thought she finally fell asleep.

Maureen Addison stood at her front window, watching. All of the younger kids were in bed, although the baby, Crystal, still cried. No problem. Maureen's ma, in her long-ago and barely remembered childhood in Vermont, said crying was good for babies. Strengthened their lungs. Maureen was the second of nine children, and Pa and Ma Yates watched a lot of lungs get strengthened in their time.

She'd lived with Cleve Addison for twenty-five years, and had been subjected to nearly every kind of physical and emotional abuse at his hands, and later at the hands of her older two sons. Only now, as she stood watching out of her window, for almost the first time she contemplated what life would be like without him. It had crossed her mind once or twice before, in the first year of their marriage, once what little charm he had evaporated. The first serious beating happened six months, almost to the day, following their marriage. She had thought of killing him then. Even prison seemed preferable to looking down into her future, like looking into a hall of mirrors, and seeing everywhere she looked her pitiful body covered with the purpling shadow of bruises.

Then Jim had come, a beautiful little boy baby, and for a

while the horror seemed less. Cleve beat her less while she was pregnant, and that was one reason she never went on the pill. He would certainly not have objected—he couldn't have cared less about any of the kids. Ten children later, however, she wondered if that had been the right path to take. Maybe she should have killed Cleve while it had still been possible.

Wild fantasies flashed through her mind. Trent was gone, gone somewhere. Now Jim, Andy, and Cleve were off, too. Maybe they'd never return. She pictured her husband and her two oldest sons in a horrendous accident, and images of them mangled beyond recognition hung before her watery eyes. It brought no sense of pity into her, only wild hope and longing.

Which meant it wasn't gonna happen.

She watched for nearly two hours, hardly moving. The house and the sky darkened around her, and eventually Crystal decided her lungs were sufficiently strengthened for one night and went to sleep. Finally Maureen, too, gave up her vigil, and went to bed herself, the last one on Swenson Road still awake.

It was two hours later—just past one in the morning—when Malachi Swenson woke suddenly, flinging out his arms and legs, his heart thudding wildly in his ears. His movement was so sudden he almost overturned the rocker he had been sleeping in. He looked at his father's bed, wild terror in his eyes.

Carl Swenson—what was left of him—was sitting bolt upright. His body was all pure white now, and scraps of tanned skin, like a film of tissue paper, lay on the sheets under him and on the blankets. His smooth, porcelain-like flesh glowed faintly in the dark. He had his hands clapped over his ears, and his mouth gaped. A thin, spectral hissing sound, almost too high to hear, was coming from his throat. He—it—shrieked and thrashed on the bed.

Malachi grabbed his wrist, trying to pry his hand away from his ear, shouting, "Dad? Dad, what's wrong?" but his voice only made him pull away, the shrieking hiss becoming more hysterical. Finally he ran out of the room and down the stairs, and burst into Kit's room. Kit sat up in bed, groggy and confused.

"Kit, you've got to come! Something's wrong with Dad!"

Kit jumped out of bed, and without grabbing a shirt ran up the stairs behind him. When he reached the door, he froze, staring at the ghostly creature, shining faintly in its own light, pawing at its ears and hissing pitifully.

"What's wrong with him?" he asked, and at the same time realized how foolish it sounded. He forced himself to step into the room.

Malachi sat on the bed, and had grabbed his father's forearms, and was trying to pull them away. "Dad, please, it's all right! Just listen to me, Dad, please..." He seemed not to recognize his own son's voice, and the hiss became more shrill and terrible every time he spoke.

"Wait, Malachi, wait. You remember what he said today about his hearing? He said he heard everything louder. Maybe our voices are hurting his ears!"

He let Mr. Swenson's arms go, and sat back. He started to speak, thought better of it, and looked up at Kit, tears in his eyes.

The creature's thrashings diminished somewhat, but it remained with its hands over its ears, whimpering softly.

Malachi rose from the bed and walked to where Kit leaned against the doorframe. He glanced back at his father. Kit reached over and put his arm around his shoulders. Malachi leaned against him and whispered, "What could have started him screaming? He looks like he's in such pain..." He looked around, his eyes growing wide, as sudden realization dawned. "Where's Mom?"

"I don't know. She didn't come back from the grocery store. I called the police..."

Malachi buried his face in Kit's shoulder, and his strong frame shook with sobs. Kit pulled him close and held him silently as he cried, looking past him and out of the dark window into the night.

There was a sudden flash of light in the distance, and a loud rumble, like thunder. The creature on the bed shrieked again.

"My god," Kit said softly. "What was that? The sky is perfectly clear."

They went to the window. There, over the hills, there was a second flash of light, like rainbow-colored lightning. This time the rumble was deafening. The creature gave one more thin hiss, and then fell back limply against the bed.

"Dad!" Malachi cried out, and they both ran over to the bed. Kit slipped his hand beneath the blanket, and gingerly touched the creature's skin. It was smooth and soft as a baby's cheek. No roughness, no hair, not human in the least. However, beneath the creature's chest was a steady, if fast, heartbeat.

"I think he fainted," said Kit.

"Thank God," Malachi replied.

Kit stood again. "I wonder what's happening up there. Is that where Adam's house is?"

Malachi nodded, and simultaneously there was another flash and rumble.

"We'd better call the Chief of Police."

Kit's call awakened Johnny Cole instantly. He hardly needed to even pause to wonder what part of the village it would be coming from.

That idiot Jenks better not have forgotten to check on Ann Garvey. He'd have his butt on toast if he did.

But then he heard Kit identify himself. That kid again. What was going down now?

"Chief Cole." Kit's voice was calm, but Cole could hear the tension underneath. "We… Malachi and I, we keep seeing what looks like flashes of lightning, and loud noises, coming from up the road. Near Adam's house. I'm sorry for calling you at home, but I thought someone should tell you directly, not just call 911."

"I'll go up and check it out," Johnny told them. "Probably just heat lightning, but with all that's happened this week, I'll check it out. I'll stop back on the way back down just to put your mind at ease. How's the old man feeling?"

"Worse. A lot worse."

"Any word from Helen?"

"No, nothing."

"I'm on my way," Cole's concern was clear in his voice. "Maybe I should l stop in and check on you on the way up."

He hung up the phone, quickly pulled on some clothes, and ran out to his car, and backed out of his driveway five minutes later. Another five and he pulled in at the Swensons', at about the same moment as Cleve Addison's station wagon crossed the village limits three miles to the southeast.

Kit and Malachi were waiting at the door. Malachi seemed distraught, not surprising considering the circumstances. Johnny considered telling him what Jenks had said shortly before he'd turned in for the night – they hadn't found a trace of Helen Swenson between Finn Hill and Carnahan. Then he looked at the young man's face, and decided that the bad news could wait. With his father's illness, his mother's absence was probably enough of a worry without telling him that she seemed to have disappeared completely. Poor kid— it wasn't fair how troubles came in packages.

"Are you two okay?" he asked.

Kit nodded. "It's not us, we're doing all right. It's the noises we keep hearing. It sounds like thunder. Coming from up near Adam's house. It doesn't sound… natural."

Johnny pondered what this might mean, but at that moment there was a rumble and another flash. "I'd better get up there. I'll be back—and then maybe the three of you better all come stay with me and Leslie until your mom gets back." He said it in an offhand manner, but his thoughts were in turmoil. Gets back? Gets back from where? Since when did Helen Swenson go off into nowhere, leaving behind a sick husband, her son, and some strange kid from a nonexistent city in Washington State? God above, what was happening in this village?

They watched as he got back into his car, and drove off up the road, toward Adam Thorne's house and the strange, brightly-colored lights still intermittently flashing into the clear night sky.

14. wings

. . .

Johnny Cole drove carefully up Swenson Road, and took a left on Old Church Road. He wanted to take a look at Adam Thorne's house. He wasn't sure the lights had been coming from there, but it seemed close by. In the five minutes since he left the Swensons' house, there were no more lights, and there was total silence. The moon had not yet risen, and it was completely dark. The double beam of his headlights illuminated little more than the patch of road directly in front of him.

He turned right into Adam's driveway, and almost immediately his car gave a lurch and a thump as he ran over something. He braked to a stop, and opened the door. The overhead light came on, and in its thin glow he could see something long and narrow lying across the driveway. It looked like a piece of lumber, maybe a two by six. What the heck was a two by six doing in the middle of the driveway? He hoped like mad there weren't any nails in it. Last thing he needed was a flat at two in the morning.

He pulled his car into the gravel parking strip at the top of the driveway. The headlights swung around until they were pointing directly at the house.

Johnny's heart nearly stopped.

The wall he faced was smashed. No, worse than smashed —pulverized, like some great bulldozer had crushed it into splinters of shattered wood. There was a huge, gaping black hole, and where one of the headlights cut into the edge of it, he could see fallen beams crisscrossing back into the dim shadows behind.

Johnny was not especially given to swearing. Leslie long ago cured him of that. Now, however, any other words failed him—and truth be told, the occasion warranted it.

He reached over the passenger seat and pulled out his heavy-duty flashlight. At the same time, he switched on his radio and said, in a strained voice, "Pakkala, you copy?"

Dan Pakkala, the deputy on duty, returned within a few moments, "Pakkala here. That you, Chief?"

"Yes." All consciousness of protocol was clean gone, buried under the shock. "I'm up at Adam Thorne's house. Better get yourself up here. Call Jenks. We got an emergency. Looks like someone has... God help me, Dan, I don't even know how to describe it. Adam's house is smashed to bits."

"I'll be up there in five minutes."

"Make it three. Cole out."

He quietly opened the car door, and listened. There was only the sound of crickets and frogs. Nothing else, not even a breath of wind. He turned on the flashlight and climbed out of the car.

The beam of the flashlight skipped across the side of the house. He peered upwards, and only then did he see it was not only the wall that had been damaged—the whole roof had collapsed. He walked forward, his shoes crunching on shards of glass. There were still no sounds except his own, and the small night forest noises.

He rounded the corner. The back wall of the house, and the deck standing beside it, were no more than a heap of broken and scattered boards. There was no way of entering the house. There were not even enough gaps left in the frame-work to walk between. It had imploded, as if under a punch from a giant fist. Adam Thorne's house was nothing but a pile of scrap lumber.

Was Adam inside when this thing went down? If he was, they'd have to dig out his body with a backhoe. But if he wasn't, then where was he?

There was a rustling noise, near the top of what was left of the house, and Johnny jerked his flashlight in that direction. His heart and the beam of the flashlight both bounced along uncertainly for a few seconds, as a small section of the roof broke loose from the main piece, which was jutting high above the rest of the house at a steep angle, and crashed onto the wood pile below. It bounced and slid, and finally came to rest only a few feet from where Johnny stood. He froze for a moment, staring at it, trying to make his pulse return to normal.

No surprise. With this kind of damage, it was bound to keep settling for a while. He should be wearing a hard-hat.

He scowled at his own thoughts. *Maybe the house only fell down in the first place because it was structurally unsound. Yeah, yeah, Johnny. Keep telling yourself that. Maybe Adam should have been wearing a frickin' hard-hat. Don't be dumb.*

Cautiously, he continued his circuit of the ruined house. There was no sign either of Adam or of anyone or anything else, and certainly no indication of what could have caused such massive destruction. He turned back toward what had once been the deck. The access to the ruin seemed easiest there. He supposed he had to look for Adam, futile as it seemed.

He rounded the corner when something suddenly blocked out what little light there was—as if someone threw a black blanket over him. He jumped backwards, ducked, and hit the ground rolling. Something struck the broken wall behind him with a splintering crash and he was showered with fragments of wood. Then a low, rumbling snarl. Johnny scuttled away on all fours toward a row of nearby bushes. There was a massive thump as something heavy pounded against the ground, only inches behind him as he scrambled into the bushes, the branches scratching his face and hands.

What the heck good was a bush gonna do? For a thing that just busted up a house?

Still, it did not immediately follow, nor strike at the bush, and he peered out. Whatever had attacked him was directly in front of him, and so large that it blocked out all view of anything. It was impossible to tell what exactly it was. He cowered, expecting at any moment to be flattened by the thing.

Then a siren, in the distance. Pakkala, driving up Old Church Road.

The thing evidently heard the noise of the siren as well, because in a flutter like the flapping of a giant bed sheet, it swirled upwards and was gone. It was only then Johnny realized he hadn't even drawn his gun. Probably wouldn't have done anything but make it mad if he'd shot it—like a horsefly biting an elephant.

He remained hunched up deep inside the bush for a few moments as he heard the rumble of the approaching car from down the road. Only that and the siren—all else was silent. He peered out and saw his flashlight still lying where he had dropped it near the corner of the house, its beam shining off into nowhere.

Nice flashlight. Cost him thirty dollars at the hardware store, but right now he wouldn't take a thousand to retrieve it.

He crept out of the bush, remembering how suddenly he had been attacked before. No sign of the creature. He stood, squinting into the darkness. As silently as he could, he crossed into the shadow of the far wall of the house, holding his breath, his heart thudding in his ears.

The sound of the siren grew louder, and he heard the crunch of the tires on the gravel parking strip. The siren, and then the motor, shut off. He cautiously stuck his head out around the corner of the house, along what had once been the back deck.

Suddenly there was an earsplitting rumble, and a flash of light, followed by the sound of shattering glass. Johnny thought he heard a scream, but it was swallowed up in a grinding noise, like something heavy being dragged. Another scream, this one unmistakable, followed by a second loud crash.

This time Johnny drew his gun.

And wished he'd woke up Leslie and kissed her goodbye.

He ran around the corner and along the back of the house, stumbling on debris scattered around in the back yard. He reached the corner of the house that lay near the parking strip, and flattened himself against the wall, then peered out.

Dan Pakkala's car was tipped onto its front end. The brake lights shone redly up into the air. The front bumper was dragging along the gravel, pulling piles of rock back down the driveway. Unwillingly, Johnny's eyes were drawn upward.

The brake lights illuminated only the bottom half of the thing that had hold of Dan's car, but enough to give Johnny nightmares the rest of his life—however short that'll be, he dimly thought. It looked more than anything like a great black bird, but with a bat-like fluttering, flapping quality. It seemed to shift slightly as he looked at it, going from looking like a huge crow, then an enormous black bat, then to nothing the waking mind has ever seen or would ever want to. Its legs were thick, ropy with muscles, and scaly, ending in taloned claws wrapped around the back bumper of Dan's car.

The thing gave a huge flap with its wings, and the car lifted off the ground. The front end bounced once or twice against the driveway, and then pulled upward into the night. Gravel rained off the bumper and pelted Johnny in the gusts of wind from the thing's wings. Why didn't Dan open the door and jump out? But as the car twirled in the thing's grasp, he saw Dan Pakkala's bloodied head lolling out of the shattered driver's side window. He was either mercifully unconscious, or else already dead.

After a few moments, the thing gave another burst of flapping, lifting the car another ten feet off the ground, wildly swinging it over the ruined house. Johnny stood mostly hidden by an overhanging piece of the roof, protected from the creature's view but obscuring his own. He waited until the flapping sounded like it was headed away from him and made a dash for his car. He opened the door and swung behind the steering wheel, pulling the door firmly—but quietly—shut. He peered upward through the windshield. No sign of the thing. Had it perhaps missed him? There was a red glow off to the other end of the house—probably the brake lights of Pakkala's car. He fumbled his keys from his pocket, and stuck them in the ignition.

God almighty. He was gonna have to back this car all the way down the driveway in the dark. No time to turn around. That sucker'd be on him in ten seconds. If he hit a tree or the ditch, he was a goner.

He depressed the clutch and turned the key in the ignition. The engine caught. Still no sign of awareness from the thing. At least, it was still somewhere beyond the other end of the house, to judge by the glowing of Pakkala's brake lights. Perhaps the flapping of its own wings had drowned out the sound of the engine.

Johnny put the car in reverse, heeled the steering wheel hard over, and looked back over his shoulder.

He took a deep breath, and mumbled, "God in heaven. I know I haven't always done your will, and I know you must hear a thousand prayers like this every day, from people in tight corners. But you can also see I'm in a tighter corner right now than most folks'll ever see. Place your hand over me, Lord. I just want to be able to see Leslie and Tom and Susan again, Lord, just one more time, and tell 'em I love 'em. Please, Lord, guide my hand. Amen."

He released the clutch and stomped on the accelerator.

His car peeled out, shooting gravel from underneath its tires. It skidded out from the parking strip, turning onto the driveway on two wheels. The car slewed crazily from side to side, flying down the long driveway, the branches of shrubs scraping against the doors as he got too close first to one side and then to the other. Thumping loudly over debris. Johnny knew the creature saw him and was bearing down on him, but he couldn't spare an eye for it. If it got him, it got him. Right now he had to concentrate on getting down onto the road without piling into a tree.

He was right. If he had looked, he would have seen the creature drop Pakkala's car onto the ruined house—landing front-end first, bursting the fuel line, and seconds later explode into flames. Like a nightmare glider, the thing swooped down upon Cole's car fleeing backwards down the driveway, the two in a hellish race for the finish line.

Cole beat it by only seconds, and shot out onto Old Church Road. He slammed in the clutch and the brake, skidding wildly backwards, then popped it into first gear, and took off toward the intersection with Swenson Road, only a quarter mile away.

Suddenly there was a crash, and Johnny was struck from behind by hundreds of tiny pieces of flying glass. Simultaneously his back wheels spun out, and the car heeled around crazily. He fought for control of the car and gave a quick glance over his shoulder.

"God almighty!" he screamed.

The thing shattered the back windshield, and one huge, scaly foot was sticking right down into the car. Its talons were curled around the back seat, claws embedded in the vinyl seat cover. It was pulling upwards and backwards, trying to lift up his car just as it had Pakkala's. Johnny's mind raced. What could he do against something like this? There was no way to stop it, it was far too strong. Once the car was airborne, he might as well give up.

The car lurched, its left back end tipping upwards. Johnny was slung sideways, half into the passenger seat. His foot slipped off the accelerator, and the engine stalled. Face to the glove box, his fear evaporated. Feeling the thing straining against the weight of his solid patrol car, he popped open the glove box and rummaged through it as best he could. A bottle of aspirin, a road map, the registration papers, a tire pressure gauge. *Where is it? It's in here, I know it is, where is it...*

The rear of the car kept jerking higher with each blustery flap. At last, Johnny's hand felt and gripped the ivory handle of his hunting knife.

Breathing hard, he popped the snap on the sheath, and slipped it off, exposing the razor-sharp steel blade. With one quick, lithe movement, he reached back over the seat, burying the knife to the hilt in the creature's leg.

There was a horrific shriek from somewhere in the air above him, and the car slammed back down to the ground as the talons opened and let it drop. Johnny knocked his head on the ceiling, and then did a belly flop onto the steering wheel, sending a shockwave of pain up into his gut. He fell backward and landed on his butt in the driver's seat.

He pushed in the clutch, and turned the key in the ignition. The engine sputtered into life, and he peeled off down Old Church Road. He was doing an easy seventy miles an hour by the time he shot onto Swenson Road, and only then did he slow down and look over his shoulder.

He saw, or imagined he saw, a huge, diffuse blackness like a dark blanket floating in the sky over by where Adam Thorne had lived. It was lit from underneath by the orange glow of flames. Adam's wrecked house burned wildly, and would continue to burn out of control for nearly a day. In the fraction of a second Johnny watched it, the black shape congealed into a tiny speck, no larger than a bird. It then shot off like an arrow to the right, toward the old church, and was swallowed up in the general blackness of the night sky.

15. flames in the night

. . .

Kit and Malachi watched the tail lights of Police Chief Cole's car disappear up the dark road toward Adam Thorne's house, then shut the door and went back into the living room. Malachi sat down in his father's old recliner, his face in his hands. Kit sat on the couch.

"Malachi," he finally said quietly.

He looked up, his eyes red-rimmed and exhausted.

"Your father was right. So was your mom. I have to go home."

He shook his head weakly, as if this was a question he was tired of thinking about. "How?"

"I don't know, but they were right about something else, too. It's that church—the old Methodist church. The answer, somehow, is up there. I've got to go try. As soon as it's daylight."

"Why? What can possibly be up there?"

Kit shrugged. "I don't know."

Malachi rubbed his eyes, then looked up blearily. "How can you have caused all of this? It's just not possible."

He stood up and went to the window, looking out into the darkness. "I don't know." He sighed. "Somehow when I put on those ridiculous glasses, it changed everything. I wish it wasn't true. I'd like to stay. I mean, I miss my family, and I want to go home, but I wish..." He turned and looked at him. "I wish you were in my world. I'd like to be able to be friends with you. I just don't think it's possible. We don't... don't live in the same universe, or something. Your dad was right. I'm going to have to find a way to go home, or else whatever it was I brought with me—whatever's doing all of these horrible things—will destroy all of you. Maybe me, too, eventually. Or maybe your dad was right about that, too, and I'm just a carrier. But I don't want anyone else to get hurt. Especially..." He blushed, but quickly looked back out of the window, too fast for him to notice. "Especially you. Malachi, I... like you. A lot. I don't know if you've figured it out, but... I'm gay. I mean, I don't know if..." He trailed off, unable to figure out what more to say, or if he'd already said too much.

"I wondered." Malachi gave him a tired smile, but a genuine one. "I am too. I figured you knew. After... Trent."

"I wasn't sure. People like him call anyone they don't like gay. But there were other things, and it seemed like..." He paused, shrugged. "I know that we haven't known each other for very long..."

"You don't have to defend yourself."

"If I succeed tomorrow, we'll probably never see each other again."

Malachi looked up. "*Probably*. What does that mean? This whole situation is nuts. You don't even know what you're going to try to do in the morning."

"You've got a point."

Malachi stood up. "I'm just about dead on my feet. I've got to get some sleep. I don't know how Dad's going to be in the morning, or if... when they find Mom..." His voice hitched, but this time he held back the tears. "I don't want to be too exhausted to function."

There was a noise from outside of a car pulling up in front of the house.

"Is that Chief Cole?" Malachi asked, moving to the window.

"No. It came from the other direction."

All four doors of the car opened, and a number of figures, shadows in the darkness, climbed out. Kit and Malachi squinted out into the night for a moment, and then Malachi suddenly snapped out of his lethargy. He grabbed Kit's arm. Pulling him away from the window, he ran to the door and locked it. He hit the wall switch and turned off the living room light.

"What?" Kit was alarmed.

"We've got to get away from the windows. That's Cleve Addison's car. I saw Andy in the light when he opened the door, and there's a bunch of other guys, too!"

Malachi ran into the kitchen, followed by Kit. He locked the back door as well. After a moment's thought, he opened the door to the laundry room, and pulled Kit inside.

"No windows," he said, and Kit nodded. "What are we going to do? They've come after you!"

"We should call the police." He peered out around the door, in time to see a shadowy figure look into the kitchen window. Shortly afterwards a hand turned the doorknob. It rattled briefly, then stopped.

Kit waited for a moment, and then got down on his hands and knees, crawling to the counter along the back wall of the kitchen. He reached up and slid the phone off the counter, and dialed the number for the police station.

Four rings... five rings... six. He let the phone ring ten times before hanging up. Whoever heard of there being no one home at the police station? He knew the Chief of Police was up at Adam's, but shouldn't there have been a deputy on duty?

There was a furious pounding at the front door.

"Swenson!" came a voice, slurred with alcohol. "Wake up, you skinny old geezer!"

Malachi heard his father, or whatever creature his father had metamorphosed into, wake up and begin to wail again. Tears of anger and grief welled up in his eyes. Kit froze against the counter, his heart pounding.

"Send us out that kid, and we'll leave. We ain't got no quarrel with you or your family. We just want the kid. We got a score to settle."

There was no sound but the hissing shriek of Mr. Swenson, almost above the range of hearing.

"We know you're in there!" came another voice, younger than the first. "Come out, ya coward, or we'll have to just burn the house down with you and the rest of 'em in it!"

Without warning, there was a sudden flash like lightning, and another of the thunderous rumbles from up on the hill. Johnny Cole, only a half a mile away, had just begun his tail-first race for his life down Adam Thorne's driveway. Guessing that the men outside were distracted for a moment, Kit jumped up lightly and joined Malachi in the laundry room.

"You know these people. Would they really burn down the house?"

He nodded. "Andy Addison has fewer morals than anyone else I know. He's worse than Trent ever was. And... if the same thing has infected him that made Trent crazy, he'd do anything."

Kit nodded quietly. "Then I've got to go outside."

"Kit, no!" Malachi grabbed his shoulders and looked up at him. "Kit, do you know what they'll do to you?"

"I've got a pretty good idea."

"You can't..."

He cut him off. "I also can't let you and your father be hurt because of me. I've already done enough damage to this village. And maybe... maybe if I let them kill me, I'll just wake up and find myself back in my world. Maybe that's the way home."

"No! You can't take that chance!" Malachi's voice dropped in volume, but became fiercely intense. "I won't let you." He ran out of the laundry room, and across the living room. One of the men peering through the window saw him and shouted to the others. There was a clamor of voices and a rush of footsteps up onto the front porch.

Malachi came running down the stairs carrying a shotgun. He went up to the curtained window in the front door, braced the butt of the gun against his shoulder, and pointed the barrel at the window. "Get off my porch!" he shouted, in a deep, booming voice, so different from his normal gentle tones that it was hard to believe it came from the same person. "I've got a shotgun, and I know how to use it. If all of you people aren't gone in one minute, I'm going to open this door and shoot whoever's still here."

There was a breathless silence, and then the sound of feet moving quietly down the stairs. Kit thought he could hear voices, and the sound of a quiet laugh quickly suppressed. Then everything was silent again. Malachi stood frozen, holding the gun, for nearly a minute. Slowly, the muzzle of the gun drooped, his shoulders sagged, and he began to shake with quiet, helpless sobs.

Kit walked over and put his arms around him, and he relaxed against Kit's body like a child. Kit took the shotgun from his hands and leaned it against the couch, and gently helped him down onto it, and sat next to him.

Without warning, there was a crash of breaking glass from upstairs, and another screech from Mr. Swenson. Kit heard a bellow of harsh laughter, and leapt up and ran to the foot of the stairs. He looked up the staircase, and coming from one of the upstairs rooms was the red light of flames.

"Malachi! The house is on fire!"

"Kit, Dad's up there!"

"Stay down here. I'll go get him!" He leapt up the stairs three at a time. He ran down the upstairs hall. The fire was in Mr. Swenson's room. When he got to the door, the entire room was in flames. He could see an empty beer bottle lying in the middle of the room, and he smelled gasoline. He frantically looked for a way to get into the room, but even one step inside the heat was overwhelming. And a fantastic sight—one that rivaled what Johnny Cole had seen only minutes before —lay before Kit's eyes.

The thing which had once been Carl Swenson lay on the bed, flames were leaping around it. The bed itself was burning like a torch, but there was brighter light coming from inside it than from the flames themselves, as if illuminated from within. The creature itself seemed untouched by the conflagration, almost as if it were absorbing the flame, incorporating it into itself. It was becoming less and less human, as the fire burned away whatever vestiges of humanity were left to it. Finally, its shrieks diminished and ceased altogether. It stood up on the flaming bed, like a phoenix rising from its own pyre. And then it opened its eyes.

A dazzling flood of multicolored brilliance—the most beautiful thing Kit had ever seen—poured from the creature's eyes. The flames themselves paled in comparison. The creature was no longer even vaguely human, much less Carl Swenson any more. If anything, it looked angelic. Kit had heard his Catholic grandmother once talk about cherubim and seraphim. He suddenly knew for sure he was looking at one. It raised its radiant arms high above its head, opened its mouth, and uttered a single note of piercing, unearthly beauty, and then vanished. The whole event, from transfiguration to disappearance, took less than thirty seconds.

Kit stood, astonished, in the doorway a moment before being brought back to reality by the heat scorching his face and arms. He turned and fled back down the hall and down the stairs.

"Where is he?" Malachi shouted. "Kit, where's Dad?"

"He's gone," Kit was amazed to hear himself say so simply what a thousand words would be inadequate to express.

"You left him?" He started to run up the stairs, but Kit caught him by the shoulder.

"No, Malachi. I didn't say he was dead, and I didn't leave him. I can't explain it. He's gone. I saw him... Malachi, he was like an angel..."

The other boy backed away from him, a wild, desperate light in his eyes. "You're lying, you're crazy. I've got to go to my father..."

Kit stood staring at him. "Malachi…"

There was a crash, and the front door exploded inward. Kit jumped backwards and grabbed the shotgun, which was lying propped against the couch, and pointed it at the dark figure standing in the doorway.

"You two got to get out of here!" the man outside shouted.

It was Johnny Cole.

16. toward absolute zero

. . .

Charles James Fielding, Jr., of Carnahan, New York, walked down the highway that if he had followed it for fifteen miles would have led him to Finn Hill. That wasn't his intent. At that moment, Finn Hill wouldn't have been a particularly pleasant destination anyway. The village was in an unprecedented uproar, caused by the tragic burning of both the Swensons' and Adam Thorne's house the previous night. Charles—Charlie to his mother, C. J. to his father and friends—wouldn't have cared much had he known. Such events in the lives of total strangers in the next village don't usually make a great impact on the minds of nine-year-olds.

C. J.'s mind right at the moment was on his favorite summer pastime, which was fishing in the creek west of Carnahan. This was the first summer his mom let him go by himself, which was a considerable honor, and he was determined to take full advantage of it.

Carnahan was about four times the population of Finn Hill, and to the inhabitants of the smaller villages in the area, it seemed like a teeming metropolis. It hosted the regional high school and a small vocational-technical college, as well as the county seat. More importantly, it had the only cinema within a fifty-mile radius, three restaurants, and the roller rink. This last establishment was what probably led to its reputation among the older residents of rural areas of the county as a hotbed of crime and loose morals.

Despite its standing as the local big town, C. J.'s mother, who came from Syracuse and knew a big town when she saw one, correctly considered the streets of Carnahan about as safe as streets could be anywhere in the U.S.A. She let her boy do his roaming, as long as he remained conscientious about letting her know where he was and returning on time. This morning he had awakened at six-thirty, ate breakfast, and was ready to go by seven-fifteen. His parents were just getting up when he went upstairs to let them know where he was going ("down Sugar Crik"), what he was going to be doing ("fishin'," as if there was any doubt), and when he would return ("'bout lunchtime"). His parents gave him the nod, and he raced down the stairs and through the living room with the energy only children under ten seem to have, scooping up his fishing pole, tackle box, and snack on the way. Soon he was ambling down the road under the July early morning sunshine.

It was under a mile's walk along the broad shoulder of the highway from his parents' house to Sugar Creek, and took C. J. about a half an hour taking it pretty easy. He was a fairly unusual kid—not in his enjoyment of fishing, which half his classmates shared, but in his enjoyment of solitude. C. J. was a friendly boy with a big, open smile in a face bronzed with summer tan, and a fairly unruly mop of light blond hair. A likable and well-liked kid who in his nine years had made no real enemies, but no real friends either. He was most comfortable when alone. He spent countless hours roaming by himself on his parents' 110 acres, over half of which was forested. His mom quickly gave up worrying about him—he was careful, conscientious, and seemed completely happy. He was simply a natural-born loner, content to think his own thoughts and not have them interrupted by the clamor of other people's voices.

Today, he reached the Sugar Creek bridge in just under a half-hour. The best fishing spots were a couple of deep pools about two hundred feet downstream, where he could sit for hours in the shade of huge old sugar maple trees, daydream, and watch his bobber for a sign of a bite. The easiest way to reach them was to cross the bridge and scramble down a steep trail on the opposite side. He typically removed his shoes and waded the rest of the way in the shallows. The slab-like pink granite making up the foundations of the creek bed made for easy, if sometimes slick, walking.

He crossed over the bridge. A car whooshed by, and he waved at Mr. O'Reilly, the owner of the local feed store, driving his battered Buick to work. Mr. O'Reilly grinned and waved back. C. J. turned left onto the top of the narrow trail down to the creek.

Immediately, his smile faded. The sumac and willow bushes lining the trail were bent and broken. There were tire tracks in the damp earth, leading down toward the creek itself. He had been down this trail early yesterday morning at about seven-thirty, and stayed on the creek until shortly after nine o'clock, when he had to leave with his parents to go visit his grandmother for the day. Had there been a car accident between then and now? Looked like it. He set down his gear at the trailhead and jogged down toward the creek.

At the bottom, the damage was even more apparent. The tracks reaching the soft, muddy creek bank had churned up deep ruts. Whoever did this must have been going awful fast. He reached the bottom of the trail, and pushed his way through the willow scrub at the bank, and looked out into the creek.

About midway out in the creek, but still in shallow water —this section of the creek was all under three feet deep—sat a blue four-door car. It evidently had been heading toward

Carnahan when it had gone off the road and down the bank, and then swerved to the left. Its front end was actually under the bridge, which perhaps explained why no one had seen it until now.

Heart pounding, C. J. stared out into the stream at the car. For some reason, he couldn't see into its interior. Perhaps only a trick of the shadows of the bridge and the trees. The stream chattered by, and a faint breeze stirred his over-long summer hair. He continued to stare at the car, debating inwardly whether to investigate. His mother's frequent use of the phrase "curiosity killed the cat" came to mind, but then he thought of his dad's gleeful rejoinder, "and satisfaction brought him back." He leaned forward, trying for a better view, but still couldn't see in. Anyhow, the car didn't look like exploding or giving forth mobsters or monsters any time soon. The cat side of him won. He pulled off his shoes and waded out towards it.

As he got close to it, he understood why he hadn't been able to see into it. The rear window, which faced him, was covered with some kind of scum or fog, rendering it completely opaque. The creek water swirling around his calves, he walked around to the driver's side, plunging into the shadow of the bridge.

All of the windows were obscured in the same fashion.

He stood staring at the drivers' window, wondering if he dared to open the door.

No, bad idea. All that water'd go into the car. Even though it was probably leaking in anyhow.

Half unwillingly, he raised his hand, and reached out the tips of his fingers to touch the metal door handle. Immediately he gave a yelp and took a step backwards, slipped on the creek bed and sat down. The water only came up to mid-chest sitting down, but he stood back up quickly, panting and dripping, staring at the car with a new fear.

The door handle had been cold. Cold enough to take the skin off his fingertips. Cold enough to burn.

C. J. took off his battered baseball cap, dipped out some water from the creek, and poured it over the handle. There was a sizzling sound, and when he was done, the handle was coated with ice.

"Jiminy," he said under his breath.

He leaned forward, and with a sudden start realized what all along had been obscuring the windows. Had it been winter, he would have recognized it immediately—it was the bane of any upstate New York driver who didn't have a garage. It was frost, a thick enough coat to completely block all of the windows.

As he absorbed the entirely novel concept of frosted windows in midsummer, he saw the final thing—the thing that sent him pelting back up the trail towards home, the thing that made him even forget to retrieve his precious fishing pole and tackle box. In the center of the driver's side window, frozen into the frost crystals and layer of ice on the inside of the car, was gray hair. He saw the clearly recognizable swirled hair that came from the part on the top of someone's head. Someone who was still in there, sitting in the driver's seat, leaning over, the top of their head pressed against the window. Someone who was surely frozen solid, to judge by the temperature of the door handle.

C. J. made it all the way home in a little over ten minutes.

Chief of Police Mark McLarney, Johnny Cole's counterpart in the precinct east of Finn Hill, which included Carnahan and seven villages farther east and south, was not a man who liked mysteries. He lacked Johnny's intelligence, compassion, and drive, and had built his reputation as a staunch defender of order—of the way things "should be." He ran a tight precinct, and his men were instructed daily on their duty to keep things that way. The Chief of Police was a positive terror to the kids of Carnahan. Kids, in McLarney's mind, were problems waiting to happen. Always running around screaming obscenities, throwing rocks at street lamps, pissing off bridges. Bunch of incipient delinquents.

That was why Charles Fielding, Sr.'s telephone call to the office at eight o'clock in the morning with a story of a wrecked car in Sugar Creek was bad enough. But when he added that his nine-year old son said there was a frozen body inside, it had really toasted Police Chief McLarney's fanny, to use his favorite expression. Doggone prank-playing little squirt. Now, of course, he'd have to spend his valuable time checking it out, and of course it'd turn out to be an old grocery cart or something. And if that kid was his, wouldn't he have just tanned his backside so good the brat'd have to eat standing up for a week? Couldn't believe any self-respecting father would even call up the police with a story like that.

Ten minutes later, the Chief of Police and the deputy were standing together with the water of Sugar Creek swirling around their legs, and for the first time in recent memory McLarney found himself speechless, all thoughts of toasted and/or tanned posteriors forgotten.

The water C. J. had poured from his cap onto the door handle a half-hour earlier had solidified into a row of tiny icicles. McLarney pulled out a handkerchief and wrapped it around his hand—he remembered the father saying something about "so cold it burned my son's fingers"—and tugged at the door handle. It gave way with a crunch, and chunks of ice dropped into the warm creek water and spun away downstream. The door creaked open, and a gush of cold air came from the interior, fogging in the humid summer air. It felt like it had come from the inside of a deep freezer.

The door swung open. There was a harsh grating sound, and the body of a woman fell halfway out of the car.

The deputy swore loudly and vehemently, forgetting that the Chief of Police, a staunch Baptist, didn't hold with swearing. He gave a sidewise glance at his boss, but this time, McLarney didn't even seem to have heard. They both stared dumbly at the woman.

McLarney had heard people say they were "frozen stiff" by the harsh New York winter weather, but that was hyperbole. This woman really was. Her arms were bent and outstretched, fingers curled into parallel arcs, as if she had been flash frozen while driving. There were frost crystals in her hair and on her brows and lashes. Her eyes were half closed. Her skin was mottled bluish, and looked dull, like unglazed ceramic.

Wordlessly, the Chief of Police turned, waded back to shore, and trudged back up the hill to his car. He opened the door, and sat down in the driver's seat, one foot still on the shoulder of the road, and radioed the office.

"This is Chief of Police McLarney calling the precinct office. Sheila, you there?"

"I copy, sir," came a female voice.

"Sheila, put in a call to the morgue. Get an ambulance out to the Sugar Creek bridge. There's been an automobile accident. Car ran off the road and into the creek. Driver's dead."

"Yes, sir."

There was a pause. "One more thing."

"Yes, sir?"

"Tell them the body is frozen."

Sheila did not respond for a moment.

"You copy, Sheila?"

"Could you repeat that, sir?"

"It's frozen. Frozen solid. Tell them the driver looks like she's spent about three weeks in a meat locker. I know it sounds weird, but it's the truth. You copy?"

"Uh... yes, sir."
"McLarney out."

The ambulance arrived, and the body was taken out by two young men who, despite training and several years of dealing with accident victims in various stages of dismemberment, looked to be aghast at what they had found. They had to wrap cloth around their hands, or they would have been seared by the intense cold pouring from the woman's body. Then, they found they couldn't straighten her out. Finally the body was not laid out flat, as was typical, but stayed curled up on its side in a half-fetal position on the stretcher, its arms outstretched eerily beneath the sheet. A truck was called in to winch the car up out of the creek.

Through all of this, the Chief of Police watched with a grim look on his face. The car looked almost normal now. All of the frost had melted, and both the inside and the outside of the windows were covered with condensation. It was almost like she was the source of the cold, but that seemed so impossible he dismissed the idea immediately.

A purse in the passenger seat had contained the driver's license of a Helen Swenson of Finn Hill, and the picture looked like it matched the driver's face. That meant he was going to have to give Johnny Cole a call. This would blow that old buzzard's socks off. About time he had to do some real work in that cozy little village of his.

After the car was towed, the Chief of Police drove back to his office. He poured himself a belated cup of coffee—Charles Fielding's call had robbed him of his eight o'clock cup—but he had hardly sat down at his desk when a call came in from the county coroner's office. The coroner's office was itself in Carnahan, which was the county seat—in fact, it was located only three doors away from the police station.

A voice growled into the telephone, with no preamble whatsoever, "What the devil's going on with this woman, Mac?"

"Doggone if I know, George." George Cochran was the county coroner, and one of the only people in Carnahan who could beat the Chief of Police for brusqueness. As a result, McLarney was slightly intimidated by him, and disliked the inevitable contacts with him intensely. For one thing, Cochran was the only person he knew with the nerve to call him Mac. He hated that nickname.

"I've never seen anything like it in my career, and I thought I'd seen it all. You got any idea what her body temperature was when she was brought in?"

"I didn't take it, but it was cold enough to make frost all over the inside of the car."

Cochran laughed. "It was a rhetorical question, Mac. It was also more than enough to frost the windows. Her core body temperature—as well as we could tell, you couldn't get a thermometer into any orifice in her body without drilling a hole into her with a steel bit—was 143 degrees below zero Fahrenheit. We had to dig a subzero temperature probe out of storage to take her temperature."

"You gotta be kidding."

"It gets better, Mac, it gets better. She's been lying on my table for about fifteen minutes now. You know what her temperature was about two minutes ago, just before I called? 151 degrees below zero. She's cooling off at a rate of about six degrees every ten minutes."

"How is that possible?"

Another raspy laugh. "Well, it's some process I never learned about at med school. Who is she?"

"Some woman up from Finn Hill."

"You'd better get in gear and call up Johnny Cole and find out what the devil is going on."

McLarney gritted his teeth. He hated it when George

Cochran told him how to do his job, which was fairly often. "I was just about to do that. I had to make a complete search of the car before it could be towed, and I just got back to the office myself."

"Okay, then. Let me know what you find." Click.

McLarney slammed down the phone. If he had been a swearer, he probably would have let a few ripe phrases fall. Instead, he simply flushed dark red, muttered dire predictions of what this job was doing to his blood pressure, and dialed Johnny Cole's number. He did, however, allow himself the luxury of punching the buttons with unusual vehemence.

"Finn Hill Police Station, Deputy Jenks speaking."

"Jenks, this is Chief of Police McLarney over in Carnahan. Your boss there?"

"No, sir. He's... out," he finished lamely.

"Guess I might as well have you tell him. I have a body over here of one of yours. Name of Helen Swenson. Ring any bells?"

"Jesus Christ," said Jenks with some force.

"I beg your pardon, deputy," barked McLarney into the phone.

"I'm sorry, sir, it slipped out. It's just that... things have been kind of weird over here the last few days, and the Swensons have been in the middle of it. Carl Swenson—that's Helen's husband—seemingly died last night in a house fire, although they haven't found his body yet. Helen disappeared sometime around yesterday midday, and we looked for her all over Finn Hill and round about, and couldn't find her. How'd she die?"

"There, you got me, deputy. She was found by a kid. Her car had skidded down an embankment into a creek, but the accident doesn't seem like it was the cause of death. Truth to tell, she seems like she froze to death."

"Froze to death? In July? Jesus Christ."

This time McLarney let the impiety pass. "You got it. I'd

like a word with Cole when he comes in. There's something weird going on here."

"I'll let him know."

McLarney got even with George Cochran by hanging up on the deputy without a further word, but it didn't really make him feel better. In fact, it was only a little after nine o'clock, and he felt a rotten headache coming on. It didn't look like the day was on its way to improving much.

17. ambush

. . .

K it woke up at about eight o'clock that morning on the sofa in Johnny Cole's living room. Cole had driven him and Malachi there the previous evening, when it was clear that somehow, both of Malachi's parents were gone, and the Swensons' house was beyond the help of any amateur firefighting.

By the time they left, the house was already a roaring inferno. Kit had not realized how loud a house fire was. Flames swept through the old wood frame house so fast Kit and Malachi didn't have time to gather any of the Swensons' belongings. The racing and crackling fire was like the last triumph of the strange fate which this week brought, and it was bent on erasing every trace of the Swensons from Finn Hill.

Malachi was in shock as he climbed into the front seat of Johnny Cole's car, and the Chief of Police got a rough blanket from his trunk and slid it around his shoulders. He didn't even seem to notice the car itself looked like it had been through a trash compactor.

"What happened up at Adam's house?" asked Kit, his voice rough from the smoke and from exhaustion.

"Son, I don't want to talk about it," Cole said in a tense voice. "I don't even know if I believe it myself."

Kit used an old towel on the floor in the back of the car to brush the glass off the seat, and spread it over the seat before he sat down. Cole started his car and drove off down Swenson Road in silence. There didn't seem to be much to say. There were no lights on as they passed the Addison's house, and Kit noticed Cleve's car wasn't in the driveway.

Leslie Cole got up when she heard them come in, and the horror and sadness registered immediately in her face when her husband told her about the loss of the Swensons' house. Malachi stood shivering and mute, and Kit put his arm around him. He leaned into Kit gratefully, but Malachi's eyes still registered a shocked lack of emotion.

Leslie settled Malachi down in the spare bedroom, which until recently had been occupied by Adam Thorne. She apologetically gave Kit the sofa to sleep on, and he lay down. He heard the Malachi sobbing softly in his room, and he wanted to go and comfort him, hold him in his arms and take away his grief. With a drowsy surprise, Kit realized he was falling in love with him. Moments later, he was asleep.

It seemed like no time passed at all. Kit was suddenly and completely awake, and the clock on the living room wall stood at a little past eight. Light streamed in the window. It was another beautiful day in the Adirondacks.

Kit looked around him. He had been too exhausted to notice much the previous night. The Coles' living room was a perfect reflection of the Chief of Police and his wife—simple, unpretentious, straightforward. The walls were of varnished pine paneling, a warm and pleasant orangey brown. There was a fireplace insert, and a narrow mantelpiece with pictures of two smiling people in their late teens or early twenties, a boy and a girl. Kit guessed they were the Coles' children. The furniture was plain and unadorned, but somehow suited the house exactly. The one pretense toward interior decorating was a print hanging over the sofa, depicting a garden and a pond with water lilies. It was pretty, but seemed somehow out of place. Kit wondered who had given it to them for Christmas.

A warm smell of fried sausage hung in the air, and Kit heard Leslie Cole bustling about the kitchen. Kit stretched like a sleepy cat and sat up.

Leslie heard his motion and turned. Peering back through the open door into the living room, she gave him a smile that activated lines around her mouth, though her eyes spoke a sadness the smile could not disguise. She quickly dried her hands on the kitchen towel, hung it neatly over the oven handle, and walked into the living room.

"I'm Leslie Cole." She extended her hand. "We met briefly last night, but you looked so exhausted I don't expect you remember."

Kit shook her hand. "I remember you."

Leslie sat down in an old wicker-backed rocker, and regarded him with compassion. "Guess there's no easy way to say it, and I guess you also ought to know. Helen Swenson is still missing. Firefighters have been up at the Swensons' house, and they haven't found Carl's body yet, but it's pretty clear he died in the fire. Johnny paid an early call to the Addisons', but there's no sign of Cleve or his sons and their gang. Johnny told me to tell you you should lay low here today, or at least till he finds them and brings them in."

Kit looked at her squarely. "I can't do that."

"Why not?"

God help him. Here he was, having to explain all this to another person. Wasn't this ever going to get any easier?

"I can only explain it by saying that it's time for me to try to find my way back home," he said finally. "It was almost the last thing Mr. Swenson said to me. I've got to return to the old church, where it all started." She frowned at him, and her eyes registered no comprehension of what he was saying. "I know you think what I'm saying doesn't make any sense. You're right, it doesn't. But that doesn't make it false. This whole situation is crazy. I've got to turn things back around, bring it all back in line."

"I don't understand you at all." Her voice was quiet and held no accusation.

"Mrs. Cole, I know this will be hard for you to believe, but you've got to believe me. The Swensons believed me, and I swear to you I'm telling the truth. I am not from this world. Somehow I have to get back to my own world."

She eyed him dubiously. "Kit, you can't go. Johnny told me to keep you here, so I can't let you leave."

"He doesn't understand. If he did, he'd let me go." Kit chuckled grimly. "If he understood, he wouldn't let me within a hundred miles of his house. It's the only way all of this will stop. I'm the one who started all of it—Mr. Swenson's illness, the disappearance of Christina Thorne, all of the craziness over at the Addisons'. If I leave, then things will right themselves, and it'll all go back to normal." He paused for a moment. "I hope."

She still regarded him with perplexity, and Kit realized with a dawning sense of despair that both of the people who believed him—or who had been trying to, anyway—were gone. Helen and Carl Swenson were the only adults with any credibility who could have convinced this nice woman that Kit McIntyre wasn't stark raving crazy, and God only knew where either of them were now.

"You've got to believe me, Mrs. Cole."

There was a sound of a door, and Leslie turned. Malachi Swenson walked out of the spare bedroom. He was pale, his face drawn with exhaustion. The sight of him made Kit's heart ache. How long would it be before he smiled again?

"He's telling the truth, Mrs. Cole." His voice was totally inflectionless. "Kit doesn't come from our world. He just needs to go home. You've got to help him."

Leslie's forehead creased, and she leaned back in the rocker. "This all sounds like some kind of fantasy story."

"Maybe it is."

Leslie took a deep breath, and stood up. She smoothed back her hair in a distracted fashion. "Well, neither of you are going anywhere without breakfast. I'll fix you some sausage and eggs, and it will give me space to think about all of this."

It was shortly after they had picked up and washed the breakfast dishes that Johnny Cole came back. All three froze as he walked in. Leslie stood at an open cabinet, arranging clean glasses and plates. Kit and Malachi were putting away the butter, salt, and pepper. The Chief of Police's face was grim and white. Leslie knew him well, and knew only bad news—really bad—could upset his equanimity to this degree. "What's wrong?" She closed the kitchen cabinet. Kit glanced at Malachi, whose expression had not changed.

Cole came and stood in the doorway into the kitchen. "Malachi—"

"It's Mom, isn't it?" His voice was quiet and emotionless. "You found Mom, and she's dead."

Cole's eyes widened in surprise, and he nodded.

"Oh, dear God," Leslie whispered under her breath.

"I knew it. I dreamed it last night. I saw Dad. He came and talked to me. He said Mom was dead, but I shouldn't worry, because they were together. He said I should help you get home, but not to let my grief ruin my life." He looked over at Kit. "He told me he didn't die in the fire, his body simply became something else until there was none of him left. He said it was like dying in childbirth, giving birth to an angel." He swallowed. "I'm sorry I didn't believe you, Kit."

"Child," said Leslie.

"No, it's all right. I can't cry now. Later." Malachi turned toward the Coles. "Don't you see? What Kit told you, it's true. It's all true. He's got to get home before this whole world falls apart. You've got to help us. *Please.*"

Cole looked at his wife. "What are you asking us to do?"

Kit looked at him steadily. "Just let me go. Back up to the old church, where it all started."

The Chief of Police's eyes registered a sudden stab of fear. "Kit, I can't let you do that. You don't know what's up there."

"You're right. I don't. But worse things are going to happen unless I do." Kit swallowed. "And maybe even if I'm killed, it will still work. Maybe I'm just the sacrifice—like in the old days, when they'd throw people into stop the volcano from erupting. All I know is, I've got to try."

"Kit. There's some… some *thing* up there." When Cole spoke, Leslie turned and looked at him in amazement, obviously aghast at the raw terror in his voice. "I've never seen nothing like it, not in my worst nightmares. It killed Adam Thorne and Dan Pakkala. It destroyed Adam's house, and nearly killed me. You can't think of just… just walking up to something like that."

"I have to."

"I can't let you."

"Sir, you *have* to. If you don't, you have no idea of what's going to happen. I don't know either, not really, but I *feel* it. It's like a huge brushfire. It started with a tiny spark, then spread, and soon it's going to go out of control. Whatever you saw up there—it's only the beginning. Think about that, and imagine something worse. That's what's coming, if you stop me."

"You're expecting me to let you go alone?"

"I'm not asking you to come with me."

"I can't do that," Johnny said after a moment. "You go, I'm going with you. But I gotta tell you, there's a good chance neither of us will come back alive."

"I'll go by myself if I have to." Kit met his eyes steadily. "And I have to. You know that."

Malachi shook his head. "No. I'm coming with you, too. Police Chief Cole is right. You can't go alone. No freakin' way."

"God almighty." Cole glanced out of the window. "You two half got me believing all of this."

Kit's voice was completely emotionless. "If I'm lying, then how do you explain what happened to you last night?"

There was silence for a moment. A cardinal at the bird feeder outside the kitchen window sang loudly. Cole looked again at his wife. "Leslie," he began.

"Johnny Cole," she said in alarm, "you can't mean to…"

"It's my business to check out anything strange. I'm just going to drive them up, and have a look around. I'll call for backup at the first sign of trouble."

Leslie twisted her apron in her hand, and sat down at the kitchen table. "Johnny—"

"I'll be careful."

"You be more than careful. Johnny, are you sure—"

"No. Not sure. But I've got a feeling, and I've got to see it through." He looked up at Kit. "I had a feeling about you, from the first time I met you, up there at Adam's the night Christina disappeared. Like you don't belong here. You don't strike me as a lying runaway. I guess if I believe that feeling, I've got to act accordingly." He leaned over and gave his wife a kiss. "Don't you worry any more than usual, now, Leslie." He walked over to the door, and motioned to Kit and Malachi. "Come on. If we're gonna do it, let's do it." They followed him to the door. Kit turned, and looked at Leslie, still sitting, looking small and worried in the brightly lit kitchen.

"Thank you for everything. I'll probably... probably never see you again. But I'm glad we met. I wish I could stay here. You're such... such good people."

Leslie's voice was strained. "Good luck. I hope..." she paused, and managed a thin smile. "I hope you get home, Kit."

"Me too," he said, as he walked through the door.

They climbed into the Chief of Police's car, and he backed down his driveway and onto the road. The road from the Coles' house wound around a good bit, but finally struck the highway east of the village. Johnny Cole sat with his elbow propped on the frame of his open window, driving with one hand. Only his eyes betrayed his apprehension. Neither Kit nor Malachi knew of the huge, black, winged creature which was haunting him, into whose talons he now felt he was delivering them. Kit stared out of the passenger side window, looking lost in his own thoughts. Malachi was mute as well, his hands on his knees, looking forward through the windshield.

They passed the first of the side roads, which intersected the road they traveled on from the left. A rusty blue station wagon was stopped at the intersection, but after a moment it pulled out behind them. Instinctively, Johnny glanced in the rear-view mirror.

"Uh-oh."

Kit turned to look at him. "What's wrong?"

"Your buddies are back."

Kit looked back over his shoulder, and his heart began to thud in his chest. Behind the wheel of the station wagon, Cleve Addison's fat face was clearly visible, his teeth exposed in a vicious grin. Andy Addison was in the passenger seat, and looked like he was cradling a gun.

Several other people could be seen as shadows in the back seat.

"I think one of them has a gun," said Kit. Malachi let out a faint moan, but did not turn.

"They won't try anything as long as I'm with you," Cole said soothingly.

Simultaneously, Andy Addison leaned out of his window, let out a high-pitched war whoop, and shot out one of the squad car's tires.

The car immediately slewed to the right. Johnny and Malachi both swore, saying exactly the same word at the same time, something that under any other circumstances would have been funny. The front right tire slipped over the edge of the shoulder, and the rear end of the car swung around, gravel flicking out from under the tires. Johnny hit the brakes, but it was too late. The front end of the car plunged over the edge of a five-foot drop off, the rear end up like the Titanic going down for the last time. The car flipped over, skidded downhill for about twenty yards, then lay still.

Cleve screeched to a halt, and Andy and Jim jumped out of the car. Andy grinned wildly. They waited for a moment, but there was no sound or motion from within the Chief of Police's car.

"We got 'em all," Andy said. "All three of 'em. Cole, too."

"I hope that kid's still alive," said Jim grimly. "Gonna cut him up good."

Andy jumped over the embankment, and Jim followed. Cleve and one of the other men got out and stood, watching, as they walked down the hill. Leaves crunched under their run-down sneakers. There was a sudden *chunk-chunk* as Andy re-cocked his gun. Still no sound came from the car.

Andy's gait became stealthy, and he brought his gun up to his shoulder. He was only about five feet from the driver's side window, which was open. He could see Johnny's back. His left arm seemed injured. Blood stained his sleeve, and his body was motionless, still hanging upside-down from the shoulder harness.

"Looks like all of 'em are dead, or knocked out!" Andy called up to his father, but not taking his eye off the car. "Don't care, gonna have some fun. Blow some holes in 'em. Startin' with Cole. I owe him from way back." He took aim at Johnny Cole's head.

Johnny turned and brought up his pistol, held firmly in his right hand. Aiming a pistol upside down was not something he'd ever been taught, but he did it admirably. The bullet caught Andy Addison squarely in the chest. He pitched backward, and his shotgun went off. The shot went nearly vertical. The kick slammed him into the ground. A small amount of blood trickled out of his mouth, and he died without uttering a word—although the surprise in his staring eyes spoke volumes.

Jim Addison swore under his breath and ran for the shotgun. Johnny Cole shouted, "Don't, Jim, or you'll join him. I have an open channel to the station, and they know what's happened. My deputy will be here in minutes. I suggest you get yourselves out of here, fast." Jim looked up at the figure of his father, standing white with rage above them, then back at the Chief of Police. Finally, he turned and sprinted up to the station wagon. There was a hasty conference, and they heard the sound of screeching tires, heading for the highway.

Johnny Cole let out a great breath. "Now, we gotta get ourselves out of these harnesses. You kids okay?"

Both answered in the affirmative.

"Kit, you wanna turn on that radio and give a call in to the station? Better get someone out here."

"You mean what you said about an open channel..."

Johnny smiled wanly. "Stop your jawin' and do it, kid." Kit obeyed.

Kit was dubious when Cole told them to stay silent, swinging upside-down from their seats, after the accident.

Neither he nor Malachi was hurt, and every instinct told him to get out of the car and run. He had looked upon the Chief of Police before as being a nice, if rather rustic and hick-country, policeman, and now he found himself in a state of somewhat awed admiration at his savvy.

"Hold on tight when you hit that belt release, or you'll land on your heads," Cole said when Kit finished the call to the station.

Kit maneuvered out of his belt, and Malachi did the same. They clambered over to Cole, who was still stuck in the harness. Only then did they see the blood.

"What happened to your arm?" Kit tried unsuccessfully to keep the horror out of his voice. The arm was twisted into some improbable shape, and blood seeped through the sleeve. It was obviously badly broken.

"It got caught outside the window when the car went over."

Kit and Malachi got under him and tried to cushion his fall as much as possible, but even so he cried out involuntarily as he was maneuvered to the ground. "God almighty, that hurts. Don't know what Leslie's gonna say."

"She'll probably tell you she's glad you're alive," said Malachi. Kit pulled the door release and the door ground open, creaking harshly on its bent hinges. They pulled him, as carefully as they could, from the wrecked car.

"Chief Cole..." Kit began.

"I know. You've got to go on. Do it, son. God knows why, but I believe you. Maybe after last night I can believe anything. But I believe you're right about the time. It's almost up. Go take care of it, son." His white face looked into Kit's. "I would have helped you if I could have. But I can't go anywhere now." He partially sat up, wincing at the pain. "Don't go through the woods. The thing almost got Adam there. Go through the village, but look out for the Addisons."

Kit nodded and stood. "Malachi, stay with him."

Malachi sat, cradling the Chief of Police's head, and his eyes locked on Kit's.

"Take me with you. I've got nothing left here."

A wild hope leaped up in Kit's heart, but he immediately pushed it back down. His response came from somewhere even more basic, and he knew he spoke the truth. "I can't. What if you did to my world the same thing I did to yours? Our worlds are... incompatible. I don't know why, but that's just how it is." He looked down at Malachi, and tears stung his eyes as well. "I don't understand how it can be, that our worlds can't coexist, because I... I love you, Malachi Swenson. I know it's only been a few days, and you probably think I'm crazy. But I do. I love you. I don't think I'll ever be able to look at another boy now..." He leaned forward, and kissed him softly on the mouth. "I've got to go. It's got to be now. Goodbye. Just remember I love you and I will never forget you."

Kit walked back toward the road. The body of Andy Addison stared at him with unseeing eyes. He tried not to look, but out of the edge of his sight the crazy, wild glare still shrieked horrifically at him. Finally, it was behind him. He walked up the hill, and reached the sheer drop that had flipped the Chief of Police's car, and climbed it.

"Kit!" Malachi called to him, and then he turned. He looked so vulnerable, sitting in the middle of the sunlit woods, still holding Johnny Cole.

"I love you, Kit!" Malachi's trembling voice came up clearly from the bottom of the hill.

Turning away from him was the hardest thing Kit had ever done.

18. tsunami

· · ·

Kit followed the road up from where he had left Cole and Malachi. In a moment he heard sirens, and quickly ducked off the pavement into a bush as an ambulance zoomed past. He didn't especially want to be seen right now, but was glad help had come for Police Chief Cole. He liked Cole, and hoped his injury wasn't too serious.

Not that Kit would ever see him again. One way or the other. Either he'd be back home, or he'd be dead. But he hoped that whatever happened to him, the nightmare ended for these nice people.

The leaves rustled overhead, casting dappled shadows on the road. The beginning of another idyllic summer day in the Adirondacks. But now he was alone, and aware of something else—a high, almost inaudible whirring sound he couldn't be quite sure of. It was faint, but now that he heard it, he was nearly certain it had been there ever since he had arrived, a constant undercurrent to this whole weird, dreamlike week. He could feel the energy of something, something powerful, and was sure it lay ahead of him. Past the village center, up by the old church. That was the epicenter, that was the principal focus. That was where, for good or ill, he was going to try to stop this tidal wave of irrationality pouring down off that hill, engulfing first the Thornes, and then the Swensons, Addisons, and Tony Gallagher, and now which headed toward the village like a silent, invisible tsunami.

He had just reached the intersection with the highway into the village when the ambulance tore past again, this time heading up the road. Police Chief Cole, and, he guessed, Malachi Swenson taking a trip to the clinic in Carnahan. He looked up and down the highway. No sign of Cleve Addison's battered station wagon. That was fortunate. What they would do to him now, alone and on foot, now that Trent was missing and Andy dead—well, it didn't bear thinking about.

Kit turned right, toward the village center. There was the usual swish of cars along the highway, the speed of their passing fluttering his hair. He saw no one he recognized from his short stay in the area, but that didn't strike him as odd. The sun was now high in the sky, and shone down into his face.

He reached the village limits, which were demarcated by a wooden sign: "Entering Finn Hill, New York, est. 1792." A small brass plaque screwed to one post stated the sign had been erected by the Finn Hill Garden Club three years earlier. Geraniums, zinnias, and marigolds flowered in brilliant profusion around the signposts. It looked just like any ordinary, peaceful upstate New York village.

In fact, it looked a whole lot too peaceful. Kit gazed down the road. There was no activity in the village that he could see. On any given day in Finn Hill, there were usually at least thirty people, not counting those in cars, easily visible from any point on the village center's periphery. Villagers stopping at the Nice 'n' Easy, the hardware store, the post office, shopkeepers sweeping the walks, old-timers trading farm news, speculations on the weather, and gossip, out-of-towners stopping to ask directions. Now, Kit seemed to be the only person in town, other than drivers of cars passing through.

The first awning cast its deep shadow across his face as he stepped onto the sidewalk. Christensen's Bakery. A sign in the window said "Open" but there seemed to be no one home. The next shop, T.K. Equipment Rentals, was dark inside. Its brilliant scarlet sign, seeming somehow out-of-place in such a quaint village, indicated that it didn't open until one o'clock anyway. And then the next door, to Parker's Antiques. Kit turned and looked into the shop.

He gasped loudly and took a step backward, bumping into a street side wastebasket in a box-shaped cedar housing. Mr. Averill Parker, the sour-faced antique dealer who had given Kit the eye only a few days earlier, stood behind the door of his shop, pounding furiously on the glass. He was red and dripping with sweat. His mouth kept moving, "Let me out! Let me out!" but Kit could hear no sound. Kit stared for a moment, heart pounding, and then gingerly walked to the door of the shop. He reached out his hand and turned the old-fashioned brass doorknob, and swung the door open.

And Mr. Parker swung with it. Kit looked at the door, his face a mask of perplexity. From the other side of the door, he saw the back of Mr. Parker, his shoulders heaving as he pounded on the glass, pleading for his release. Kit ran around to the outside, as if he thought he was the object of some strange magician's illusion. On one side of the window was the front of Mr. Parker, and on the other side, his back. Kit waved his hands in front of the old man's face, but he seemed not to notice, and continued his futile pounding.

Averill Parker was trapped, sandwiched in his store-front door window.

Kit's natural compassion made him stop, and force himself to think of what he could do to help the old man. Break the window? That would probably kill him. He rubbed his hands over the glass.

"Mr. Parker!"

There was no response. The antique dealer continued his silent shouting and pounding.

Kit looked around. There was still no one on foot in the village. The emptiness began to seem frightening in and of itself. Where was everyone? And how could he help Mr. Parker? How, for that matter, could anyone help him? Shouldn't he just go on, continue on his errand?

Kit stood, torn by indecision, watching the trapped antique dealer.

The whirring sound in the distance intensified, and the ground shuddered. Borne on the light breeze came a second noise—a sizzling, somewhere between an electrical discharge and bacon frying.

"What the hell *now*?" Kit said quietly.

Then he turned and saw it, and had no idea what he was seeing.

None of the descriptions his mind generated were sufficient. A puddle of molten glass. A flowing, sentient blob of water. A mobile optical distortion. An enormous amoeba. Something halfway between transparent and visible. It reached out feelers as it slipped downhill toward him, moving as easily across a road surface as it did grass. Behind it, it left a charred path of blackened foliage and melted blacktop.

The whole thing was almost ten feet in diameter.

The sizzling intensified as it approached. What was it looking for? Food? He remembered from his biology class that amoebas ate by engulfing; is that what this thing did? Was the soot and ash it left behind some kind of residue after absorbing whatever nutrients it could from organic matter it passed across?

It was fifty feet away, and closing fast, heading right for the row of buildings that made up the main storefronts of Finn Hill.

His breath whining in his throat, Kit turned and ran.

The transparent creature responded immediately, veering from its course—probably saving Averill Parker and whoever was left in the village—and pursued Kit.

How was it tracking him? Sound? The vibration of his footfalls? Whatever it was, the thing was *fast*. It was gaining on him, slowly but steadily. Kit was a good runner but couldn't keep it up indefinitely.

If he faltered or fell… he'd be cooked alive.

He'd been prepared to die when the Addisons had attacked Malachi's house. He half believed what he'd told him, that if he died maybe he'd just wake up back in his own world, safe and sound. But dying this way?

Even thinking of that kept his feet slamming against the pavement.

Ahead of him was the Nice 'n' Easy and Kwik Fill, where he and Malachi had taken shelter from a thunderstorm. It seemed like ages ago. Like the rest of the town, there was no one in evidence either using the pumps or staffing the mini-mart that stood behind it. A germ of an idea began to form in Kit's mind, but it would depend… it would depend on so many things, not to mention a good dose of luck…

He forced his aching legs to sprint up the low hill to where the gas pumps stood. Ran between them, then—as quietly as he could—crossed the narrow gap between the pumps and the door.

The creature slowed. Heat haze shimmered up from it. Beneath it, the asphalt melted to a glistening black, the acrid smoke of burning tar prickling the back of Kit's nose.

"C'mon," he breathed. "A little closer…"

The pumps were now directly between him and it. It was still moving forward slowly, tentatively, reaching out a feeler, trying to figure out which direction its prey had gone.

Okay, time to tell it what it wanted to know.

Kit stomped on the ground, then flung himself through the door and crouched down behind the wall.

The creature surged forward, struck the nearest gasoline pump, and with an earsplitting report, it exploded.

The concussion was a lot louder than he'd expected. All of the front windows of the mini-mart shattered simultaneously, spraying the interior of the store with glittering shards. But he was on his feet again, running down the aisle to the service entrance at the back, bursting through it a door with a sign saying, "This Door Is To Be Used By Staff Only. An Alarm Will Sound If It Is Opened By Unauthorized Personnel."

Let the alarm ring, my friends. He sprinted across the alleyway behind it, then circled back around to the road.

Would an explosion kill something that burned that hot? No way to know. Perhaps the blast had shattered it, ruptured whatever served as a cell membrane, leaving it to ooze out its life onto the slowly cooling pavement. Only after he'd gotten a hundred yards farther did he venture a look over his shoulder at the gas station, the pumps still fountaining flame and smoke. If the thing wasn't dead, at least Kit had slowed it down.

There was no sign he was being pursued.

If what Police Chief Cole saw up at the old church was worse than that thing, God help them all. As for Kit, he wasn't sure if he could face it. He slowed to a walk, and finally sat down on a bench in front of the post office, face in his hands. Then the thought crossed his mind that instead of trying to go back home, maybe he should just get out of Finn Hill. Carnahan was only ten or so miles up the road—he could walk that far in a day. He was pretty sure he could hitchhike a lot farther than that. Clear out, leave this weirdness to someone else.

He looked up, and turned toward the east, where Swenson Road met the highway. Did he have it in him to face whatever was up there? He stood, and only then noticed there was a man walking toward him—the first other pedestrian he'd seen that day. The man hailed him.

"Kit! Kit McIntyre."

The man had an unmistakable face and walk. Once you'd seen it, you wouldn't forget it. Kit had seen it before. The voice calling was also familiar, and at the same time it was an impossible voice, one he never thought he'd hear again. It had only been a week since he last heard it, but the events before that week seemed more remote in the past than his own birth was, and less real than a dream. Kit stopped walking and stared dumbly. There, walking down the sidewalk of Main Street, Finn Hill, New York, was Philip Amirault.

"Philip?" he finally croaked.

Philip looked pale, but whether with fear or some other emotion, Kit could not tell. "Kit, I didn't think I'd find you. It seemed impossible."

A car drove past. Kit thought it was one of the deputies who had helped to look for Christina Thorne on his first night here. The deputy slowed as he saw the inferno at the gas station, and from the wide-eyed expression on his face, seemed to be wondering just what in the heck had happened. Kit's eyes followed the deputy's car down the road, watched it turn into the police station, thinking, *buddy, you're not the only one.* He looked back to Philip. After only one week, the town was what seemed familiar. Philip was the one who seemed out of place. If all the events of the last week were a jigsaw puzzle, Philip was a piece from a different puzzle.

Kit walked toward his old friend, and then all the horror of the last few days suddenly coalesced into a single, focused thought.

This was the person who started it all. He was the one who sent Kit here. He was the one to blame for all that had happened.

"Philip, why did you do it?" Kit's voice was cold. "You did this. You sent me here. You sent me all alone to a place where our town doesn't even exist..."

"You must believe me," Philip began, his voice cracking. "I never meant you to come to any harm."

"Tell me!"

"Kit, you've gone behind the frame."

"And what is that supposed to mean?"

"You're inside a story. You've gone into a world which exists in our world only as a fiction."

"What?" Kit's gray eyes were narrowed to slits. "That isn't possible."

"I'm telling you it is."

"You're lying."

"No. Not lying. Believe it. That's what the glasses do. They open a hole between different frames of reality. I figured that out when I put them on at first, but my eye is so bad I couldn't see it clearly, and I took them off. I thought—I honestly thought— all they did was allow you to *see* inside. It was like an author's dream come true, to be able to see the worlds he and others had created come to life." He swallowed. "I guess I was lucky. I got them off before the hole opened completely, so I didn't get pulled inside. You did. God, forgive me for not telling you." The old man's eyes were watery, and he mumbled. It crossed Kit's mind that perhaps he had gone insane. "I thought they just showed you pictures from other frames. Honestly didn't know you'd go into the hole, Kit. God, forgive me."

"You're crazy," Kit hissed.

The intentness returned to Philip's one sighted eye. "Then you tell me how you got here."

The point hit home. "You mean... none of this is real?"

"Not in our world. Kit, you are inside a falsehood. I know this." He paused, swallowed. "I know because I wrote it. None of this is real."

"You *wrote* it?"

"Yes. Finn Hill is a place in one of my earliest stories. It was modeled after a little town in the Adirondacks where I spent some engaging times in my youth."

"But the people…"

"Characters. They're fiction, Kit. All of them." He looked at Kit, who stared back at him in disbelief. "The Swensons. The Addisons. The Thornes. The Darnells. They're all characters in my story." He glanced around him. "Although it seems like there are a good many more people here than I'd thought originally."

"No." His mind shrieked at him, *Malachi's not real? This place, these people, not real? How can that be?* The horror of finding himself here a week ago was nothing compared to the horror of losing it all this way, even now that it all seemed to be falling apart. He had set out that morning to risk his life for an illusion? He had held in his arms, kissed, fallen in love with a shadow? Kit shouted, and tears streaked his face. "No, you're lying! You're lying! This is real! He is real!"

"He?" Some of Philip's old asperity came back. "There's a he? God help us."

Kit took a deep breath. "Malachi. Malachi Swenson. He… Philip, he's real."

"You and Malachi Swenson?" Philip gave a half smile, which quickly vanished. "Oh, of course. I should have guessed. He's a good match for you. But he's not real, Kit. Not in the same way you are. While you're here, he's real to you. And I suspect while you're here, you obey the laws of the world you're in. If you die here… well, I'd guess you'd be dead, and never seen again in *our* world. But Kit, what you must understand… your coming here… it's opened a gateway from other frames. These other things, they're not supposed to be here. They come from other places. Perhaps from a book somebody's writing, or a myth, or a drawing, but whatever it is, they're not supposed to be in here. Neither are you. Neither am I." His voice cracked. "This place only existed in my imagination until you put on those glasses. And your being here has linked this world with other places, let in other realities. It's torn up the barriers keeping the worlds apart."

"None of this makes any sense," Kit said desperately.

"They don't even obey the same laws of time. In our world you have only been gone for a few hours. Your mother doesn't even know you're missing."

"That's not possible."

"In your heart you know it is. You've got to come home. I've come to bring you back."

"No." He was certain now—he couldn't face it. Somehow Philip's assertion that this place had no reality was worse than what this Finn Hill, the one he was coming to love, was becoming. Kit was backing away from him. "I won't go. I'm going to get out of here, as far as I can, but I'm not going near that church again."

"You have to go." He gestured at the destruction around them. "I saw the burned out buildings on the road up there. The ashes are still warm." He nodded toward the gas station, still belching black smoke. "And a fire ahead is still burning. You see what your presence is doing." He paused. "This whole world will burn if you stay here."

"I'm not responsible for what has happened. If anyone is, it's you, not me." He choked back a sob. " And anyway, if none of this is real, what does it matter?"

"We both are responsible, even if we didn't mean any harm.. Your arrival tore a hole in reality. And the people here, they may only be characters in a story in our world, but to themselves, they're real. In their frame, they love, they laugh, they hurt, they bleed, they die. You have allowed all sorts of things to infiltrate their frame from all the other frames. If you don't seal it by returning to our world, they'll all die. It's too late for all the ones who have already died. But you can save the rest of them. You can save Malachi."

"I can't do it!" Kit sobbed.

"You have to." Philip wiped the back of his hand across his lips. "God, I'll never write again. I never thought I was creating a real world somewhere else in reality when I wrote. But now, you have to come back. Seal the hole."

"How?"

"Go back to where it started. The Methodist Church. That's where I landed when I jumped through. It must be the focal point. The hole is still there. You have to find the glasses, put them on, and jump into the portal. I have a pair, the pair that brought me here," he patted his jacket pocket, "and I'll need them to get home. I'll follow you in. We both have to return home. It's the only way."

Somewhere in the distance behind them, there was a huge crash and a scream, which echoed up from the valley to the south. Philip grasped Kit's right arm in one tough, liver-spotted hand.

"Kit, you're not stupid. You know it has to be now. Look at what's already happened." He gestured around at the empty village. "In a few more hours, it will all be gone, and then the destruction will spread. Things are getting in, Kit, things which should be contained within their own worlds, worlds where they can be managed. Things from other places—all the stories, drawings, myths ever conceived. They're all pouring into here, and this world can't handle them." He paused, and swallowed. "Think about it. Imagine some of the horrors you've read about. Imagine some of the hideous things you've seen painted. Now imagine what some of these things could do if they got into this world. You can stop it from happening, Kit. If for no other reason, for him—for your Malachi."

Kit turned his tear-streaked face over his shoulder, toward the forested area where he had last seen him. He imagined Malachi's face, as Kit had last seen it—small and distant, as he called out to Kit. Was Philip right? Would his presence ulti-mately destroy this world, Malachi's world? Why in the hell couldn't he hang on to some piece of what he'd found here, to the promise of a relationship that for the first time made him feel whole? He felt as if he were being forced to turn his face away from happiness toward abject fear, and look at it straight on. He writhed, teetering on the edge of indecision.

After some minutes in which Philip stared at him in silence, Kit turned and faced the east, the direction in which the church, and the hole between the frames, lay. Without looking at Philip, he began to walk toward the intersection with Swenson Road.

"All right," he snarled. "All right. If we have to do this, let's do it."

Philip turned to follow. "And pray God we're not already too late."

19. a doorway into deep space

. . .

While Kit walked along the highway toward his encounter with the glassy, superheated predator in the streets of Finn Hill, Ann Garvey followed her summer routine.

Ann looked upon her two-and-a-half month respite from Finn Hill Elementary School as an opportunity to recharge her batteries. From the first day of student teaching—a hundred or so miles south, in Anderson, New York—she had thrown herself into it heart and soul, and the result was by June, she was usually exhausted both physically and mentally.

She had grown up an only child. Her younger sister, Susan, had been born with severe birth defects and had only lived a few days. By the time her career had begun, both of her parents were dead—her mother of pancreatic cancer during Ann's high school years, and her father of a sudden, catastrophic stroke during her second year of college. When she stepped into her first classroom, she had already decided the children would be her family. She taught them as if they were her own, and in a sense they were. She loved her students, and in turn was one of the most loved teachers in the school.

Ann had long ago developed routines for all of her chores, so she could divorce her highly active and academic mind from the boring small matters of life. The result was that from the outside, she seemed to live a repetitive and colorless life, especially in summer, when she was not immersed in the daily chaos of elementary school. No one saw, and few would have guessed, the mousy-looking second-grade teacher with the thick eyeglasses was also an accomplished linguist—largely self-taught—a fine classical flutist, and had enough correspondence credits in history and literature for a second major in each.

Her favorite avocations were reading and gardening. The morning of Kit's trek through the nearly empty village, she had just finished a leisurely breakfast of oatmeal and orange juice, and prepared herself to sit for an hour or so with a book. She usually waited until all of the dew had burned off before going out, preferring the late morning and early afternoon for working outdoors—she gardened in sneakers and disliked wet feet. From the sunshine streaming in the sliding glass door at the back of her living room, it looked like a fine morning in the making, although the weather forecast the previous night had said thundershowers were likely by this afternoon.

Ann's living room was simple but comfortable. She had a large wicker-back rocking chair that was her favorite spot for reading. A crocheted afghan purchased at a summer fair several years ago tumbled over the seat and back. Ann had just sat down and arranged the afghan cozily around her when she heard a sizzling noise. It didn't sound mechanical. It sounded like frying meat. Ann got up and went to her front window, peering myopically out toward the road.

Flowing down like water, the predator came down the hill from the direction of the Swensons' burned-out house, heat haze rising from its translucent surface. It scorched its way across Tony Gallagher's front yard, upsetting a birdbath, and leaving a blackened strip of grass behind it. It made a right-hand turn and came across the ditch and into the road. At that point it was coming straight for her house and garden. Ann caught her breath.

What was that? It could totally destroy her yard!

She was on the verge of running outside, intending to try somehow to keep it away from her brilliant flowers, when the thing suddenly veered away back downhill, toward the highway and village—fortunately for her.

It was only when its sound died away to the south that Ann went outside. She was barefoot, and even in the morning sun the dew was cold. She walked to the edge of the charred strip that it had created, and stood staring at it. Seized by a sudden impulse, she knelt next to it, putting out one finger gingerly to touch the soot-covered leaves of a dandelion.

It crumbled into ash under her touch.

Ann had always had an acute sense of smell, perhaps to make up for her poor eyesight. She was immediately struck by a harsh, acrid odor. Like the ozone after a lightning strike. Whatever had done this...

...it was completely separate from the living things she knew of. A few weeks ago, she had watched a documentary about evolution, and that all life on Earth is related. Even the most different species come from a common ancestor; an ant and a grizzly bear and a palm tree all have a common ancestor if you traced their lineages back far enough.

This thing, though? It was entirely and unquestionably alien.

The thought filled her simultaneously with wonder, fear, and a deep curiosity. She looked at its path, leading down Swenson Road toward the village. Why wasn't there a scientist here, someone who could study this, perhaps explain it?

At that moment, she heard the sound of an explosion

coming up from the village. The distance only served to magnify its horror. Ann shivered, and turned her head toward the source of the sound. It wavered in the light breeze, and then subsided to a dull roar.

It seemed a good time to go back inside.

She brushed the ash off her fingertips and returned to the warm and safe confines of her living room. Even once inside, though, she found her senses heightened to the breaking point. She was listening… for what? Only the faintest thread of the sounds came up from the village below, but still she stood stock-still, breath held.

There was something unaccountable coming down out of those woods up past the Thornes' house. It was all tied together, somehow—this alien creature, and the miserable tragedies striking first the Thornes, then Tony, then the Addisons, then the Swensons. She settled herself back in her rocking chair, and picked up her book. She thought about Kit, whom in her mind she had begun referring to as "Malachi's boyfriend." She hoped he didn't think life was always like this here. It was a pity he didn't visit when things were normal.

And then the strange thought entered her mind that maybe Kit, too, was another piece of this puzzle, and perhaps he knew more about how this all tied together than she did.

She'd have to give that more thought.

She opened her book. The drowsy summer sun spilled over her shoulders and cascaded onto the old braided rug in the center of her floor. The silence, after the earlier uncanny noises, was uncomfortable, and she couldn't get herself lost in her book as she usually did.

The morning wore away. She heard the old mahogany grandfather clock in the hall chime ten-thirty. The sound made her look up. It was time to be getting outside, time to finish weeding the border of zinnias and marigolds along the front sidewalk.

What if the alien came back, though? What if something else was out there, something worse? What if…

That was when she noticed the hissing sound. It was so quiet that it might have been going on for a long time, unnoticed, but it was impossible to know. It was almost inaudible even when she attended to it, a faint, continual hiss, like air slowly leaking from a small hole in a child's balloon. There was no way to determine its source. It was quiet, and seemed to come from all directions at once.

She closed the book and set it on the small table next to the rocker, and stood up. The sound was ever-so-slightly louder now. She walked into the kitchen to check if she had left one of the gas jets on when she heated up the milk for her oatmeal. All of them were off. Of course—she would have smelled it had she left one on. And anyway, the sound was now distinct enough she could tell it didn't come from the kitchen. It was noticeably softer there.

She returned to the living room. There was nothing there she knew of that could cause such a sound, and a second search of the room turned up nothing. By this time it was again a little louder, a little more distinct.

Ann's eyes fell upon the block of sunlight on the floor, the light coming in through the sliding glass door. It looked dim.

Darn it! It was already clouding up. She should have gone out earlier, alien or no alien.

But a glance out of the window showed a clear blue sky, and the ash tree in her back yard cast a clear, sharp shadow against the lawn. She walked to the sliding door, and suddenly became aware that it was not the sky, or the sun that had changed. The glass in the door had. It was slightly gray, like those old-fashioned photo-gray lenses that darken when exposed to light. She looked closely at it, and as she watched, it continued to slowly darken. And when she put her face close to the glass, she realized it was the source of the hissing sound, as well.

She backed away, and a flutter of icy fear danced down her backbone.

It had caught her, too. Whatever was coming from up there past Adam and Christine's. Now it was here, in her house. She'd get swallowed up by it, too, just like all of the rest of them.

She thought about leaving the house, about running away, but then she remembered the charred path in the road. The unaccountable was already well past her little house. It was all around her. There was no running away. There was nowhere to run to.

The window had now darkened enough to be immediately obvious to anyone entering the room, and the hissing sounded like a rapidly deflating tire. Ann swiveled the rocking chair around to face the window, and sat down. Her fear was still tempered by a good dose of curiosity. She had read some about so-called supernatural events, but had always been skeptical. One of her unfulfilled wishes was to be a witness to an unequivocally paranormal event. Now, it seemed, she had a good chance to observe the supernatural without leaving her rocker.

Okay. Go ahead. Do whatever you want to. I'm ready.

The window continued to slowly darken, pale gray to gray-blue. She could still see the familiar objects of her back yard—the ash tree, her hammock, the vegetable garden— through a kind of blue haze. Superimposed upon it all she began to see tiny spangles of light, like stars floating in the air.

There was a fluttering noise behind her, and she turned. She had a music stand near the opposite wall, with a thin sheaf of sheet music on it. Her flute sat in its case against the wall behind it. The papers had fallen off the stand, twisting through the air as if in a breeze. With a start, she realized there *was* a breeze, almost too soft to feel. Her spider plant in its macramé hanger was rusting gently. She stood, and placed her hand near the sliding glass door. There was air flowing there, outward, through the solid pane of glass.

The darkening accelerated to blue, to indigo. The breeze picked up. The afghan on her rocking chair flapped and tumbled to the floor. Her book, sitting on its table, flipped open, and the pages riffled with a whir. When the last page turned over, the fingers of the wind picked up the cover and snapped it shut. The book slid off the table and thumped onto the floor.

Ann's fear was rapidly overtaking her curiosity. The window was almost black now, and the points of light didn't just look like stars—they *were* stars. Her back yard was clean gone. She looked out into a vast, velvety blackness, pierced by millions of unfamiliar constellations. They looked unusually hard, cold, and sharp, starlight unmellowed by a trip through earth's warm, moist atmosphere.

This is what the stars must look like from the space shuttle.

In a flash, she understood. All of the events of the past week were connected, and she knew how. Her quick mind, even in the midst of her fear, snapped the pieces together neatly. The strangeness, the unaccountable—it was coming into Finn Hill from the *outside*. Somehow someone had created an interface between here and there, wherever *there* was. Kit—it had to be Kit McIntyre, he was the only odd piece in the puzzle. And the interface moved down the hill from its source. Of course, of course! How had she not noticed the pattern before? The Thornes, the Swensons, the Addisons— she had heard about Trent's disappearance from Marie Bedford of the Nice 'n' Easy the previous afternoon—Tony Gallagher, and now... her. All of them eaten up, one after another, by something from outside the well-ordered world Ann Garvey knew. She didn't know specifically how each of them had died, but the otherness was ultimately responsible. The unaccountable, flowing down the hill like a river.

And now her sliding glass door was being turned into a gateway between the earth and deep space. Somehow, her doorway was a portal between her living room and… nothing. She looked at the black sky where her familiar back yard should have been, staring dumbly at the impossible constellations hanging across her door. The wind was stronger now. She put her hand out and touched the window glass. It felt spongy, porous and elastic.

She teetered on the edge between fascination and terror. The air in the house was leaking away. Soon the window would be gone, and the house would decompress. With a jolt like an electric shock, she realized it all could go. Maybe once the door opened into deep space, the whole village would get sucked through. Maybe the whole world.

Fear tipped the scales. She backed away, turned to run, but it was too late. The music stand fell over with a crash. The breeze turned into a gale, then a hurricane. Ann's ears popped, as if she were going up in a jet liner. The wind made her t-shirt billow like a sail. She was able to manage two steps, but then a plant in a heavy blue Delft pot flew off the mantelpiece with a grinding sound. It swung end over end, grazing her scalp, and soared out through the door and vanished. Ann gave a cry, taking a step backwards as the windows of the kitchen and front door imploded, scattering sparkling shards over the floor.

The timbers of the house creaked and groaned with the strain. Her hair stood out straight behind her. The bookshelf in the hallway fell over with a crash, and a stack of *Horticulture* magazines flew rattling into the air toward her.

She half turned her head to avoid them, and the wind took her glasses off, pitching them through the now jet-black doorway.

Ann Garvey shrieked, "No!" and reached out to catch them. Her voice sounded thin in the nearly airless room. The window was now almost all gone, and she felt the air being sucked out of her lungs. Her oxygen-starved mind was unable to command her legs to hold her up, and she fell, the world spinning around her. She was immediately caught up in the last of the gale, and flung toward the window.

With her last bit of strength, she flailed her arms wildly to save herself, and by some strange fortune, her left hand caught the door frame.

She was suspended there, her body stretched out horizontally like a flag in a hurricane. Her neck arched backwards, her hair streaming out behind her, her sightless eyes bulging with terror. Some kind of unconscious instinct made her hold on, but slowly, her hand was slipping from its tenuous grasp. And when it did, Ann Garvey would plunge out into the cold vacuum of space, and the unaccountable would have claimed one more victim in Finn Hill.

20. the road to the church

. . .

Kit jogged lightly up the shoulder of the highway toward Swenson Road. By this time there was a line of cars at a dead stop, pointed toward the village center, unable to pass because of a fire crew blocking the road, dealing with the still-smoking pumps at the gas station. The drivers of the first few cars in the line had turned off their engines and surveyed the situation, wondering how they would detour around the problem. As Kit passed, he saw one man said, in annoyance, "What the hell is going on here?" Kit could have told him, but didn't take the time.

As he ran, Kit heard Philip puffing behind him. He knew he was going too fast for the old man, but didn't slow.

"Kit!" Philip finally gasped.

"What?" Kit asked without turning.

"Do you still have the glasses?"

Kit stopped, and turned. "No." Through his anger, he felt suddenly afraid. "Why?"

"You have to have them to get back through the hole. Where are they?"

"I threw them into the window of the church right after I got here."

"Then they're still there?"

"I would guess so."

Kit turned and began to jog again.

"Kit," Philip wheezed.

"What?"

"You must know how sorry I am."

Kit rounded on him again, eyes blazing. "Well, you know what? That really doesn't make a whole lot of difference now. You jerked me around, Philip, you know that? You used me. And because of it, a bunch of people are dead, including both parents of a boy I happen to love. You understand me?" He turned away. This time, he started off at a fast walk. "Maybe if we both get home, I'll be able to forgive you, but right now I don't feel in a very forgiving kind of mood, you know what I mean?"

Philip was silent for a moment. "You're going to need a flashlight."

Kit didn't stop. "What?"

"When you get into the inside of the church. It'll be dark, right? You'll need a flashlight. Do you know where you can get one?"

Aw, crap. He should have thought of that.

"I think there are a couple of flashlights in the outbuildings behind Malachi's house... where his house used to be. I saw them there when I helped Mr. Swenson a few days ago."

They turned up Swenson Road, past the maple tree where Kit had his first run-in with Trent Addison. It seemed like decades ago. Today, once they got away from the jammed-up highway, everything was quiet. The only sign of strangeness was the blackened path of the alien zigzagging down the road.

They reached Ann Garvey's cottage. The front yard was empty. Ann had just returned inside from examining what the alien had left behind and was trying to get involved in her book, unaware that a far greater adventure was less than a half-hour away.

Behind them, a voice called out, "Kit! Wait!"

Kit turned, and saw Malachi Swenson running up the road toward him. "Kit, are you okay? What happened down in the village?"

He caught Malachi in his arms, and held him for a moment, as he regained his breath. "I'm okay. It was something... something from another world that caused all that damage in the village. Not my world. I've never seen anything like it, and I hope I never do again." He shuddered. "How's Police Chief Cole?"

"The ambulance came for him. He'll be all right. His arm is broken, but that's it. He told me to follow you." He looked into Kit's eyes. "He said to make sure you made it okay."

"He knows a lot more than he lets on."

Malachi nodded, and then his eyes fell on Philip. "Who are you?"

Kit smiled in spite of himself. Even the traumatic events of the past days couldn't dull Malachi's natural bluntness. "This is Philip Amirault. He comes from my world. He's the one who is responsible for my being here."

Malachi looked at Philip. "You and Kit..."

"We come from the same place," said Kit.

"I too am here to make sure that Kit gets back," Philip added with some urgency. "We need to go. Before it's too late."

"Too late for what?" Malachi asked.

"Before the damage to your world becomes irreparable."

Malachi absorbed this in silence. He reached out and took Kit's hand, and they turned and resumed their walk up the road. Their walk toward... what? What waited up there in those woods?

Malachi pointed off to the left. They were approaching Cleve Addison's house. Kit scanned the land to the right of the road. "Is there any way of getting past that house without being seen?"

"There are only cornfields off that way," Malachi answered. "There are woods further on, on the other side of the fields, but Police Chief Cole told you to avoid them, remember?"

"I remember. I just wonder if the woods aren't safer than passing right by the Addisons' front door."

Kit motioned them off to the right side of the road, and they skirted the edge of the cornfield. It was impossible to go along a row—the rows ran perpendicular to the road—but at least they were farther from the house itself. Kit noticed, with rising horror, Cleve's battered station wagon was parked in the driveway.

They almost made it. A clump of sumac stood on the north side of the driveway. Only a little farther on and it would obscure the view from the window. They were nearly out of sight when there was a sound of a door opening, and Kit turned, his heart thudding in his chest. A man walked out onto the front porch, leaned against the porch railing, and spat into the yard. Then he looked up, saw Kit, did a double take, and their eyes met.

It was Jim Addison.

Immediately he whirled around and ran back into the house. "Pa! Pa!" Kit heard him bellow. "It's him! The kid! And Malachi Swenson! Walkin' right up the road together! Holdin' *hands*! Pa, come on!"

"Run!" Kit yanked on Malachi's hand and pelted off up the road. Philip did not understand the necessity, but saw the fear in Kit's eyes, and ran as well as he could after them.

The Swensons' house was nothing but a pile of blackened timbers. The heat had scorched the flowers along the walk and blistered the paint on the mailbox. The outbuildings still stood intact, however, and Kit ran around to the back. A large metal tool shed stood next to the barn, and he pulled on the rusted door, which grudgingly scraped open. There were two heavy-duty flashlights standing on a shelf. Kit grabbed them, and handed one to Malachi. "Let's go."

At that moment there was the sound of a car, passing slowly by. They flattened themselves against the wall of the shed. Kit looked out through a rusted hole in the side. Cleve's station wagon cruised by. Besides Cleve and Jim, there were at least three other men inside. One of them had a shotgun. They peered out of the window, looking for signs of Kit, knowing that he couldn't have gone far.

They waited until the sound of the engine had faded into the distance before coming out of the shed. Kit looked with one eye around the edge of the outbuilding, and up the road. There was no sign of the Addisons' car. He silently motioned to the others, and they followed him.

"We should stay off the road as much as possible," Malachi said. Kit nodded.

North of the Swensons' property there were more trees. Malachi led them out, and they passed from tree to tree, staying as much as possible in the shadows. It was about ten-thirty and the sunshine was brilliant, making it hard to be inconspicuous. Cleve's car had passed up the road toward the church, and had not returned yet. Every step made Kit more nervous. What if they had ditched the car and hunted them on foot? What if he was right now in the sights of the shotgun?

What if Malachi was?

He remembered what Philip had said. *In their frame, they love, they laugh, they hurt, they bleed, they die...*

No. He'd caused so much damage here. He would save Malachi, even if he had to die himself doing it.

The land began to descend rapidly toward the creek at the bottom of the hill. There were thickets of scrub willow and alder, better cover but harder to get through. Kit ventured a look back at Philip. He was pale and sweating.

Hard on a man his age.

At that moment, he realized he did forgive Philip. At least a little.

They splashed across the creek, hoping the bubbling of the clear water over the rocks would mute the sounds of their feet. All of them were becoming increasingly jumpy, even Philip.

Kit realized, of course he knew the danger. He invented the Addisons. He knew how crazy they were.

There was still no sign of the Addisons, but it seemed far too much to hope that they had given up the hunt. Only a few feet past the creek, they scared up a grouse, which exploded out of the underbrush with a whir of wings. Kit jumped backwards, tripped on a tree root, and sat down hard. He remained there for a moment, unable to stand, wondering privately how long it would take for his heart rate to return to normal. Malachi extended a hand to help him up, and they walked on.

The bushes came to a sudden end about fifty feet past the creek. Kit went forward and peered out. All clear. He motioned to the others to follow.

The intersection with Old Church Road was just ahead. Kit could see the road take a right-hand bend around a cluster of maples. Malachi leaned over to Kit, and whispered, "We can cross around behind that bunch of trees and cut off the corner. Shorter. There's a path." He ran lightly down a shallow slope away from the road, down into a rough lane of tall grass and poplar saplings. It cut off to the northeast, the direction they wanted to go. They waded through the grass, the dry stalks swishing around their knees. Kit gently squeezed Malachi's hand.

"Don't ever forget me."

"I won't."

Kit felt sudden tears well up, but he fought them down. "I wish things were normal. That we had just... you know, grown up together. That I could have asked you out. That we could have... well, had classes together, been lab partners, gone to football games together, gone to dances." He laughed. "Even though I'm a lousy dancer."

"So'm I."

"I'm so sorry about everything that has happened."

Malachi looked straight ahead. "It wasn't your fault. I don't blame you, so don't blame yourself. Right now I just feel numb. I can't really think about it, not yet. We have to see this through, first."

Kit looked at Malachi, his eyes filled with concern, and gave him another light squeeze of the hand. Then they both turned toward their destination.

The lane ran up a hill, meeting Old Church Road about a hundred yards west of the church. The top of the hill was treeless and exposed to view.

"Is that safe? Don't you think we'll be seen?"

Malachi looked around, his brow furrowing. "I don't think so. I've never had to think about it that way. But I believe the only really clear view is up the road toward Adam Thorne's house."

They came out of the last clump of bushes. Now for the last stretch. They climbed up the hill, and saw the road swinging away in front of them. Kit's eyes followed it to the left.

"Oh, crap."

Cleve's car pointed down the road, straight at them, less than a half a mile away.

"Come on!" Kit began to run again. At the same moment they heard the car peel out, spitting gravel from under its rear wheels, and come flying down the road toward them.

"There it is! Philip! The church!" Kit turned his head. To his dismay, Philip was about twenty feet behind them. His face was gray, and he gasped hoarsely. Kit swore under his breath and turned back. He ran to Philip, and grasping his arm, helped him up the low slope toward the abandoned church. They turned on their flashlights and darted inside the doorway. Philip leaned against the wall, his breath coming in huge, rasping gulps. Kit reached up and unbuttoned the top button of the old man's shirt.

"Okay," Philip wheezed. "I'll be okay. Just give me a moment."

The dusty interior of the church, with its overturned pews and rotten floorboards, did not seem as spooky to Kit as its exterior had several days earlier. The feeling it evoked in him was hopelessness. Kit now saw that when he had thrown the glasses into the church window, there were hundreds of places they could have gone. They could easily have skittered under a pew or into a dark corner. Worse, they could have fallen through a hole in the floor, and at this moment be underneath the church. The flashlight beams bounced crazily over the floor, resting on mildewed hymnals, strings of cobwebs, broken plaster from the walls. At any moment, Kit expected the Addisons to come crashing through the door, shotgun blazing.

"We'll never find them. Philip, you have to go back without me."

"No," Philip panted, still out of breath. "No good. Two people have to go back through the hole, or it won't seal. Two went out, two have to go back."

"At least you'll get home safely!"

Philip was about to respond, when Malachi shouted, "I found them!" He was kneeling in the far corner of the church, and held up a pair of wire-rim glasses. One of the lenses was cracked, but otherwise they seemed sound. He ran and gave them to Kit.

"Now," Philip said. "I think the hole is about ten feet in the air, above the front door of the church. At least that's how far I fell when I landed here. We should try to get above it, and jump down into it. Isn't there a window up in the steeple?"

"I think so."

There was the sound of a car door slamming, and then angry voices. Philip turned toward the door. "I think the Visigoths are about to sack Rome."

"Come on!" Kit thrust the glasses into his pocket, and pelted up the stairs to the choir loft. The other two followed. The wooden floorboards vibrated beneath their feet as they ran, booming hollowly. Kit reached the small door leading up into the steeple first, and slipped inside.

Kit shone his flashlight up into the dusty darkness, illuminating the old staircase that wound its way up to the top, to the window overlooking the front entrance. Several of the stairs were cracked or had gaping holes. He wondered how Philip would make it up them, but Philip and Malachi came up behind him, the old man still wheezing.

"Can you get up there?"

Kit looked up. From where he was, he should have been able to see the window. He frowned. "It looks like something is blocking the stairs, further up."

He took a step forward, and pointed his flashlight straight up. It was large and dark, and the flashlight beam did not illuminate it. It seemed to swallow the light up. And it moved downward, toward them.

"What is that?" Kit shouted, as it coalesced into a dark, winged form, eyes glittering with an intelligent, all-consuming hatred, claws outstretched, needle-sharp talons pointing toward them. They did not know it, but they were seeing the last thing that Christina and Adam Thorne had seen before they died.

21. through the portal

. . .

Kit froze. Malachi shouted an obscenity and backed down two steps. The thing was upon them in a moment. One huge claw grabbed Philip Amirault by the face, and lifted him off the ground. The old man struggled feebly, his legs dangling in mid-air, kicking spasmodically like a hanged man. Kit grabbed the creature's scaly leg, the one holding Philip. It immediately swung its other leg up and brought the claw slashing across his arm. Kit felt a lightning bolt of searing pain, so intense for a moment he almost blacked out. It lifted its leg to strike again. Malachi reached out to grab it, and caught hold of one hideous toe. Instantly the thing turned its birdlike face toward him, its beak poised to stab at him. He still held the thing's toe, and its movement threw him off balance. He lurched sideways just as the huge beak arced down, and it missed him by inches. Kit heard the sharp *thuk!* as the beak glanced off of the wall.

It was killing Philip. It wasn't even real, and it was going to kill him, and then there would be no way to fix all this. It wasn't real... it wasn't real...

And with that thought echoing in his ears, suddenly Kit knew what to do.

He plunged his hand into his pocket, and pulled out the glasses. The thing seemed to sense what was happening. It dropped Philip, who crumpled to the floor, senseless, and gave a harsh croak of anger. Kit saw the shining, hate-filled eyes, and claws reaching out for his throat. Then he put on the glasses.

This time, there was no soft, molasses-like bending and twisting. The alteration was sudden and complete. What hovered over Kit was no longer a diffuse, winged blur with a beak, eyes, and talons. It was flat and almost motionless. It looked like a nightmare drawing, floating in space. The grotesque mouth gaped. Its eyes glittered with fear and anger, as if it wanted to escape its two-dimensional prison, and rend and tear whoever had imprisoned it. Kit reached upward and took hold of it. It felt like thick, soft cardboard, but it vibrated with concentrated hatred.

"You murderer. You killed Adam and Christina." Kit grasped it with both hands, and tore it down the center.

There was a hideous wailing shriek, almost above the threshold of hearing. Kit looked at the thing in his hands, and the two halves of the drawing seemed to fall apart into black flakes of ash, like burned paper. His hands were dark with soot. He reached up and removed the glasses. The creature was gone.

Philip lay on the floor, nearly unconscious. He had two deep gashes on his head, and his face was covered with blood. Kit's own arm was bloody, and ached like fire.

"Come on, Philip," Kit begged. "Come on." He reached his good arm under Philip's body, and pulled him to a sitting position. "Philip! You've got to get up."

"Can't. Thing almost killed me."

"You're not dead yet." Malachi knelt down on the other side of him. "You've got to get up!" They hauled him to his feet, and together began to half push, half drag him up the narrow staircase.

"No! Don't understand... you don't... too late. My heart."

Kit whirled around. "What?"

"No use. Can't make it." Kit shone his flashlight in the old man's face. His blind eye was wandering uselessly, and his lips were purplish. Blood still streamed from his wounds, running in thin trickles down his neck. His shirt was spattered with red stains.

"What about sealing the hole?"

"Can't help that." Philip's voice was hoarse and thin. "Can't do it."

"Oh, man," Kit mumbled to himself. "Then what's the use of anything?"

Malachi whispered, "They've found us."

There was a sudden increase in the volume of the angry shouts from outside. In the midst of the roar, a clear voice—Kit thought it was Cleve Addison's—said, "They're up there in the church! I see their tracks!"

"Come on," Kit demanded. "You've got to make it, Philip." They began to push the old man up the stairs again. Philip himself seemed galvanized by the noise outside. He began to lift his feet, one step at a time, although his face was ashen and drawn with pain, and his breath came in uneven, ragged gasps.

It seemed forever before they reached the window. A square patch of light came through it and struck the wall behind them, the only bright thing in the dusty dimness. There were three intact pieces of glass in the frame, but no latch. Kit pulled upward on the frame, and to his alarm the whole thing fell out, tumbling into the sunlit air and landing with a dull thud on the grass below. The people below sent up an excited yell.

"They're in the steeple!"

Kit slipped on the glasses again, and stepped out onto the sill. The realization flooded over him... it had all happened before. The evening breeze ruffled his hair, caressed his face. He looked down at his feet standing on the old wood. People on the ground, yelling for him to jump. It was all familiar, from a dream he had an eternity ago.

And then he saw it, about halfway between himself and the ground. He had never seen anything so beautiful and so frightening at the same time. He knew he had to act, now, but for a moment all he could do was stare.

It was a spinning hole, a vortex in mid-air. Through it he could see, gem-like, thousands of worlds. They were clear near the center, but became smaller and more indistinct on the edges, blending into a rainbow of brilliant colors. Inside the hole he could see glimpses of people, landscapes, creatures familiar and unfamiliar. One scene melted into another almost too quickly to register. The whole thing was silently whirling at a fantastic speed. From it, tiny sparks were being thrown off, like splinters of iridescent glass.

Suddenly, in a blinding flash of clarity, Kit understood. This tear between the worlds threw off bits of itself into this world, fragments of realities so different from this one they had turned Finn Hill into a horror story. What other worlds, other realities, other universes had mingled with this one to create the horrid bird thing that had killed the Thornes and nearly killed Philip Amirault? In what place was it normal for a human to change into a luminous being who could stand in the center of an inferno of flames but remained unburned? From what kind of world had the fiery-hot glass predator come? Here, Kit realized, here was the source of all of the answers, if one only had the time to investigate all of those worlds that met in this iridescent, spinning vortex.

As Kit watched, a shower of sparks scattered from the spinning hole. One of them struck a maple tree nearby, and it shuddered, and the trunk twisted around slowly, creaking and rustling, and then two deep-set and shining eyes opened in it, the bark peeling back to expose them like corrugated eyelids. One of the men down below noticed it and began to scream.

Another spark flew into the air, toward another of the men who still stood in front of the church, but on the side away from the transformed tree. He didn't react when the spark pierced him, but immediately Kit could see the beginnings of a change, a change Kit knew would accelerate until it consumed him, as it had Carl Swenson. Kit recalled the morning of his first day in Finn Hill, when Mr. Swenson had winced in pain and blamed it on stiffness and lack of sleep. Had that been the moment a spark had entered him, and begun to alter him into the half-angelic creature he ultimately became?

Kit looked down at the man who had just been pierced. The man had seen him standing in the window and shook his fist at him. Kit saw just the faintest hint of flexion in his arm, as if his bones had become slightly rubbery. Then the man heard his comrade scream on the other side of the church, the one who had seen the tree. He ran to see what had happened, and again, as he ran his legs bent in a way just a little too flexible to be normal for human bones. Kit shuddered at what the outcome would be in two or three days or less. A worm, some kind of squirming invertebrate human that writhed and wriggled and could not stand up? A helpless invalid, crushed by the weight of his own body against bones that had turned to jelly? As Kit looked, more sparks scattered from the hole, flying over the trees toward the village. Each one of them, he now knew, was the seed of some other world, something that didn't belong here. No, Philip was right. It had to be stopped.

"Jump, Kit." Philip gasped for breath. "You know you must jump."

"So do you, Philip!" Kit shouted. He heard footsteps on the stairs, rushing up behind him.

"No, Kit, I don't," Philip said. Kit turned as much as he could, in time to see out of the corner of his eye the old man's trembling hands placing his pair of glasses on Malachi's face. "It only has to be two people. Two people came here, two have to go back. It doesn't matter which two."

"How do you know that?" Kit demanded. "How can you be sure?"

"I'm not." Philip staggered back, his voice becoming weak. "But we have no choice but to assume this is the way the story ends."

"Philip, no!" Kit shouted, but Philip fell, his eyes rolling upward in his head, and he vanished into the shadows behind the window. There was a thud and a groan in the darkness on the stair. And then Kit lost his balance, and fell too, but forward, outward, into the empty air.

And just as in his dream, Kit felt a warm, strong hand close over his, and he pulled Malachi out into space with him. But this time he could see Mal's face, his brown eyes obscured by the ridiculous glasses, and narrowed against the rush of the wind, his t-shirt fluttering and snapping as they fell. Together they were flung outward, spinning as if they were caught in a whirlwind, and he felt Malachi's hand slipping from his. He tightened his grip, but the pull was impossible to resist, and their hands separated. They tumbled separately through space, the gale in the vortex wrenching Kit's cry of anguish from his lips and tossing it carelessly aside, as he lost sight of Malachi and fell, alone, through the gateway.

It takes time to tell, but the sensations all registered in less than a second, and then were swallowed up in blackness.

At that moment, the people standing on the ground heard a sound like a high wind, although the trees were still and they felt nothing move. Then it was swallowed up, and silence reigned once more at the abandoned Finn Hill Methodist Church.

All through the village and beyond, the change was felt. Kit never found out why the village had been nearly empty that morning, but the events of that day would be remembered by almost everyone within a five-mile radius of the church, even those who didn't know much about exactly what had happened during the previous week.

Marie Bedford, cashier of the Nice 'n' Easy and Kwik Fill, had been enjoying a cup of coffee before going down and opening up the store, when there was a noise at the front door. A kind of grunting and snuffling. She lived on the south side of the village, not too far from the Coles, and one of her neighbors kept a few pigs. One of the pigs, a sow named Daisy Belle, was an accomplished escape artist, and she figured the fat old thing had gotten out again and was rooting around in her petunia bed.

Marie smacked down her coffee cup, stomped to the front door, and threw it open.

"Doggone you, Daisy Belle..."

Except it wasn't Daisy Belle. A small, swarthy figure dressed in heavy plate mail was pulling tomatoes off the vines in her garden and cramming them into its mouth. It was only marginally human. It was thickset, hairy, and two teeth rather like tusks came up from its lower jaw. Marie, hardly ever at a loss for words, stood and stared.

When the thing heard her voice, it turned and regarded her from small, glittering, piglike eyes. There was a ringing sound of steel, and Marie saw with horror it had drawn a long, curved sword. Then, it shouted, *"Bazgush marzad vakhun!"* and came at her, sword upraised.

Marie raised both hands to the side of her face and shrieked. At the same moment there was a whickering sound, and an arrow flew past her, so close she felt the wind of its passing. It skewered the throat of the creature, which gave a hideous, bubbling cry, and fell face down on the lawn. She looked in the direction from which the arrow came, and there, sitting on a huge gray stallion, was a tall man wearing a travel-stained green cloak. He carried a long wooden bow, and a quiver of arrows was at his back. A straight sword in a black sheath hung by his side. His face was weather-beaten but still somehow commanding. His hair was shaggy, black/gray, and gave him a rather wolf-like appearance. He regarded her with pity from his high position. She looked back at him, her eyes popping out of her head. Then she gave a weak sigh, and fainted dead away.

When she came to, there was no sign of the man or the creature, but her tomatoes were still gone, and there were hoof prints in the lawn.

Anders Christensen, owner of Christensen's Bakery, had gone in early that day, as he always did. He did the majority of his baking in the early morning. He turned the sign in the window to "Open" and went into the kitchen in the back of the shop. He had opened up his bins of flour and sugar when he realized he had not yet donned his apron. A fastidious man, he went to the closet to fetch it before going any further.

The closet was closed by a sliding pocket door. He slid it open, and looked in. To his amazement he was not looking into the dark interior of the closet at all. He was looking into his own kitchen. It was as if the door was not a door, but a mirror. Stifling an exclamation, he leaned into it, and looked around.

Anders was the son of Norwegian immigrants, and his parents had taught him to maintain his calm when faced with difficulties. He stepped back, and closed the door, and opened it again, and peered inside. It still looked the same. He stepped through the doorway, and as he did so, he saw ahead of him someone stepping into an identical door on the other side of the room. He wasn't sure—he'd only had a glimpse—but the back of the retreating man had looked an awful lot like himself.

"Uff da."

The kitchen-within-a-closet looked just the same as the one he had just come from. There were the bins of flour and sugar, their tops off, and there was the door into the front of the shop. He humphed, and walked toward that door, and swung it open. He was not too surprised to find himself looking into his kitchen again. On the other side of this new kitchen was the back of a man looking through a swinging door.

"Hey." His voice echoed, reverberating like a voice in a cave. He turned and looked behind him. One of the echoes sounded like it came from that direction. He turned, and simultaneously the figure in the new kitchen turned.

Now he was facing a second figure, back turned toward him. He squinted nearsightedly through the open door framing him, and faintly glimpsed, receding through the door beyond, another kitchen—then another—then another. Had Mr. Christensen been a frequenter of carnivals (he wasn't), he would have recognized the effect at once. It was like a house of mirrors. He stepped through the door and let it swing shut. His double did the same, vanishing from sight into the room beyond. Anders Christensen was alone in the room.

"Well."

He spent a few more minutes, trying various closet doors and shop doors, until he became convinced they all led to his kitchen, one way or the other. Finally he decided that if he was stuck in his kitchen, he might just as well bake his bread.

At precisely 10:42 that morning, he was busily making cream cheese Danish. How exactly he would get them out into the shop when he couldn't get out of the kitchen, he hadn't yet figured out, but might as well make them anyway, right? A job's a job. However, at that moment he heard a sound like a rushing wind, and there was a series of flashing lights through the slats of the swinging door into the shop, and under and around the sides of the closet door. He stared at it for a moment, humphed again, wiped his hands on a towel, and walked to the swinging door. He reached out and pushed the door open.

His shop was back. "Okay, then," he muttered to himself, shaking his head, and brought out a tray of buns to place in the display counter.

Ricky Spence was a second grader who lived just off the main highway, in a neat little Cape Cod along with his mother, father, and two younger sisters. He was a rough and tumble type, with more energy than his sisters and parents combined. They all seemed perplexed by his infinite tolerance for running, jumping, throwing, and yelling. Despite the fundamental lack of understanding on the part of his family, Ricky was still a basically happy kid who enjoyed every day fully.

But even so, the morning of Kit and Malachi's disappearance was one of the milestones in his life up to that point.

He woke up at five-thirty, long before anyone else in the house did, and his eyelids popped open with their typical unstoppable enthusiasm. The sight that met him, however, was not one he expected, even in the furthest reaches of his imagination.

Peering into his bedroom window was a dragon. It was a sleek, shiny copper-red and green, and it regarded him with a steady, unblinking gaze from slit-pupiled eyes the color of honey. Ricky bounced out of bed, shouted "Awe-SOME!", ran to the window, and threw it open.

The dragon docilely rested its chin on the sill, and Ricky

scratched its scaly head just behind the ears. This was evidently pleasant to it, for it chuffed a smoky breath from its circular nostrils and gave a shiver, thrusting its rough nose playfully against Ricky's shoulder.

Well, that was all it took. Ricky clambered eagerly out of the window, and within moments he was up on the dragon's back, clad in light blue and white striped pajamas and grinning with an exuberance unusual even for him. A pair of dark, bat-like wings unfurled, and they were airborne. Ricky had never flown in an airplane, but this was better anyhow. He got to see everything from above, with no sound but the flutter of the dragon's wings and the whoosh of the wind in his ears. The flight lasted for three hours, with only one quick stop for Ricky to pee discreetly behind a bush. Then they were up again, soaring and dipping over cornfields and forests and towns. Several people on the ground saw them, resulting in two fainting spells and one man who swore off alcohol for the remainder of his life.

Ricky turned up missing at breakfast time, and his mother and father flew into a panic, especially when there was no answer when they called the Finn Hill Police Station. Their trauma was relatively short-lived, however. It was shortly after ten o'clock when he reappeared, still pajama clad, with a story of flying on a dragon's back. His father's anger and his mother's relieved tears were not sufficient to dampen his enthusiasm, and he dragged them both outside to see the dragon, which he said was curled up by the big pine tree in the back yard.

Of course, by that time it was gone. Ricky was devastated, and his parents looked at each other and nodded knowingly. He, however, maintained it had really been there, and no amount of cajoling would persuade him otherwise. After seeing their son would not change his story no matter what dire consequences were threatened, Mr. and Mrs. Spence considered having him evaluated by a psychologist, but after talking to some of their friends—and finding out they were not the only ones in Finn Hill who had unaccountable experiences on that strange morning—they decided to try their best to simply forget about it, and hope that Ricky would do the same.

Mr. and Mrs. Spence succeeded. Within a few weeks, the event was neatly tucked away among "cute things that Ricky has done." Within a year, they had forgotten all about it. Ricky, however, never did. For the rest of his long life—and he lived well into his eighties—whenever he thought of anything as fun, he always weighed it mentally against that glorious ride he had taken through the clear skies on the back of a real dragon when he was eight years old.

About forty-five minutes after Johnny Cole had left, Leslie decided to take her mind off her worries by busying herself repotting one of her house plants. Afterwards, she turned on a faucet to wash her hands. The sink backed up, and she couldn't turn off the water. It overflowed onto the floor, all over their new linoleum—just installed last year, darn it all. She ran and got a set of pliers to turn off the water underneath the sink, but even with the pliers, the handle wouldn't turn. By this time, there was an inch of water all over the kitchen floor, and it was spilling over onto the carpet in the living room.

She ran to the phone, and dialed the number for Shannon West, her next door neighbor. There was no answer.

She called the police station. Maybe her husband was finished helping those kids on their strange errand, and was back there. No answer.

Bill Stern, the plumber. No answer.

Fred Carlucci at the hardware store. No answer.

Now she began to get scared. There were several inches of

standing water all over the kitchen and living room. The carpet was surely ruined, and the furniture would go too, if she didn't do something. She splashed over the floor to the front door, and tried to open it. The doorknob turned, but the door wouldn't open.

The sliding glass door was similarly stuck, but at least that was breakable. She took the metal meat tenderizing mallet from a drawer in the kitchen, wrapped her hand in a towel, and struck the glass. Instead of breaking the window, the mallet rebounded, the recoil hurting her wrist, and she dropped the mallet with a splash into the rising water.

She looked around her, and felt the panic rise in her throat. She fumbled desperately with the latch to the slider, but it wouldn't budge.

She was going to drown. The house was going to fill up like a fishbowl, and she was going to drown.

But at that moment there was a high, rushing sound, like gale-force winds, although not a leaf stirred. Immediately afterwards there was a gurgle as the drain came unplugged, and the water in the sink ran out. The waterfall over the edge of the counter slowed to a drip. She tried the slider latch again, and it opened easily, and the water cascaded out across the deck and into the back yard.

Leslie walked slowly across the wet kitchen floor, reached out a hand, and shut the tap off. She stared at it for a moment, frowning.

The phone rang. Its bell sounded shrill, and Leslie whirled around, slipped on the wet floor, and almost fell. Heart pounding, she staggered over to the phone and picked it up.

It was the admissions nurse at North Hamilton Regional Hospital in Carnahan, calling to tell her that her husband had been admitted with a broken arm. He was otherwise fine. The nurse also added, with some asperity, she had been trying to reach her for the past twenty minutes but there had been no answer.

There were over fifty odd occurrences the morning Kit McIntyre and Malachi Swenson vanished, never to be seen in Finn Hill again. There was a lot of speculation as to what had happened to them, most of them centering around some sort of murky plot for revenge by Cleve Addison. Cleve, his son Jim, and two of their friends were arrested shortly afterwards for arson and attempted murder. The police tried to add charges of murder for the deaths of Carl Swenson and his son, but forensics specialists never were able to find a trace of either one's body in the ashes, so the murder charges had to be dropped. Cleve was not able to put up much of a defense, especially since his cronies were all too eager to sell him and his son up the river in exchange for a lighter sentence. And actually, Cleve's memory of the events following Trent's disappearance was hazy at best, as if someone else had been operating his body in the absence of his conscious mind. Of course, he didn't articulate it this way, even to himself. In the end, he and Jim were both sentenced to fifteen years in state prison.

Maureen, for once in her life acting swiftly and decisively, had her few meager belongings and her remaining children packed up within two weeks of the verdict, and was driving east in the family's rusted station wagon to Vermont, to live temporarily with her sister.

After that, what next? She could go anywhere. She could. She was not afraid of hard work, and after all it was a big old country. There were lots of places where she could go where Cleve would never find her when he got out.

Lots of places.

And she began to smile, for the first time in a long, long while. She smiled for most of the rest of that car ride, and for quite some time thereafter.

At eight o'clock, George Cochran in the Hamilton County Coroner's Office checked the temperature of the body of Helen Swenson, and found it had dropped to a horrific 298 degrees below zero Fahrenheit. Clouds of mist rolled off it when he opened up the locker, and the temperature in the room plummeted. He was still undecided on what to do about it. He considered calling up a colleague in Watertown, but hesitated. He didn't like being called a fool, which was pretty likely considering the circumstances. He decided at about eleven-thirty to check on the body one more time, and found that the temperature had begun to rise. By noon, it was back to 200 below.

By the next morning it had warmed up to right about the freezing point, and George was pretty glad he hadn't messed about with calling Watertown after all. Whatever mysterious aberration had frozen the poor woman was evidently over. She was back to being an ordinary dead body. That, he could deal with.

Besides, he had other things to think about. The previous afternoon, someone had reported yet another dead body, this one sprawled on the stairs of the steeple inside the old Methodist church in Finn Hill. It turned out to be an odd-looking old man, probably in his seventies or eighties, and no one knew who he was. He had no identification, but had a peculiar set of injuries—several deep cuts and scratches, although clearly nothing that would be life-threatening, even to someone his age.

Cochran autopsied him that afternoon, and found a fairly serious blockage of the coronary arteries. Heart attack. He first contacted Johnny Cole's deputy, and then Chief of Police McLarney, but neither was able to turn up any information on missing old men. He tagged the body *John Doe*.

And, of course, no one ever did find out who the body

belonged to. It was eventually buried at the state's expense in the public cemetery in Carnahan.

A whole crowd of amazed spectators witnessed the spectacular reappearance of Averill Parker from the window of his shop door. Mostly they were drivers of cars who had been unable to pass through the village and had turned off their engines and gotten out to see if anyone in Finn Hill could direct them how to detour around it. The old man had resumed his futile and silent pounding, unaware an increasing and horrified audience watched his antics, with only a few breathed comments such as, "He's stuck in the window!" and "How we gonna get him out of there?"

Then the windless wind rushed by, and Averill was thrown bodily through the window, landing flat on his face on the sidewalk. He stood up, red and sweating, bleeding from a scrape on his balding head and the palms of both hands, his wire-rim glasses askew. He stood up, brushed himself off, and squinted sourly at the crowd of astonished people.

"What the devil are you all staring at?" His voice was hoarse from shouting. "You people think we like to be stared at here? It's a village, not a zoo!" He turned and walked into his shop, and slammed the door, leaving a speechless group of "outsiders" gazing through the now-empty glass.

The last breath of air pulled against Ann Garvey's nerveless hands. She held on by only two fingers now, and her consciousness was rapidly slipping away. She couldn't cry out, couldn't scream. She felt her ribs compressing as the last of the air in her lungs was forced out.

Her hand slipped off the wall.

There was a huge blast of air, and she flipped head over heels outward. The force of the rush threw her almost twenty feet. She landed on her back, skidded for a few yards, and fetched up against the edge of her raised bed garden. Looking up, she saw bell peppers hanging over her, about two inches from her eyes. They looked like fuzzy green blobs, but at this distance she recognized them. Her lungs filled with grateful gulps of air, but it took her mind over a minute to catch up, and figure out that the stars were gone, and she was still in her yard. Except for the birds, everything was silent.

She sat up, then stood. She cautiously felt her way back to the sliding glass door through which she had been thrown. It was shut—locked—and the glass was intact.

After a few moments, she began calling for her next door neighbor, Nina Cook.

Nina was inside the house, but Ann had a strong and confident "teacher voice." Nina heard the calls and came running, and found Ann standing in the shade of her eaves, calling for help, in trouble but not seeming especially frightened. After what Ann had been through, being stranded without glasses in her back yard seemed almost like an opportunity to relax.

Ann told Nina only that she had somehow simultaneously lost her glasses and gotten locked out of the house, and Nina —a sweet woman but not the world's brightest—apparently believed her. She ran around to Ann's front door, which was unlocked, and let Ann in. Ann had a spare pair of glasses, and after finding them and placing them on her nose, thanked her neighbor and apologized for the mess in the living room and kitchen, a mess which included the shattered remains of Ann's front door fanlight and kitchen windows.

"Land o' Goshen," Nina said in a hushed voice. "What happened? This place looks like it was hit by a tornado."

She never found out how close she had come to the truth.

Neither did Ann Garvey ever see her blue Delft planter or her other pair of glasses again, and several of her *Horticulture* magazines were nowhere to be found. She pictured them floating out somewhere in the chill dark between the stars, in a place so distant even the constellations were different, and shuddered.

Somehow, at the moment, the loss didn't seem all that important.

22. a homecoming, a crash landing, and a phone call

. . .

Kit landed with a thump on his stomach. He was face down on a dark, dingy carpet. The room was dimly lit, and he still looked through the smeared and cracked lenses of the magic glasses, but it didn't take him more than a few seconds to realize where he was.

He was underneath the dinner table in Philip Amirault's apartment.

He crawled out from under the table, took off the glasses, and stood up. It all looked the same as always, like the interior of an old attic. Their teacups were still on the table. Kit's was lying on its side, a thin trickle of chamomile tea dried beside the edge. Stacks of books and typed manuscript pages were scattered over the table. The box with the three remaining pairs of glasses was sitting, still open, where Philip had left it. The Swiss cuckoo clock on the far wall showed three o'clock. Good—if Philip had been right, and it was still the same day, then Kit's mom wouldn't be back home from work yet. Explaining to her where he had been was a task he didn't like to think about.

Kit stood there, gazing around the room. Somehow being back here made his adventures of the previous days seem like something he had read about, but not experienced. And, after all, wasn't that what Philip claimed they really were? Fiction. Not real. That thought made him half expect Philip to come walking out from behind a bookcase or out of the bedroom, and tell him to stop daydreaming and get back into the real world. Instead, nothing happened. Philip's stuffed coyote looked at him through its glass-bead eyes.

"Philip?"

No answer.

"Malachi?"

The apartment was silent, although there was the familiar sound of traffic from outside, muffled by the closed window and Philip's tapestry. Kit's arm hurt like crazy. He looked down, and saw the gash the talons of the bird-thing in the church steeple had torn in his forearm. Whatever Philip believed, it had been real. This injury was no fiction. Suddenly, it was too much for him. After all he had been through, it was just too weird to be here again. He quickly walked out of the apartment, and shut and locked the door behind him.

He walked up the stairs to the third floor. Where was Malachi? Hadn't he gone through the gateway with him? When their hands separated as they fell… perhaps he had been thrown clear of the vortex and had been left behind in Finn Hill?

If Philip was right about how these things worked—and just how would he know for sure?—if he hadn't come through with him, there would still be some sort of cosmic imbalance. The hole wouldn't have sealed. Which meant Kit might have brought back the terrible interface between the worlds to his own world. No—not just to his world, to his own apartment building. Now *that* was a scary thought.

Or maybe Malachi had been thrown into a different world, one of the ones they'd glimpsed while looking down into the vortex. There had been millions of them. Was the vortex a portal to all of them? If so, Malachi might have been thrown into a completely different universe, and he'd bring the interface along with him, as well. Their bumbling attempts to get Kit back home might doom more worlds than just his.

He turned his thoughts to Philip. Was he dead? He'd looked close to it the last time he'd seen him, gray faced, bleeding, vanishing backwards into the shadows. That didn't seem possible, to lose Philip too. He wondered what would happen when people here noticed he was missing. There would probably be an investigation. Well, good luck to them. They wouldn't ever find him. Dead or alive, he was trapped in a book somewhere, or a painting, or something. He was still behind the frame.

He got home to find that Laurie was gone. She had left him a note saying, "Gone to Mary Jo's. Be back by 4:30." Good. If Laurie saw the gash on his arm, there'd be no way that she'd let him go without a complete explanation. Now at least he'd have a chance to clean it up and put on a long-sleeved sweatshirt before she got home. Although that in itself might raise an eyebrow. Kit usually went shirtless when the weather was hot, and whenever there was no good reason to put one on. Oh, well. If she noticed, she noticed. But he'd still take every precaution he could. That kid was getting just too observant for her own good.

Kit went to the bathroom, stripped off his t-shirt, and gingerly washed his arm. The cut was long and ragged but fairly shallow, and didn't look life-threatening. He pulled up the bandage on his chest. The cut there was healing up cleanly. He switched out Malachi's loaned t-shirt for a long-sleeved one of his own, went back out into the living room, and sat down in the recliner, looking out of the window and thinking about Malachi Swenson.

Why? Why couldn't he have been from his world? It just was not fair. Why couldn't he have come here with Kit, and made this world a little less colorless?

He was quickly descending into a sadness that was unusual for his normally placid temperament, and he finally decided to go down to the high school soccer field and see if any of his buddies were still there.

He told himself he'd get over Malachi. And he remembered what he'd told himself while he was there. If his life here was colorless, it was because he'd chosen to let his life lack color. If he wanted to, right now he could choose to add color to it himself.

Maybe that's why he met Malachi. Maybe he needed to learn that he could write his own story, and create his own colors.

At that moment, the telephone rang, and Kit walked over to the counter and picked it up.

Hazel Roy walked out of the screen door of Yann's Drug Store, and down the steps. Three-thirty. Hottest time of the day. Why in the good Lord's name Miss Bertha couldn't find a more decent time to send her out was beyond her, but doggoned if she didn't always pick the middle of the after-noon for discovering she needed a bottle of aspirin, or a box of Ex-Lax, or that her high blood pressure medication had run low. And then, of course, it was, "Hazel, go down and pick me up a little something down at Yann's." *A little something* always meant it would take at least a half hour, between walking down in the blazing hot Louisiana summer sun, waiting for Yann Dubois to fill the prescription or find what-ever it was Miss Bertha needed, paying for it, and walking back. Officially, Hazel was supposed to be off for home by four o'clock, but it never seemed to work out that way.

She stood for a moment in the shade of the awning, glad to be out of the direct sun for at least a few minutes. This time it was a box of cough drops, and that could wait. Wouldn't hurt the old biddy. If a sore throat'd just affect her tongue, now wouldn't that be a blessing?

The thought made her feel remorseful at her own ire. Bertha Scott was known throughout the town as having a tongue sharp enough to carve a turkey with, but she was a fair enough employer and never treated Hazel any differently just because she was Black. More than you could say for some people.

But she could still find a better time to send her off down the street after a box of cough drops, that was for darn sure.

Hazel took a handkerchief out of her purse, and mopped the sweat off her forehead. She slid her cat's-eye glasses up the bridge of her broad nose, and was just about to start walking back up Morgan Street toward her employer's house, when there was a huge crash on the corrugated tin roof of the drug store, and then a sliding clatter. Hazel jumped back against the wall, one hand pressed against her ample chest, her heart thumping wildly.

The clatter got louder, and a dark shape plunged over the edge of the awning. It fell, but caught somehow on the gutter, and just hung there, swinging. Hazel screamed.

It was a boy, surely no more than sixteen or seventeen, tall, athletic-looking, with curly brown hair. He had somehow grabbed onto the gutter as he slid down the roof. Fortunately, as it had saved him a fall onto the concrete sidewalk. The boy's glasses—round glasses, like that wizard kid wore in the movie all the kids liked so much—weren't so lucky. They flew off, struck the sidewalk, and both lenses shattered. Hazel stared at her, her eyes popping out.

"Lord a'mighty, child, you scared me half to death! What was you doing up there?" Hazel went and helped him down. He looked shaken but seemed otherwise unhurt.

"I... I don't know."

Hazel's glare softened. The fall had evidently scared the life out of the youngster, and he wasn't in his right senses yet.

She stooped and retrieved the ruined glasses, and handed them to the boy, who slipped them into the pocket of his shorts. "What's your name, child?"

"Malachi Swenson."

"Where're you from?"

"Finn Hill, New York."

"New York! Where are your parents?"

Malachi swallowed. "They're both dead."

Hazel's broad forehead wrinkled up in sympathy. "I'm real sorry, child. You here visiting somebody?"

At this point, Yann Dubois came out from the inside of his shop. Yann and Hazel were a study in contrasts—a tall, gangly White man, so thin and pale it looked like he had no meat to speak of on his long limbs, and a short Black woman, round and dark in all aspects. "Were you playing on the roof, young man?" Yann said in a nasal, unpleasant voice.

"No, I wasn't. I don't know how I got up there, I really don't."

"Mr. Yann," Hazel stammered, "I swear, I was just standing here and all of a sudden he just came down, almost on top my head."

"You kids," Mr. Dubois sneered. "Last week it was those Romero boys on their skateboards, just about knocking down my customers. Now it's you. You live around here?"

"No, sir."

"Lucky you don't, or I'd take my belt to your hide and apologize to your folks afterward. Now get."

He turned and stomped back into his store, and the screen door slammed.

Hazel reached over and took Malachi by the arm and propelled him down the street. Miss Bertha's cough drops could wait. "Now, don't you worry. He's just like that. He don't like anyone that ain't like him." She glanced over her shoulder to make sure he hadn't followed, and added, "Skinny, white, and ugly."

Malachi laughed.

"I'm gonna bring you over to Miss Bertha's house. I housekeep for her three days a week. Gotta warn you, she don't much like kids either, so just stay quiet. You look like you could use some lemonade and to get out of this sun for a while. Then you can go back..." She paused. "Who you visiting?"

"I'm not visiting anyone. I..." Malachi trailed off. This was just too weird. He had heard this conversation less than a week ago, but had been on the other side of it that time.

"You a runaway, child?" Somehow he knew this would be the next question.

"No, I'm not. And this will sound really strange, but where am I?"

At that point, Hazel thought she understood. Poor child had scattered his wits, maybe knocked his head on that roof when he fell. "You in Broussard, Louisiana, honey," she said, her voice calm and a little condescending.

They turned up a long driveway, alongside a huge old Georgian-style house with a massive front porch at the top of a wide, rather rickety set of stairs, a high gabled roof, and enormous, ornate windows. A gigantic oak tree, bearded with Spanish moss, overshadowed the driveway, but even under the shade of its branches, the air was stiflingly hot and humid. Hazel's dark face was beaded with sweat but she didn't seem otherwise troubled by the heat. Malachi, on the other hand, felt like he was walking through a sauna. How did people actually stand living here?

They entered the house from the back, and Hazel took her into the kitchen. The room was huge, painted white, and everything in it seemed old—the cracked linoleum, the rust-stained sinks, the old-fashioned gas stove. It had impossibly high ceilings. Malachi wondered how on earth they changed the bulbs in the light fixture.

The house was quiet except for the ticking of a clock.

Hazel retrieved a glass carafe out of the refrigerator. She poured some lemonade for Malachi, into a thick, heavy glass containing about eight ice cubes, and made him sit and drink it all. As he did so, an overfed black cat slunk into the room and began to rub against Malachi's leg.

"Now, honey." Hazel pulled up a chair. "Who you staying with?"

At that moment, there was the sound of someone entering the room. Malachi turned his head, and Hazel popped up out of her chair, quickly for someone of her girth. Standing in the doorway into the next room was an old woman, probably nearer eighty than seventy, but ramrod straight, and close to six feet tall. She looked down on both of them with alert, and stern, eyes of a rather surprising China blue. Her hair was steel gray and curly, but was cut short. No concessions to conventional femininity.

"Who are you?"

"My name is Malachi Swenson, ma'am," Malachi said. Here was someone, Malachi sensed, who could exceed Upstate New Yorkers' bluntness by a mile. Best to be on company manners.

"He almost got hurt right by Yann's, Miss Bertha," Hazel added quickly. "I just thought he looked like he needed something cold to drink to ease him."

"Well," remarked Miss Bertha. "That's as may be. Where do you come from, young man?"

"New York state, ma'am."

One of Miss Bertha's eyebrows lifted. "A city boy, hmm?"

"No, ma'am. My village is as small as this. Maybe smaller."

"Oh." Miss Bertha considered this for a moment. "I always thought that New York was all city. Be that as it may, you'd best be getting along before your folks get worried about you."

Malachi took a deep breath. Kit had explained his situation to Malachi's parents. That seemed like an easy task compared to explaining the reverse situation to these two. A sudden thought struck him.

"Ma'am, before I go—" Malachi took a deep breath. "Do you have a road atlas I might look at?"

Miss Bertha's eyebrow lifted higher. "Reckon I do. Old one, my nephew left it here last time he visited. I don't even know that they make road atlases any more, with computers and GPS and whatnot. Hazel, it's in the bottom drawer of the writing desk."

Hazel trotted off into the recesses of the house, leaving Malachi alone with the old woman. Neither of them spoke, but it was clear Miss Bertha didn't care for this unwelcome interruption of her late afternoon routine. Malachi tried smiling at her. The eyebrow simply lifted further. He wondered how high it could go, and if it would eventually simply merge with her hairline.

Hazel came back a few moments later with a battered road atlas, and set it down in front of him. He eagerly opened it, and turned to the page for New York.

And there it was—or, more accurately, there it wasn't. Where Finn Hill and Carnahan should have been there was just an expanse of highway. Other towns, towns she'd never heard of, lined the road. Raquette Lake, Indian Lake, Sabael. Watertown was still there—that must exist in both worlds.

Then she turned toward the back of the atlas. Wyoming —that was too far. Wisconsin, West Virginia. Washington State.

Where did he say his town was? Somewhere east of Seattle. She looked closely at the map, and there, right on Interstate 90, she saw it.

Issaquah. Kit McIntyre's home town.

Malachi looked up, his eyes shining. Miss Bertha noticed it. She later told her best friend, Mrs. Ida Peck, "Doggondest thing. When that young man looked at the map, he lit up like a Christmas tree. He looked like you did last year when you won first place for best dessert at the Broussard fair."

Ida peered at her friend through her thick eyeglasses. "What do you think he was looking for?"

"Beats me," Bertha replied. "Whatever it was, it musta made him pretty happy."

Malachi looked up from the road atlas, eyes glistening with tears that came from some undefinable mix of elation, grief, love, and sorrow. He pulled out his cellphone. "No service." Not that he expected it. His phone server was in a different world—can't get much farther away than that.

But it was impossible to quell the rising excitement in his heart. "Can I use the telephone, please?" he asked.

"Call to where?"

"Issaquah, Washington."

Hazel looked up at Miss Bertha, and then gave a warning glance at Malachi. "Honey, you can't call the state of Washington. You know how much that'll cost?"

Miss Bertha glared at her. "Now, Hazel Roy, who runs this house?" She turned to Malachi, and looked at her appraisingly. "Who do you need to call?"

Okay, time to take a chance. "I need help. My parents are both dead, and I have some family in Washington state who might be able to help me. I need to call them and let them know where I am. It'll be quick, I promise." Well, it wasn't the whole truth, but it wasn't bad for a start.

Miss Bertha looked at Malachi down her long straight nose. "It's on the table just the other side of that door."

Malachi stood and walked into the next room. Two pairs of curious eyes followed her out.

The telephone sat on a small mahogany table with intricately carved legs. The telephone book—*South Central Bell:*

Lafayette, Broussard, Youngsville, Milton, Duson, and Surrounding Areas—was underneath the phone. He opened the phone book, found the area code, and then dialed information.

"What city, please?" an inflectionless female voice asked.

"Issaquah, Washington."

"Go ahead."

"Kit McIntyre."

There was a pause. "There's an Alison McIntyre in Issaquah."

He shivered. Why was he scared all of a sudden? "That's it." The automated voice began reciting the number. He picked up the pen next to the telephone, and wrote it on his hand. Then, after some thought, he retrieved his shattered glasses from his pocket, and dropped them into the wicker wastebasket that stood next to the telephone table.

Wouldn't need those any more.

He carefully depressed the receiver, waited for a dial tone, and then with a trembling finger, dialed Kit's number.

It rang once, twice, and then there was a click, and a sweet, familiar voice.

"Hello?"

"Kit, it's me. It's Malachi." He felt like laughing and crying at the same time, and fought back both. "Is there some way you can come pick me up? I landed in Broussard, Louisiana."

about the author

Gordon Bonnet has been writing fiction for decades. Encouraged when his story "Crazy Bird Bends His Beak" won critical acclaim in Mrs. Moore's 1st grade class at Central Elementary School in St. Albans, West Virginia, he embarked on a long love affair with the written word.

His interest in the paranormal goes back almost that far. Introduced to speculative, fantasy, and science fiction by such giants in the tradition as Madeleine L'Engle, Lloyd Alexander, Isaac Asimov, C. S. Lewis, and J. R. R. Tolkien, he was captivated by those writers' abilities to take the reader to a fictional world and make it seem tangible, to breathe life and passion and personality into characters who were (sometimes) not even human. He made journeys into darker realms upon meeting the works of Edgar Allen Poe and H. P. Lovecraft during his teenage years, and those authors still influence his imagination and his writing to this day.

This fascination with the paranormal, however, has always been tempered by Gordon's scientific training. This has led to a strange duality: his work as a teacher, skeptic and debunker on the popular blog *Skeptophilia*, while simultaneously writing paranormal and speculative novels, novellas, and short stories. Gordon explains this, with a smile: "Well, I do know it's fiction, after all."

He blogs daily, and is never without a piece of fiction in progress—driven to continue (as he puts it) "because I want to find out how the story ends." From historical fiction (*Kári the Lucky*), to murder mysteries (the Parsifal Snowe Mysteries, beginning with *Poison the Well*), to paranormal fiction with a humorous twist (*Periphery* and *Lock & Key*) to the truly terrifying (*Gears* and *Descent into Ulthoa*), Gordon's fiction has something for all tastes!

Find him conversing with his dogs (and perhaps his wife) in Trumansburg, NY, or the following platforms:
- YouTube *https://youtube.com/@skeptophilia1509*
- Skeptophilia blog *http://www.skeptophilia.com/*
- Books and stuff *http://www.gordonbonnet.com*
- Twitter *@TalesOfWhoa*
- TikTok *@LittleBustardBooks* and *@gordonbonnetauthor*
- Instagram *@skygazer227*

Or, ya know, the Google.

Please help other readers find Gordon on social media: likes, comments, and shares go a LONG way, as do reviews! If you liked this book, please tell the world! Thanks.

also by gordon bonnet

The Communion of Shadows

Sephirot

Descent into Ulthoa

The Shambles

Kári the Lucky

Kill Switch

The Fifth Day

Gears

Lock & Key

Snowe Mysteries *(beginning re-releases 2023)*

Book 1: Poison the Well

Book 2: Dead Letter Office

Book 3: Face Value

Snowe Mysteries *(available now)*

Book 4: Past Imperfect

Book 5: Room for Wrath

Book 6: The Obituary Collector

Book 7: Slings and Arrows

The Boundary Solution Series (stay tuned for re-releases)

And More…

Stay tuned for releases *(and re-releases for ones you may have missed)*

Sign up for Gordon's Little Bustard Books Newsletter and Obscure Weird Tidbits at his website: http://www.gordonbonnet.com